TEXAS
COMEBACKER

Also By John S. McCord
in Large Print:

The Baynes Clan: Montana Horseman

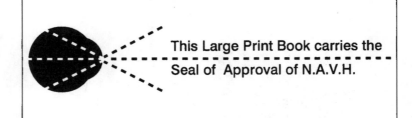

This Large Print Book carries the
Seal of Approval of N.A.V.H.

The Baynes Clan

TEXAS COMEBACKER

John S. McCord

WHEELER
PUBLISHING

Published in 2002 by arrangement with P.M.A. Literary and Film Management, Inc.

Wheeler Large Print Western Series.

The text of this Large Print edition is unabridged.
Other aspects of the book may vary from the original edition.

Set in 16 pt. Plantin by Liana M. Walker.

Printed in the United States on permanent paper.

Library of Congress Cataloging-in-Publication Data

McCord, John S.
    Texas comebacker / John S. McCord.
      p. cm. — (The Baynes Clan)
    ISBN 1-58724-306-7 (lg. print : sc : alk. paper)
    1. Baynes family (Fictitious characters) — Fiction.
2. Texas — Fiction.   3. Large type books.   I. Title.
PS3563.C34439 T4 2002
    813'.54—dc21   2002028081

To my Joan, who does everything
with consummate good taste,
even her selection
of elegant and loving parents,
Mr. and Mrs. J. M. Tuggle.
I call them Tug and Eve.

ONE

I suppose every country boy knows on sight the smoke of a burning barn. Something deep inside me turned my horse toward that rising column of tragedy. Maybe the climbing smudge in the brassy, breathless hot Texas sky called up a pale old memory. A hundred hard-earned lessons crowded my mind, cautions that a wise man tends to his own business. Still, once upon a time, I'd had a home and neighbors who felt duty-bound to help each other.

Boyhood days stay with us forever, and those times were only five years or so behind me when I turned my horse on that fateful day in 1868. Only twenty-three years had passed since Pa wrote my name and date of arrival in the family Bible, but I'd seen more meanness and treachery than most who die of old age.

A fierce fight goes on in a man's head when he aims to do what seems right but, by doing it, goes against lessons he's learned the hard way. My mustang gelding, a bead-eyed, snake-headed lineback dun, pointed his scarred face toward that smoke on account of my memory of neighborly responsibility, but I kept him at a walk. His slow pace came from my feeling I should tend to my own affairs and ride away. It never fails; when a man does something with a divided mind, he does it half-assed.

When I rode to the edge of a thick grove of live oaks, the barn was already in roaring torment, the roof going through the dying groans and snaps of the last seconds before it perished. The sucking breath of the towering flames, only a hundred feet from where I stopped at the edge of the wood line, made such a commotion I almost didn't notice three men nearly under my nose.

Two of them saw me at the same instant. Both jumped as if beestung. Quick as a scorched tomcat, one came up with a rifle. Peeling out of the saddle when a man wearing a gunnysack over his head levels a smoke pole isn't a thing I had to be taught. That reaction comes normal to everybody but half-wits. I hit the dry weeds face down and with such a thump I hardly heard the crack of the bullet. I took a big bite of Texas dust when I flopped out of the saddle, and I didn't like it.

Being a man sensitive to insult, I pulled my Navy .36 and shot that fellow holding the rifle. Seemed to me my answer came off dead slow, with me half stunned and blinking through a faceful of soil, but my lead reached him before he could get off a second shot, so I guess I didn't do too bad.

When he dropped his rifle and spun around from the force of my bullet, the second man grabbed him and pulled him out of sight. Since the trees grew so close together in that spot, both men managed to duck out of view after about two jumps and a stumble.

The eye being drawn toward motion, I couldn't help but take my first good look at the third man. He minced around and around in a single spot, a queer, slow, straining step, like an agonized Mexican hat dance, clutching feebly at a rope around his neck, the toes of his boots barely touching the ground.

I wriggled to the base of a nearer tree, leaving the dun ground-hitched. He didn't worry me. That horse and gunfire knew each other just fine; he wouldn't bolt. I stared wistfully at the stock of my rifle in its boot, but I didn't dare try for it.

Cursing the noise from scattered dry leaves, I crawled to the next tree and silently spat dirt about six times. Finally, my teeth came together again without grit making my head thunder. When I licked the tickle on my upper lip, the taste told me my beak-first crash from the saddle had also given me a bloody nose.

The dancing man's performance showed less and less spirit. He spun around to face me, but my bet was he didn't even know I existed. His eyes rolled frantically toward the sky while he tried to grow a foot taller to ease the pressure on his throat. His extended tongue, rigid features, and even his hands had taken on a dismal blue cast.

I'd get to him, in my own good time, if it could be done without getting myself shot. Hell, he was no kin of mine. This business had nothing to do with me. My quick reflexes and a dash of luck were all that kept me from being a chunk of dead meat over there by my grazing mustang. Only a dunce kept expecting little dashes of good luck to come when needed.

The barn roof fell in at the same moment I heard horses and caught a glimpse of two sack-headed riders. One rode close to hold the other in the saddle. That's all I got, just a glimpse, before they were out of sight again. They gave me no chance for a shot, even if I'd had my rifle.

The dancer's hands fell away from the rope, and his boot toes settled loosely in the dirt. I tore out from behind my tree for a sprint past him, took a hop to grab my knife from the top of my legging, and cut the rope down low where it was tied around the base of a sapling. The freed rope whipped off the high oak branch above him, and the dancer flopped to the ground, limp and loose as a pile of hog guts.

My landing wasn't much better. A black-berry bush embraced me with a hundred thorny branches when I dove in face first, but I didn't get shot at. Nor did I find any more sack-heads when I thoroughly searched through those trees. That little job took me more than half an hour.

When I circled back to him, the dancer had fought loose from the rope and started crawling toward a little house, fortunately located a good distance from the fire-gutted barn. The wind, what there was of it, saved the house by blowing most of the soaring sparks away from it.

On his hands and knees, making progress a few inches at a time, he swung his whole body, crablike, toward me when I led the dun up beside him. The poor devil couldn't turn his head on a neck black with bruises and so rope-burned that little drops of blood kept oozing out.

I saw now he hadn't simply been strung up. His attackers had nearly beaten him to death before using the rope. They probably used something more than fists to batter his face that badly. He pointed a bloody finger with a broken nail toward the shack, using a frantic jabbing motion.

"Can you talk?"

I couldn't tell whether the dancer tried to speak or merely to shake his head. Anyway, he shuddered, stiffened, and grimaced with pain. I found myself rubbing my own throat at the sound of his wheezing effort to breathe. He pointed at his mouth and then jerked his head back and forth in a negative motion. His bloody finger jabbed toward the shack again.

"You worried about something in the house?"

His hand tightened into a fist for a moment to show I'd guessed right before the finger resumed its jerking motion.

"I'll take a look."

The dancer slumped to the ground, his open hand waving me forward even as his body went slack.

Navy .36 in hand, I circled the house. With four rooms, two on each side of an open dogtrot, it turned out to be bigger and more solidly built than it looked from a distance. Flower beds all around and glass in the windows surprised me. All four doors leading to the rooms from the dogtrot stood open. Nobody hid inside to shoot at me, which was lucky, because the house was fancy and had a wood floor that creaked with nearly every step I took. The sack-heads must have left the house alone; everything looked clean and orderly. I didn't see anything to upset the dancer.

Then I did. At first, I took it for a pile of dirty clothes thrown carelessly into a dark corner. Then I saw a woman's high-top shoes with a rope around the ankles.

"Oh my God." My voice broke into a hoarse croak as two thoughts hit me at the same time. I realized why the dancer was so frantic in spite of his own pain, and my stomach turned at what might be lying there. The meanness done by men to each other can make even a cynic like me a little queasy, but that done to women and children always made me the sickest.

But when I spoke, she moved. I shoved a table aside and looked down into the damndest pair of eyes ever graced a woman's face. Nobody who's ever looked into an enraged cougar's features close up needs to know more. Those eyes scared the hell out of me, set me back a step, caused me to raise my .36 like a spooky kid. I nearly shot a tied-up woman.

When I took that step backward, I made a dumb noise. It's the same noise I used to make when one of my brothers surprised me with a poke in the ribs.

I came forward again, but I couldn't look away from those eyes. "Ma'am, are you all right?"

"Can't you see I'm tied up? Put that gun down and untie me this instant. Where's my brother?" Her voice reminded me of a rusty file on iron. My bet was she'd done a sight of howling and screeching before I found her lying so quietly.

"There's a man outside. I guess he's your

13

brother, ma'am. He's a mite raggedy, but I think he's worth repairing."

"Don't just stand there mumbling. Untie me!"

I holstered the .36 and again pulled the knife from the knee-high legging on my right leg. That being my shaving blade, I had the ropes off her wrists and ankles with one stroke for each tie.

She sprang to her feet but gave a little half scream half groan and swayed like she was going to topple over. I grabbed her arm to steady her. Quicker than I could see, she slashed her fingernails across the back of my wrist.

Those wild eyes put me back a step again, rubbing a scratched wrist. That crazy woman looked forevermore like she planned to spring on me and sink her fangs in my throat.

"Keep your hands to yourself."

"I'll do that, ma'am. A man can take a lot of simple pleasure from not touching you." My face burned hot as the smoking ruin of that barn when I backed toward the door. Fact was, I feared to turn my back on her and was glad to get away. First time I ever met a woman who could scare me by looking at me. Besides, I figured the dancer needed my help more than she did.

"Where you going? Come back here."

"No more of that, ma'am," I said glancing down at the blood-beaded furrows on the back of my wrist. "I got chores to do." Once outside the door, I kept moving. The dancer lay where I'd left him, my dun standing ground-reined nearby. "That your sister in there?"

Dancer's eyes had swollen shut, so I couldn't tell if he had cat's eyes like the woman. His hand went up and down in what I took to be a yes signal.

"If that's your sister, she was tied up. I didn't see anything wrong with her except she was probably stiff and sore. She was pleasant as a hornet's nest. Is it safe to be around her?"

He seemed to take a little time to think about that before giving an up-and-down hand movement.

"She isn't crazy or something like that, is she?"

His grimy hand gave a quick wave back and forth.

"I can either carry you to the house or help you walk. What's your preference?"

Two fingers made walking motions.

I got him to his feet as gently as possible, only to face a wobbly woman bearing down on us.

"Oh Win, poor Win. Those animals, how could they do such a thing? Let me help you."

Her voice was so different, so gentle, I wondered if this was the same witch or if another one had just arrived and dismounted from her broom. I found myself looking down at a thatch of wild red hair that didn't come high as my shoulder. Skinny as a fence rail, she probably didn't weigh more than a sack of feathers, but poison mostly comes in small jugs.

"Keep away, ma'am. Don't get in the way. Go back to the house and get things ready. I'll need a place to put him down when we get there."

"Yes, yes, I'll get things ready," she said, and did a better job of walking as she hurried back to the house. She was fast getting over looking so wobbly.

We made an awkward job of it. Win stood six or seven inches shorter than my six three. When he tried to put his arm across my shoulders, I had to bend my knees and walk like a constipated duck. Finally, I asked him to put his arm around my waist, and that worked better.

She ran out on the dogtrot and pointed. "In here."

I eased Win into a straight chair in front of the fireplace. She'd put kindling afire already and had a kettle of water hanging to heat.

"He's all bruised around the throat, ma'am. He can't talk, and I don't think he can see through all that swelling around his eyes. I think he tried to ask if you were, uh, hurt."

"No, I wasn't, uh, hurt," she said, mocking

me. "After all, they just tied me up and left me lying on the floor for hours and hours." I got a flash of those eyes again, but they didn't look so savage this time.

"Your eyes startled me at first, ma'am. Must have been the light in here. Now I see they're just that odd blue or gray that people with red hair sometimes have to make do with."

She paused and gave me another hard look, so I gave her a fake grin while holding myself ready and keeping a safe distance. If she made out to claw me again, I didn't figure to get caught by surprise a second time. Seemed to me she crouched, but she didn't spring. Instead, she wrung the water out of a piece of cloth and started swabbing Win's face.

He made writing motions, and she ran from the room for a moment, returning with a scrap of paper and a stubby pencil. She went back to removing blood and dirt from her brother, glancing down once in a while to read what he wrote.

"I can see a little," she read aloud, and patted him on the shoulder. He wrote again.

"Did I hear shooting?" she read. "Yeah," I answered him.

She wrung out her cloth again and asked sharply, "Well?"

"Well, what?" I asked.

"Is that all you're going to tell him?"

I shrugged. Silence fell for a long moment, so I added, "That's all he asked."

"Did you drive those men away?"

"Can't drive men," I answered. "You Texans think everything acts like cattle. They decided to leave."

"Because you were shooting at them?" she asked. "Might've made 'em feel unwelcome."

"Did they beat you up too?"

"No, ma'am."

"How did you get so bloody?"

"Fell off my horse." I rubbed my nose and looked at the black flecks on my hand. Being a clean-shaven man, I figured I must look like a clown, probably had a dried-blood mustache.

"On your face?"

"Yes, ma'am, I fell on my face."

"Do you do that often?" The question came in the same tone of voice a woman would use to say, "Poor baby," to a whining child. I decided to ignore it. The ceiling was so low I had to stand all hunched over, so I stepped outside and looked around for a while. I never was contented inside walls. Besides, the sack-heads might decide to come back.

I made a good long study of the tracks left by the sack-heads. By the time I headed back to the house, I knew nothing more about the men, their sign being so mixed and blurred on the hard dry ground, but I'd memorized those horse tracks.

I found a well around back, cranked up a bucket of water, and washed my face.

After tying my dun to the rail in front of the house, I took another tour around the place, inspecting the roof of the house for falling cinders and watching the dying fire. Even a complete burn-down leaves the metal parts of harnesses and tools behind, but the barn still burned too hot to get near it. No loss is ever so bad that there's nothing worth saving from it. Those who think otherwise have never seen real hard times, have never faced that grim moment when there's no choice but to save what you can and start over, no matter how bad the setback.

Finally, I sat on a bench in the dogtrot where I could see the two of them through the door but not feel trapped.

"You need any help?" I asked.

Without glancing at me, she shook her head. Win scribbled on his scrap of paper again. She read, "I think you saved my life. Did you cut me down?" She looked startled. "What does he mean, cut him down?"

"I found him dancing at the end of a rope. He looked like he was tired of it, so I cut him down."

She drew a sharp breath and seemed to shrink, which was quite a trick for a runt like her. "That's why his neck is so torn? They tried to hang him? Is that what you're saying?"

"No, ma'am."

"Well, what then? Can't you speak plainly?

19

What do you mean?" She glanced around the room, and I had the feeling she wanted something to throw at me.

"I mean they didn't *try* to hang him. They did it. Your brother danced on the tips of his toes till I could get him loose. Those men were too mean for their own good. That's what really saved his life. They strung him up in such a way he'd take a long time to die, fighting that rope until he was too weak to hold himself up to breathe. If they'd hanged him decently, I'd have been too late."

"I can't believe they'd just ride up here and commit murder."

"Ma'am, you're welcome to believe what you please. Fact is, they didn't even tie Win's hands. They wanted him to last awhile, and they wanted to stand there and watch him suffer. Somebody hates your brother in the worst way."

She shuddered, wrung out her cloth again, and pointed at the basin of grimy water. "Throw this out."

Not being in the habit of wasting water, I pitched it into the flower bed where it would do some good and brought the basin back to her. She poured more from the kettle and went back to work.

I said, "You're welcome," but she paid me no mind.

Win wrote on his scrap of paper again. She paused to read for a moment and said, "He wants to know what kind of Indian you are."

"Scotch-Irish, English, and Spanish," I answered, and walked over to the fireplace to stand in front of him. It seemed insulting to talk to the back of the man's head, like he was a post or something.

I swear, aside from being clean, his face looked better already. She'd stitched the bad cuts over both eyebrows with black thread while I was outside, and it looked like a tidy job. Win held a hot pack in place around his throat with a hand that was now clean.

"I thought so," he said slowly in a strained whisper after a couple of failed efforts. "You speak like an educated man, and you're way too tall for an Indian. Could you stay around a couple of days till I feel better?"

"I don't mind. You know who those men were?"

"No. I'm Winston Mill." He lifted a thumb in the woman's direction. "She's my sister, Cris."

He stuck out his hand and we shook before it hit me. "Ha, I get it now. She calls you Win, Win Mill." I chuckled, watching the slit of one eye I figured was the one he could see through. "And she's Cris Mill. Sounds like gristmill. Wind Mill and Grist Mill, that's dandy."

Cris stepped forward. "Don't make him talk. It's not good for him."

I had a gutful of that woman's insulting

21

tone of voice. She spoke to me like I was a shuffle-butt slave every time she opened her mouth. Still looking at his one almost-good eye, I asked, "Did you say this is your sister or your mother?"

"I'm his sister, and you keep a civil tongue," she said in her harpy voice.

"Your sister doesn't like me, Win Mill. I just had a second thought on it. Best for me to ride on."

"She's upset. I'm sorry." He ran a finger into his mouth and carefully explored with it.

"Lose any?" I asked.

He gave me a palm-up gesture with his free hand, indicating he wasn't yet sure if he still had all his teeth, leaned forward, and spat bloody stuff into the basin. I would have needed to be a brass statue not to feel sorry for the poor devil.

"I might stay a day or two, just to help out till you get on your feet, Win, and just in case those men with sacks over their heads come back. I might think about it, but she's got to do the asking."

Even his swollen mask of a face didn't conceal a trace of a smile. His sister wasn't amused.

"Win! I can't ask a strange man to hang around here. That would be . . . I won't do it. It's your place to do things like that." She stood straight as a ramrod, blushing as only a redhead can, looking like a regular female for

22

a change. In fact, I could imagine where some might think her passable handsome, if undersized.

Win, moving very slowly and carefully, raised both palms in my direction, a helpless gesture, and I swear his slit of an eye held a wicked glint.

"Well, I reckon I'd better get on with my own doings," I said, and walked to the door.

"I don't even know your name," she protested.

I spoke over my shoulder. "Milton Baynes, ma'am."

Her startled flinch tipped the tin basin of water off the table, and it made a rattling spin or two on the floor before it settled down. Bloody water splashed on her skirt, but she made no move.

"Did you say Milton Baynes?" she asked. Her voice was different, mighty different.

Win sat unmoving, but Cris's hands twisted and balled the cloth of her apron.

"Yes, ma'am, that's my name."

"Are you from Louisiana?"

"Yes, ma'am."

"We've heard of you, I think, Mr. Baynes."

The dropping sun stretched cool shadows across the parched land, causing the crickets to start nighttime gossip. A man can hear things like that when people hush up and hold real still.

TWO

The silence stretched past awkward to embarrassing before I said quietly, "Pleasure to meet you folks," tipped my hat to Cris, and walked away.

I grabbed the cheek strap of the meanest mustang ever born and shoved his head aside before jerking his reins from the rail in front of the house.

"Mr. Baynes." Cris had followed me as far as the edge of the dogtrot.

"Yes, ma'am?"

"My brother and I would be pleased to have you sup with us. We don't want you to ride away hungry at this late hour."

"Don't trouble yourself, ma'am. You got all you can look after. No need to bother with fixing victuals for a stranger. I'll make out just fine."

She stepped off the porch and walked toward me. Remembering her reaction to my name, I spoke in a low tone when she drew near. "I understand, ma'am. I really do. No call for you to feel bad, none at all."

I set myself to jump into the saddle, but she plucked at my sleeve and said, "Wait."

Without thinking, I turned back toward her. That damned mustang, catching me in a rare unwatchful moment, reached around and clamped onto my left buttock like a fanged dragon.

I jumped forward. Hell, any man would jump when surprised by a vise attached to his rear end. Naturally, Cris just had to get herself perfectly underfoot, so I bumped her. and she gave a little shriek on the way to plopping down in the dust.

Desperately, I swung a downward and backward roundhouse as hard as I could to knock that gnawing dun loose from my backside. But he saw it coming and snatched his head back. When I hit thin air, I lost my balance for a minute, spun half around, stumbled back a couple of steps, tripped over Cris's feet, and sat down hard, all 195 pounds of me, right in the middle of her.

She made a squashed little noise.

I rolled off quick as I could and came to my knees. She sure enough looked mashed flat for a couple of seconds before she curled up in a ball. I knelt there for a bit, afraid to touch her, rubbing my own thighs and saying dumb things like, "I'm sorry," and "Are you all right?" and "I didn't mean to hurt you," with her not saying a word. All she did was make those strained little jerks people do when desperately struggling to draw breath back into tortured lungs.

Finally, afraid she planned to die right there, I started to gather her up, saying,

"Here, let me carry you inside."

Cris sucked in air like a startled grizzly, shoved me away, and hollered, "No you don't. Don't touch me, you clumsy blockhead. You might kill me."

She jumped up, quick and wingy as a covey of quail, and fluttered around knocking dust off herself and flailing me at the same time.

I kept saying I was sorry and she kept saying things like clumsy oaf and stupid lout.

That went on for a good long while.

Every time I'd try to apologize, she'd come up with more unkind words and come swarming at me. After she'd backed me around the hitching rail a time or two, she got a little breathless and slowed down some, so I got off to a safe distance.

When my eye chanced on that damned mustang, standing like a statue where I'd dropped the reins, I reached back to check the tender place which was still distressing me, and that wild woman burst out giggling.

"Are you hurt?" she asked, and went to giggling again.

"Not so's you'd notice."

"No, I suppose I wouldn't notice there," she said, and snickered some more.

"Ma'am, if you don't mind, I think it's time for me to go."

"I have stew left from yesterday. You'll be no trouble at all. I insist you stay. It's too late to be riding." She stood between me and the dun.

"Don't concern yourself. I ride lots at night." I tried edging to one side, thinking to get around her without getting close.

"As clumsy as you are, you'll fall on your face again, and that horse will eat you." She edged in the same direction, cutting me off.

"I rode that horse all the way down here from Montana Territory." I tried the other direction.

"Stay until my brother feels better. At least he can help you get on without hurting yourself." She cut me off again.

"This is a hard luck place, ma'am. I got shot at and fell off my horse; you pounced on me and let my horse bite me and then swarmed all over me. I've been chased by hostile Indians friendlier than you. You stay mad at me no matter what."

"I'm not mad at you anymore. I never stay mad long, and I didn't pounce on you. I just touched your sleeve to get your attention. You're a natural-born clown. It was worth a mile walk under a hot sun to see the expression on your face. Tell the truth, who are you? What's your real name?"

"I already told you."

"You're no outlaw."

"I never said I was."

She turned toward the dun and I warned, "Look out, that's a bad horse."

Cris gathered up the reins and walked over to the hitching rail with my mustang trailing along like a friendly puppy. She tied him and said, "No more talk. Go inside. It's suppertime."

It was either that or go find a sharp stick to keep her away while I got in the saddle, so I went in the house. The first thing she did was to light the coal-oil lamp and put it on the table. I leaned forward and turned it out.

"What on earth? Why did you do that?" she blurted.

"I'll eat in the dark a hundred times rather than be shot once in the light."

Cris put bowls and things on the table in the dark and asked me to give thanks, since her brother's throat was sore. I did so with the ease of familiar routine and picked up my spoon when Win's hand on my wrist stopped me.

Win, with his pained and hoarse voice, said quietly, "We thank you, kind God, for Milton Baynes. Amen." He squeezed my wrist, then took his hand away.

For a minute or two, I couldn't move, just sat with spoon in hand and let my mind spin while tears came to my eyes. Never in my life had anybody said anything which shocked me so completely. This redheaded little rooster of a man had been beaten nearly to death, but I'd never even heard him groan. Would it be proper to say thank you when a tough man mentioned you in his prayers? It didn't seem so, so I just sat for a minute while they both started eating as though nothing unusual had happened. Finally, not wanting to appear rude, I did the same.

She seemed surprised when her brother, even feeling poorly, ate twice as much as I did. I never was one to eat heavy. Besides, no telling what kind of potions a red witch like her might have handy.

After the meal, I stood up, said, "Thank you. Good night," and walked out. Sometimes a surprise move like that can cut off unwanted conversation, and it worked that time. I topped my dun and headed for the nearby woods before the red witch could say a word.

In deep shadow under the trees, surrounded by dry leaves to warn me should anyone approach, I watched the picketed gelding graze in the moonlight and did some thinking.

Win Mill lived in a clean, well-built home with a wild-eyed, half-crazy sister. Short, skinny, and rude, she'd die a spinster, probably. However, she cared for him with open affection. And tidy little flower beds, sparkling glass windows, and a spotless wood floor all showed pride backed with hard work. If Cris had a pleasant side, she'd decided on sight that I wasn't worth showing it to.

How could it be that, during all the hours Win's barn burned, nary a neighbor nor a friend came to help? That smoke could be seen for miles. His prayer for me cut deep. A man who'd do a thing like that must be the sort who valued friends and remembered favors.

Could Texans be that different from Louisiana folk? For heaven's sake, in Louisiana, neighbors would ride to help put out a fire in anybody's barn, even an enemy's. They might even risk ruining a good horse to get there in time.

Win Mill had done something terrible, I decided. He'd done something so bad that his friends deserted him, and men came to hang him and burn his property, men who covered their faces like vigilantes.

What could I do about it? Nothing. Win Mill had to outrun his own wolves or be pulled down. I'd stay a day or so, long enough to see him back on his feet. Decency required that. It troubled me to wonder if his name had been unjustly smeared like mine, but I had my own work to do.

Somebody, somewhere near my old Louisiana home, dared to spread lies about my family, charges so foul that a shocked Cris Mill shuddered and knocked a basin off the table upon hearing my name. Those lies spread clear to Montana Territory and made men blink and draw back when a Baynes introduced himself. I rode all the way from Montana for a single reason, to face any who dared to spread lies about the Baynes family. Whoever they might be, they had better prepare for a high-stakes game.

I wouldn't run from my wolves. I planned to find them, quiet their howling, or shoot them.

THREE

Cool darkness still covered the land during most of my morning stalk. I always made a circuit around my campsite of a morning, just a funny habit picked up somewhere. A traveling man eats a better breakfast if he knows nobody came close to his camp in the night. My pa used to say the best ambush was set on a man's front doorstep. Anyhow, nothing gives me greater pleasure than to surprise somebody who's planning to surprise me.

I came across a couple of fine horses, wandering free but carrying a lightning bolt brand. Maybe Win Mill took his initials and put them together to make that jagged design. If so, he showed good sense. A proper brand should present a problem to those who might want to alter it, and they'd have a tough time with this one. Those two horses, if they were his, were lucky not to have been in Win's barn yesterday.

I checked around the Mill house too, just so I could approach the place with a quiet mind, knowing nobody was in there but the two of them. While I was watching things, Win came out to the outhouse, walking stiff and slow. Later, Cris took the same path, showing no sign of alarm.

After shaving with water from my canteen, I went ahead and saddled the dun. If the red witch threw another harsh word or hard look in my direction, I'd just keep riding. My patience was worn down to a nub, and I saw no point in wading through her surly nature to do favors. Maybe she'd already grown too mean to train by the time Win took charge of her. Or, maybe he had no idea how to explain ladylike behavior to a willful sister. Back home, folks would say that girl was raised on sour milk.

Cris met me with a big smile when I swung out of the saddle. "Good morning," she said, friendly-like, as if she'd never aimed a harsh word at me in her life. Damned if she didn't look nice, wearing a fresh dress and with her hair combed. She didn't even have freckles, or at least, not very many.

"Morning, ma'am. How's Win?"

"Beat up and black-faced, thank you, but he can see through both eyes this morning. Come on in. I've been waiting for you to get here before I put breakfast on the table."

"You knew I wouldn't ride away, did you?"

Cris looked down at her shoes and said, "You aren't the kind to ride off and leave people in trouble. I told Win you'd be here this morning."

"You got me all figured out, haven't you?"

"A little bit. You left so quickly last night I didn't have a chance to ask you to stay."

I said, "Um, well, I . . ."

"I know why you did that."

"Oh you do? How could . . . ?"

Cris showed no intention to let me say much of anything. She rattled on. "You were afraid I wouldn't ask. Then you'd have to leave, because you said you would, and that would make you feel bad, but you'd go anyway, because you're like that. You don't give many people second chances, do you?"

"Aw, I . . ."

She cut me off again. "But you gave me a second chance, and that was awfully nice. You knew I was frightened silly, and that I was upset, and that's why I acted the way I did. You knew that, didn't you?"

"Well now, I . . ."

"I'll ask you to stay right now. Will you please . . . ?"

"Stop." This time I interrupted her. I put my hand on her arm before giving it proper thought, but she didn't bite or scratch or coil up to strike this time. Her high color and fast speech showed how embarrassing she found the job she'd set herself to do.

I took my hand away, and she finally raised her gaze from her shoes to my face when I said, "You don't need to ask me. I was just having fun."

"Thank you, Mr. Baynes."

"My Christian name is Milton. My friends call me Milt. I'd ask you to call me Milt, if you'd promise not to take it as being forward. No need to turn into fangs and claws about it. Just say no if you feel it's not proper."

"Fangs and claws? My goodness." Then she saw me glance down at my wrist. "Oh my, I'm so sorry about that. Really, I am."

I sniffed. "Something burning?"

"Oh!" She ran toward the door about three steps before she stopped abruptly and flashed a smile back at me. "I set everything off the fire to wait for you. You have an odd sense of humor, don't you, . . . Milt?"

"No, ma'am, it's just . . ." I kind of wobbled to the house and sort of propped myself against the wall.

"What is it? What's wrong?" She stepped close and put a steadying hand on my arm. Little though she was, when she latched on, a man knew somebody'd laid a grip on him.

Halfway doubled over, with my hand on my stomach, teeth clenched and groaning, I struggled to the dogtrot and sat down, kind of collapsed like I almost didn't make it. She hung on for dear life, trying to keep me from falling flat.

"What is it?" she pleaded. "I didn't know you were hurt. Tell me what's wrong."

Between clenched teeth, I groaned, "It's nothing, ma'am. It's just . . . when breakfast is so late . . . I get so hungry."

Cris blinked a couple of times before she

caught fire. "Oh, it's a joke! A dumb, silly joke!"

I moved as fast as ever I did, but she kicked me on the leg before I could get out of reach. That Cris Mill could move plenty quick if she took a notion.

Win stepped from the door and watched me, standing at a safe distance, grinning at his sister. But she was grinning too, and it looked good on her.

After breakfast that morning I checked the remains of the barn, but it was still too hot to sift through the ashes looking for things to save. So I rounded up the milk cow, banged together a temporary water trough for her, cut and sank posts to close the part of the corral left open on the barn side, patched the chicken coop and chased half-wild chickens. Win helped here and there, but he was still pretty weak. Cris was the best chicken chaser. The day went by fast.

We sat out on the dogtrot talking and enjoying the evening breeze that night after supper. Win told me that he and Cris hailed from Kansas. After he came home from soldiering for the Union, he found his father dying and his neighbors still fighting the war. Then, shortly after his father died, unknown neighbors burned his barn and shot through his windows at night a couple of times. Fearing for Cris's safety, and not having a clue who was responsible, he decided to sell out and move.

Faced with the responsibility of providing for a young sister, Win came to Texas where he had relations living in Victoria. From there, he did some long riding and found this place a few miles from Goliad.

"I bought a solid title to this place dirt cheap," Win told me. Then he chuckled and said, "No pun intended." Although still hoarse, he showed less discomfort when he spoke.

"All I see in Texas is people with lots of land and no money," I said. "Seems to me a man with a little cash could buy half the state if he wanted it, but what would he want it for?"

Win laughed with me and said, "Horse country, cattle country, some good farmland too."

I answered, "What market? Who's buying anything?"

"Nobody much, but I hear talk. Things won't always be like now. In a few years, we'll drive out the carpetbaggers and get honest law. Those who can last till then should do pretty well. Cris said you rode from Montana Territory."

At my nod, he asked, "You going home to Louisiana?"

"Yeah."

"Not meaning to pry, but coming way down here doesn't seem the best way to get to Louisiana from Montana."

"I didn't get lost and wander into these parts. I took a side trip to Mexico. My brother won a piece of Mexican property in a horse race. He asked me to go down there and sell it for him."

Win's battered face showed no expression. "That'd be either Luke or Ward?"

"Ward," I answered, raising my head and lifting an eyebrow.

"And your daddy's name is Darnell?" Cris's question was the first time she'd spoken since clearing the dishes. She caught my inquiring glance, even in the darkness, and added, "I told you we'd heard of you."

"All bad, I suppose?"

Neither of them answered, so I went on. "No Baynes man ever slighted a woman, stole anything, or harmed any man who didn't come looking for trouble. That's why I'm heading back to Louisiana. I come from a respectable family. A bunch of lies need clearing up. People heard about the Baynes clan clear up in Montana. Can you imagine that?"

Cris shrugged. "Why do you care? Do you plan to live in Louisiana?"

I blinked. The idea of picking a place to live didn't have anything to do with it that I could see, and I said so.

They both sat so quietly I took it as a signal they wanted me to explain, so I went on, "Everybody thinks staying in one place is wonderful. Not me. I like wandering. Seeing new things every day, that's my pleasure. Nothing gets tiresome; a man never gets bored. I jump up every morning wondering what new sight I'm going to find over the next rise."

"So you're a wild Indian after all," Cris said.

"By nature, I guess, if not by blood," I said.

"Even wild Indians have families."

"Yes, ma'am, I'll find me a wild Indian woman someday, I suppose."

I heard Win laugh with me, but I suspect women don't find such remarks amusing, having a more straitlaced attitude. If I'd found something that irritated Cris, I couldn't pass up the chance to feed the fire.

"Up north, the country is empty, nearabouts, cooler and cleaner. A man can find a place close to the mountains where he never needs to worry about good water. The Indian women are taller and a whole lot better looking up there too. Nothing prettier than a nice tall, dark woman."

Cris jumped off her bench and walked inside the house.

Win asked abruptly, "Milt, you remember that rifle you brought up, the one that fellow dropped when you shot him?"

"Yeah."

"Cris cleaned and reloaded it this afternoon. I think she just went after it."

"*Hasta mañana, hermano,*" I said quickly, and slid out into the darkness toward my dun.

On the third day, we were setting posts for a new barn when Win asked me, "Do you always wear that gun?"

I touched the grip of my Navy and nodded.

"Maybe I should buy one myself. Those two caught me away from the house. I keep a rifle, but I had no chance to get to it."

I dropped the posthole digger and walked to my saddlebags, which hung on the rail of the corral. When I came back and handed him my spare Navy — belt, holster, and all — he stood blinking for a moment before he asked, "How much you want for it?"

I shrugged aside his question and said, "You'll need reloads. It's loaded now, and I'll leave you all the spare ammunition I have. Still, you'll need to buy more next trip to town."

He handled it in such a way I knew he was no stranger to a handgun.

I stayed five days after that. Win didn't need that much time to recover, since he had no broken bones. Fact was, working around the place pleasured me. Win shared a lot of the habits Pa had instilled into me. No ax should be put away without a proper edge and no harness hung up unmended.

An easygoing man, Win never seemed to move fast, but he kept moving from daylight to dark. Rather than stop to rest, he'd turn to doing something else for a while, doing light work while resting from the heavy. That meant he was never caught idle while the day gave him light to work. I could have been teamed with one of my brothers.

When the swelling left his face, sure enough, he had the same eyes as his sister. In his case, those gray eyes set in a sun-darkened face gave him a piercing, unsettling expression, much like my little brother Ward's.

I'd heard people say they knew Ward was a killer the minute they saw him up close. Seemed unfair to me, Ward being the handsomest boy in the family. He only got testy if conditions were right. Threaten his family or pull a gun on him, that's what it took to get Ward started, but once kindled, he made a hot fire. Otherwise, though, he was as good-natured a man as could be found.

Win was small like Ward, and that revolver slid into his hand like an old friend. If Win turned out to be like my younger brother in other ways, I might have started a riot in the local circus. I'd opened the cage for the tiger.

FOUR

The sun had just peeped over the hills when I said goodbye. Win asked me to drop in if I happened by those parts again.

I laughed and said, "Thanks for the invitation, but I look for new country. That means I don't ride back much over trails I've already seen. Don't look for me."

Cris said, "If anybody says anything about your family, I'll tell them quick that we know one of the Baynes. He's a friend of ours and a gentleman."

"Thank you kindly, ma'am. Good luck to both of you."

The dun hit a choppy gallop in about three jumps to show how eager he was to go. I was obliged to ride carefully for an hour or so till the extra frisky wore off. That horse got meaner when he wasn't working, having plenty of time to stand around, eat his head off, and think up evil tricks. He tried twice to reach back and bite my knee.

A little Mexican boy followed a fat goat along the twin ruts of the dirt road. When I overtook him, I slowed the dun and spoke to him. *"Buenos días."*

"Buenos días, patrón," he answered respectfully. My Spanish, learned from my mother,

was that of the educated, aristocratic class. All the boy needed to hear was my greeting, and he assumed I was somebody important. I continued in Spanish.

"Where do you take your fat goat, little brother?"

"I take her home, with your permission, sir. She ate through her rope and ran away last night. I just found her."

"You live near here, little brother?"

"Yes, sir, just around the next bend and off to the right, not far."

"What's happening around here? Anything interesting?"

"Ride very carefully, sir. A few days ago banditos with covered faces rode past our house in broad daylight."

"Vigilantes?"

He shrugged, not inclined to debate the difference between bandits and vigilantes. "They have many guns. They told my father to stay inside that day, to go nowhere or he would have great misfortune."

"Did you see smoke that day, like a barn on fire?"

"My father said not to talk about it."

I took off my hat to draw a sleeve across my face, saying nothing.

The little fellow hesitated while he watched me from the corners of his eyes, but he probably felt he could speak because this tall rider spoke his language so well and didn't look like a real gringo.

"We saw smoke, like you say. We were afraid to go see. Did a barn burn?"

"Yes. It belonged to the *norteamericano* named Mill. Your father is probably right. Be careful what you say to strangers. That is always wise."

The boy's expression saddened, so I added, "But a man tires of talking only to a mama goat all morning, no?" The dun loped ahead, and I turned to wave my hat. The boy returned the salute with the flash of a smile showing clearly in his small dark face.

I rode into Goliad, a sleepy little village, shortly past noon. With most of its Mexican citizens abed for siesta during the worst hours of the brutal Texas heat, the town looked almost empty. Giant oak trees shaded the town square and the scattered houses. Few places could look more peaceful.

Figuring the saloon was good for a cool beer and, maybe, some crackers and cheese, I tied the dun in the shade and pushed through the swinging doors. The broad-shouldered bartender eased the front legs of a straight-backed wooden chair to the floor and stepped behind the bar. The greasy spot behind his chair told of the hours he'd spent tilted against that wall.

"Got any cool beer?" I asked.

"Cool as a July noon in Texas."

"I'll try one."

"Indians and Mexicans go down to Pedro's. Got him a cantina down yonder aways in the trees. You'll probably have to wake him up."

"You about to pour me a beer?"

"Don't give me no trouble. I see how big you are, but the sheriff's office is just two doors down. All I got to do is holler."

"Which you going to do, holler or pour?"

"I'll pour." He grinned, swabbed his face with a gray towel, and reached for a glass mug. The doors swung inward again as three men eased into the shadowy room. "No need for me to holler. That's the sheriff right there."

Still grinning, he put the mug of beer carefully on the bar in front of me, stuck out his hand, and said, "I'm Charlie. Welcome to Goliad." My attention divided between him and the three newcomers, I fell for the oldest trick in the book. I took his hand and found mine trapped in an iron grip, pulling me half across the bar. A wicked blow to my head set me to seeing flashes of light. I barely saw the heavy glass mug in his left hand in time to lift a shoulder to deflect the second blow.

One of the other men lifted my .36 from its holster about the same time I stabbed fingers at Charlie's eyes. He screamed, ducked, and turned loose my right hand, but when I tried to spin away from the bar, a man on each side grabbed my arms and shoved me back against it. From behind me now,

Charlie smashed that mug into my skull with an explosive crack, filling my head with thunder. My knees buckled, but men on both sides kept me erect and pinned to the bar. Vaguely, I saw the mug, without its handle, bounce across the room and roll against the wall.

Dimly, I heard Charlie's voice. "Hardheadedest son of a bitch I ever saw. Did ya see that? Broke the damn mug." His huge form came vaulting over the bar, an amazingly nimble move for a man his size. "This is gonna be fun."

His first six or eight punches came from so far back I had time to duck or roll with them, but then he got tired of missing and aimed his roundhouse blows for the body. The men holding my arms were like dead weights, and hard as I fought, I couldn't shake them loose or get my back away from the bar. I tried kicking him away, but Charlie pounded my midsection till I had no wind left. My back jammed against the bar, I couldn't give with the blows, had to soak up their full force. Now, with my legs gone limp, the two on each side had to hold me up.

Charlie, streaming with sweat and gasping for breath, grabbed one of my arms and said, "Okay, I got him ready. Your turn, Dutch."

Dutch, a short, broad, dark man stepped into view, ran a finger across a heavy mustache over a broad smile, and started pounding my sagging head and body. With an unmoving target, he worked methodically, pacing himself, pausing after each blow to set himself for the next.

By now, I felt almost detached from it. I wondered if I was still going to be conscious when I died, but I must have passed out. I found myself on the floor, choking and blowing beer they'd thrown into my face. They might as well have stuffed burning matches up my broken and bleeding nose. The sting caused a flood of tears to spill from my burning eyes.

Charlie said, "Okay, get him up. It's your turn, Sully."

When they pulled me to my feet, I saw a slim man in a white shirt seated in a chair against the wall. Mostly, I remember a thin-lipped smile, pale blond hair plastered to his head, a meager little Vandyke beard, and the star pinned to his shirt pocket.

Then another man, full-bearded, stepped in front of me, and the pounding started again. I felt a grim contempt. An arm puncher, he wasted a lot of energy, didn't know how to get his weight behind his punches. Being too groggy, I suppose, to feel much pain, I watched him get winded, stop three or four times to wipe his sweating face with the towel, and finally quit.

Charlie said, "Jesus, this is hard work in this heat. I'm plumb wore out. Throw that son of a bitch out in the street."

I guess they did, but I didn't feel it. Later, I felt dirt under my cheek and wondered how long I'd been outside on the ground. Sweat rolled off me in streams, and panic gripped me. I felt sure a barn was burning around me, the fire taking away all the air. I was burning, but I couldn't move, couldn't breathe. Everything faded away again.

Next thing I knew Dutch asked, "Is he dead?"

Charlie's voice, "I don't know why, but he ain't. You can see him breathing if you look close. My hands are so sore, I can hardly hold this here mug of beer. Look how they swole up."

Dutch said, "It's getting dark. He's laid out in the sun all afternoon. We gonna just leave him there?"

"Naw, let him die and stink up some other place. Sully, go get that sorry-looking mustang over yonder. It must be his. It brought him to town, let it carry him off somewhere."

"He say who he was, Charlie?"

"Don't make a damn. The word I got was to look out for a tall Indian. Go over yonder and get that horse like I told you."

"He ain't no Indian."

"That don't make a damn neither."

I heard the scuffle of boots in the dirt departing and then returning accompanied by horse hooves.

"How you want to do it, Charlie? Tie him across the saddle?"

"Naw, tie his feet together under his nag." Charlie snickered, "But put him on backwards and pin this here on him."

"What's that?"

"Just a sign. Says, 'Vigilante lesson.' "

I set myself for it, but I still almost cried out when they lifted me. Lying face down in the dust of the street, the front side of me had turned into a solid cake of mud from sweating in the sun. Searing pain like I never felt before drove daggers through me. I dared not try to take a proper breath; it hurt too bad. I'd heard pain from broken ribs made a man want to stop breathing.

I also didn't dare try to open my eyes. If they saw that, they might take a notion to beat on me some more. They tied my hands behind me to the pommel of the saddle and ran a rope under the dun's belly to tie my feet. Somebody slapped the dun's rump, and he jumped to a gallop.

I thought that was more than I could stand, but when he slowed to a trot, the bouncing was inhuman torture. I figured that damned dun would kill me, and it would be finished. But that vicious, stupid beast slowed to a walk before I could die. Every step raked through me like another punch and gave yet another jerk to ropes gradually sawing off my hands and feet.

Pain held me rigid. But then I knew I'd been out again, because I awoke to pain worse than ever. I blinked at a black world. My neck cramped and fought to stay bent at an awkward angle, then popped like breaking bones when I raised my chin from my chest. Had I slept or passed out? Was it night, or were my eyes swollen shut? A glance upward showed me stars.

So it was night. I always liked the night and the stars. I liked the notion of being alone to die. Even a dying man has pride, and I wanted to be dead before anybody saw me like this.

Now, on top of it all, thirst hurt worse than all the rest. My dried-out throat hurt with every breath. I tried to work my tongue around to collect enough moisture to spit. Although my lips split and blood trickled down my chin, I couldn't spit. So, I would die with a mouth caked full of dried blood and mud. I would die a nauseated, sour-mouthed death.

My stomach spasmed, bringing an agonized groan and a spray of bile out of me at the same time. Now bitter bile mixed with blood and mud. Miserably, I pondered how nothing is so sour it can't get worse. Pity the poor man who is so dry he can neither swallow nor spit.

I tried moaning through my nose, so as not to hurt my throat, and it seemed to help for a while. Then, I felt a stab of fear. What if the dun took alarm from my noises and started to buck, or tried to run under a limb and knock me off, or rolled on me? My dry, swollen eyes blinked with surprise. A man feels himself blink very plainly when his eyes hurt as bad as mine did. Yeah, I thought, I'm surprised to be afraid the dun will kill me. Silly foolishness. Hell, a dying man should have lost all fear of being killed.

A whole new idea came to me. I changed my mind. Never mind that dying. I was hurt, but not dead yet, not dead yet, ha, ha. Charlie, sweaty-faced Charlie, maybe I'll find a way back. You too, mustached Dutch. You too, bearded Sully. I took a deep breath and damned the pain.

Most of all, I wanted that sheriff, the pleased watcher who didn't sweat a drop, just leaned back in his chair and enjoyed the show. My head swam with ecstasy as I dreamed how it would feel to twist the elegant, white-shirted, grinning sheriff's head, listening to the neck bones crack. I'd rub his pretty little beard and pat his pink cheeky-cheek-cheeks until his eyes bulged and set in a death stare. The others, one by one, would face me. No guns. Bare-handed. Each would face me for a whole afternoon and night, without water. One by one.

Thinking about that, I began to hum a happy tune through my nose. Had my throat not been so dry, I would have sung a merry song. But humming was good enough for a man with festive thoughts.

My chin bobbed against my chest and woke me again. Mustn't sleep. Mustn't pass out. The saddle might slip around under the dun's belly. I'd be dragged to a sure death. Must stay awake. Just hum my way along till a hand or a foot pulled off to set me free or somebody turned me loose.

Never should a human man have to endure a headache like mine. Pain ran down a neck stiff and creaky as a broken board when the pieces won't pull apart. Agony ran like searing, molten lead into eyes I couldn't bear the thought of opening.

My skull roared and popped with pressure, trying to explode. That'd be sweet relief. If I could just smash my head against something, bust it open, let the pain out. I forced my eyes open. Maybe the dun would walk close to a tree. Maybe I could swing my head out far enough to bash it open so the agony would ease.

The night was growing lighter. Dawn. I needed to look for somebody to turn me loose. Nobody in sight. Oh well. I just had to hum along awhile yet. No hurry. What song should I hum to meet the dawn? No, that was too hard. The same note over and over sounded fine, no need to make a better tune than that.

Somebody screamed, or somebody drove knives into my ears, right into the center of my head. Which? I puzzled on it until I felt hands on me. My eyes opened with animal cunning, just a tiny bit. If the dun had taken me back to town, I'd have to play dead, so I couldn't let them catch me peeping around.

Surely, I looked dead. If I held still, anybody but a fool would know damned well I was dead. I was dry as a mummy, so I was light as feathers. The ropes fell away, and I drifted gently to the ground. If a wind should come up, I'd have to grab a tree or no telling how far I might skitter along. I used to like the wind when I was alive, but now.

A gourd of cool water pressed against my lips. I took a mouthful and swished it around, then spat it out. I drank some, cleared my throat, and spat again. The gourd drifted back full again, so I drank till it was empty.

I lifted my hand and looked at it, a swollen and filthy claw, caked with dirt. Blood seeped from cruel grooves in the wrist below it, but it worked. I watched with wonder the way my fingers moved, fascinating, beautiful, alive.

Water poured onto my head, and somebody wiped my eyes gently with a wet cloth. I started to hum my one-note happy tune again, but water splashed hard into my face.

I looked up and stared, blinking through dribbles of water, and cleared my throat again.

My voice sounded just a bit hoarse when I said, "Hello, Grist Mill. Remember me?"

FIVE

I opened my eyes and studied rough-cut boards, not yet weathered gray. When my gaze wandered a bit, I found a pale patch of blue sky. I lifted my hand again and found it clean, bandages around the wrist. The fingers folded in gently and rubbed against the tip of the thumb. The skin felt paper thin and dry, sensitive and delicate. Curious, I lifted the other hand. It looked the same, clean, thin-skinned, dry, wrist bandaged. Then I held both up together and watched them for a while. I still lived, no question about it.

I turned my head to look when I heard a sweet, lilting voice. Cris sat in a rocking chair staring at me, her sewing across her lap, needle in hand.

She called, "Win, he's moving again. I may need you."

The dogtrot, that's where I was. I had it figured by the time Win walked into sight. He stopped beside her rocker and stood watching me.

"They like me better than you." My voice came out weak and hoarse, like a sleepy old man.

He stepped closer. "What's that?"

"They like me in Goliad. They just beat

me up. They didn't hang me like they did you. You got to learn to make friends."

He gave me an unsure grin and said, "Thank God. Welcome back, Milt. You sound like yourself again. We were afraid they'd beat you till they'd addled your brain. I never saw such knots on a man's head. You kept flopping around, trying to fight."

"Fight? Me?"

"Damn right. I almost had to tie you down to keep you from hurting yourself. We found a better way, though, by accident."

"How's that?"

"You'd get quiet when Cris sang to you."

Before I thought, I blurted, "The red witch put a spell on me."

But Cris smiled and said, "It almost worked that well. Win noticed you'd get still when I spoke, said a woman's voice must have made you feel safe. You seemed to relax when I'd talk to you. Then, when I ran out of things to say, I started singing. We found that worked best. You'd quit fussing for a while every time I'd start singing."

"Except for one time," Win said.

"That was the time he straightened your broken nose. She smiled and added, "You never opened your eyes. You just socked Win in the mouth."

My hands explored my face without finding anything familiar. Everything seemed soft, puffy, and sore.

"Feels like you got even."

"Come on now. You know I didn't hit you back," Win said.

I raised my head cautiously and looked at blue and black bruises all over my bare chest and stomach. My head fell back down quick, though, and I had an instant headache. I must have put on a pained expression, because Cris spoke quickly.

"Don't do that! Our home remedy book says that you probably have a concussion, maybe even a fractured skull. You stay flat, it says, or you'll cause yourself pain and, maybe, further injury."

"Too late. You should have told me before I did it. Now I'm going to die for sure. I'm thirsty. How am I going to drink while I'm flat on my back?"

"From a spoon. I can tilt a big spoon over your mouth," Cris said in her know-it-all tone.

"Can I have a drink before I die?"

She popped out of her rocker and came up with a great big spoon. She proved it would work, if a man had the patience to take about four drops at a time.

"How long am I going to have to stay flat?"

"Probably a week," Cris answered. She sounded pleased about it.

I've had lots of women go high-nosed at the sight of me. A man grows accustomed to that if he's rough about his dress and has long, narrow, dark features like mine. Some folks think they can see meanness or kindness in the shape or color of a man's face. Most times, though, folks relax after a while and judge a man by how he acts rather than how he looks. Cris took the prize for holding on to her strong dislike for no apparent reason.

"I think your book is wrong. Nobody in my family ever took to lazing around. Afternoon, is it? I been lying here all day?"

Cris said, "Yes. That sweet horse of yours came up to the house early this morning. He crept up here like he was walking on eggs."

"Did my revolver come back with me?"

Win said, "No."

"Rifle?"

"No."

"Knife?"

"No."

"I left here with a goodly sum of money, both mine and my brother's."

"They must have kept that too," Win said. "Everything's gone but your saddle."

"Where's my shirt?"

"Cris already washed your pants. I put 'em back on you. The shirt's clean and dry too, but she's still mending it."

We talked awhile more, but I drifted off to sleep again somewhere along the way. I guess I slept through supper, but that was a blessing. I couldn't have eaten anything, bad as my head was hurting. Sleep must have been what I needed most.

It turned out I was right, though, and Cris's book was wrong. I got up and walked a few steps that very night. Though my head was swimming and I wobbled a good bit, it didn't hurt me much. Not wanting to move me any more than necessary, they'd made up a pallet by doubling a cotton quilt on the floor of the dogtrot. Maybe it wasn't exactly a bed, but still, my mama taught me that was not a proper place to pee. I don't think Mama would have approved of Cris's flower garden either, but a man does the best he can.

In spite of the red demon's scolding, I got up the next morning and sat at the table while they ate breakfast. Cris put food in front of me, and I tried to eat, but couldn't. Didn't matter much. I didn't feel very hungry. Near as I could tell, every tooth in my head rode loose in its saddle, but none had broken off, so I hoped they'd tighten up again with time.

I drank a couple of cups of coffee, but I had to wait for it to cool to get it past my tender mouth and throat. My head started to hurt, so I retreated to the dogtrot, laid myself down, and went right to sleep again.

When she woke me for lunch, Cris had caught on that I couldn't chew. She mashed some beans with a fork to make a thick soup and chopped some greens till they were slick as pond scum. Mothers crush food to mush like that to feed their babies, but I never planned to have a woman do it for me. The grub was tasty enough, but my stomach felt undecided about it, so I didn't pack in much.

That evening, after I ate some more of Cris's baby food, she spun up a couple of eggs with a fork, poured them in a glass of fresh milk, and added a dollop of honey.

When she set the glass in front of me, I shook my head and said, "I never ate raw eggs before."

Cris replied, "I never before fixed something for a gentleman and had him refuse to eat it. You aren't eating enough. You need that." Her tone of voice and the way she came down on the word *gentleman* put me in a corner. She as much as said only a rude clod would refuse to drink that concoction.

My eyes cut over to Win, looking for some help, damn him, but he just sat rubbing his mouth and looking down at the table. A suspicious man would suspect he was covering a grin.

She hustled herself back over to the table, pretending to be helpful, and faked a sweet voice. "I cooled that milk in the well for you, but maybe you'd like me to warm it. Some like warm milk better."

"Can you cook eggs after pouring that

much milk on 'em?"

"Oh no, heavens no, I wouldn't try to cook that, but I'll warm it if you'd like."

Win got up and turned away to stare out the window. Seemed to me he held himself stiff, like a man trying not to laugh out loud.

"I'd admire to try that little idea sometime, ma'am. Maybe tomorrow or the day after?"

"It'll spoil. You know eggs won't keep once cracked."

"I'd be proud for you to have it then, ma'am. You like it, and I'm sure it's mighty fine. But me, now, I think about slick raw eggs, and, uh, well, why don't you just have that for yourself?"

"No, I made it for you."

Didn't seem to be any way to get around it, short of running from the room screaming, and I wasn't up to doing that, so I picked up that big glass and shuddered, couldn't help myself. "I never drank and chewed at the same time. I'm not sure I can do that."

"Just drink it." She'd gone harpy-voiced again. "There's nothing to chew, for heaven's sake. It's good for you, and it'll help you grow tall and strong like the big boys. If you don't drink it now, I'll make you sit in the corner till you do."

That little ball of red hair and meanness figured I couldn't handle it. I drank it fast as I could. My stomach, caught by surprise, tensed up and danced around for a minute, so I walked slowly outside to await the verdict. After some quivering and twitching with sweat pouring down my swollen face, I kept it down, which must have been a terrible disappointment to her.

She didn't know how tough I could be. Hell, once I had a chance to take stock, that concoction didn't taste too disagreeable. She'd think up something new and even more horrible if I let on I could handle raw eggs and milk, so I didn't see fit to mention that it wasn't all that disgusting after all.

The next morning, I felt pretty good, except for my nose and three broken ribs and a nagging headache. Actually, the nose didn't present any difficulty as long as nothing touched it, but having broken ribs must be about as painful as being gunshot. I did fine as long as I crept around like an old man, never took a deep breath, and didn't bend over.

If I bent forward to lace my leggings, my eyes tried to jump out, my face tried to fall off the front of my head, and my ribs drove a broad-bladed sword straight through me. I figured out a way that worked fine. I stayed on my back and scooted over where I could walk my feet up the wall to lift my legs above me to do the lacings.

Cris walked out the door and caught me in the middle of it. Her mouth fell open for an instant, of course. Then she laughed like a gaggle of blue jays and prissed back in the house with her hand over her mouth, giggling.

My teeth were beginning to steady up already, but I knew better than to clamp them together the way I sometimes do when irritated. I consoled myself by remembering that my skin must have been tougher than Win's; I had no cuts bad enough to call for stitching. Thank goodness she didn't get the pleasure of sewing on me.

After breakfast, instead of jumping up and going to work, Win leaned back in his chair and asked, "Your mind still fixed on riding to Louisiana as soon as you're able?"

"I been set upon and robbed," I answered. "A man wearing a star made himself comfortable and enjoyed watching it happen."

"Blond fellow, wears a little Vandyke beard?"

"That's what he looked like. Wears his hair slicked down."

"That has to be Sheriff Russ Mullins," Win said. "He's killed two men in Goliad since coming here three years ago, a year before Cris and I came."

I described Charlie, Dutch, and Sully, the other members of the Goliad Punch-a-Tall-Indian Committee.

Win nodded and said, "Charlie Buckner owns the saloon and general store. Keller

"Dutch" Horton is Russ Mullins's deputy. Sully's name is Kasper Sullivan. He runs the general store for Charlie Buckner."

"I'm honored," I said wanting to grin but knowing my scabbed-up lips wouldn't allow it. "It seems I was welcomed to Goliad by some of its most prominent citizens. They were watching for me, Win. I heard Charlie say they were looking for a tall Indian. Anybody else around here fit that description besides me?"

Win shook his head. "I think the ones who got me must have put out the word to look for you because you shot at them. You took a terrible beating for saving my life. Who else would do it and for what other reason? Do you know anybody around Goliad? Has anybody else around here even seen you before?"

"No, but I'm meeting people fast, people I like so well I feel obliged to visit with them again, soon's I feel up to go calling."

That misled Win about my intentions. He began to describe the situation around Goliad, how the honest men were caught in a vicious no-man's-land. On one side, outlaw vigilantes rode to settle their own scores and run small landowners and Mexicans off their rightful property. Stock was being stolen from everybody. On the other side stood corrupt carpetbagger law officers using every device to cheat honest men out of their property.

I knew the story, and I knew what Win

was leading up to. He was going to ask me to help fight the vigilantes.

Nearly every Southerner had to face the same conditions, I suppose, but I'd heard that Texans were having a worse time than most. All of that business held no interest for me. I owed a debt to a few men in Goliad, and I was raised to pay debts when due. That job done, my interest still lay in Louisiana. Nothing in Texas concerned me beyond teaching a few Texans not to gang up on Milton Baynes.

When I told Win, he looked disappointed and said, "You can't go after those men alone. But we could all help each other. I could get the honest ones together if I had somebody to watch after Cris while I'm riding. I don't dare leave her alone here after what's already happened."

"Not interested, Win. None of my affair. I have a personal score to settle, and that's all. I plan to take back what was taken from me, teach a few men a hard lesson, and ride on. Besides, I don't work with any group, not ever. I ride with my family or I ride alone."

Cris spoke quietly. "All those rumors about the Baynes clan from Louisiana must be lies. I believe you now, Mr. Baynes, if that's really your name. I believe you are not an outlaw. You don't have the courage. If you ever did, those men beat it out of you. I think you plan to ride straight away from here, and everything else is just empty talk."

"You're right about one thing, ma'am. I'm not an outlaw, and that goes for my family too. You're wrong about the other thing, though. It takes little courage to be an outlaw, if any at all. Outlaws spend their time running and hiding. I've seen 'em in singles and in bunches, and some are pretty good men who've had bad breaks. But I've never met one, not a single one, who claimed to be a hero. Most all of them try to creep up on their problems from behind rather than meet them square on."

"I think you are a coward, Mr. Baynes, a fumbling, awkward coward."

"That's enough!" Win Mill's voice did not rise, but the fury in it rang through the room. "Milt saved my life at the risk of his own. He's been savagely beaten for interfering. Furthermore, he's a guest in our home. You dishonor us both by speaking like you have."

She drew herself up and matched her brother's glare without flinching.

He turned from his sister to me and said, "I sincerely apologize for my sister's outburst, Milt. Women do not understand these affairs and should not be exposed to them. Most, at least, have the wit to remain quiet, but my sister is both willful and disturbed by recent events. I hope you can understand and sympathize.

"Relax, Win. Don't disturb yourself. Cris

66

took a strong dislike for me from the instant we met. Having me underfoot for so many days put a great strain on her at a bad time when she's worried about you. I'll be ready to ride shortly. It's a shame all your problems can't be solved so easily."

Cris turned her back and busied herself with the dishes. I stood and asked, "By the way, I need a piece of good rawhide about this big." I showed him the dimensions by hand motions. "Do you have something like that around the place somewhere?"

"Yes, of course."

"And a sharp knife," I added.

SIX

Maybe because he was so embarrassed, Win brought me a steer hide and a butcher knife before he did another thing that day, but my work went slow. As soon as I sank the board-stiff hide in the creek, weighted down with a couple of rocks, I wandered through the woods near the house till I found a fine oak branch.

Two different times, in the middle of carving the handle I wanted out of the branch, I found myself stopped, still as a statue, staring off into space. Both times I had no idea how long I'd been sitting there, asleep with my eyes open. At least, my mouth didn't fall open too, so I didn't drool down the front of my shirt. But lapses like that clearly signaled that something inside my head hadn't had time to heal. For the first time in my life, I worried about myself.

After supper, I sat in the dark, still whittling by feel on the handle I needed. Cris spoke only once, her voice impersonal in the darkness. "Why don't you rest? You were so tired you could hardly make it up from the woods to the house."

Ordinarily, I'd have made some smart comment, like how restful it is for a man to do work he really likes, but I wanted to avoid trouble with her until I could leave for good. I put down the knife and wood, without saying a thing, and laid myself down on my quilt. Nobody said another word that night.

Next morning, before first light, I took up my work again. I carved a smooth oval handle, two feet long, and just the right size to fit my hand. With the carving finished, I scraped the hide to remove the hair. After cutting out the brand, which always leaves a brittle spot in the skin, I covered the handle with wet rawhide, stitched tight. The hide would draw even tighter as it dried. One end I cut into strips to braid into a loop to go around my wrist. The other, I cut into longer strips which I braided into a strong but flexible whip, about a foot and a half long.

I found a nice round creek stone, about the size of my fist, and covered it, too, with stretched-tight rawhide. Next, I attached it to the end of the plaited whip. When finished, I had a pogamoggan, an Indian mace, a skull-crushing, bone-breaking war club that made a tomahawk look like a child's toy.

Sometimes Indians carried coup sticks, essentially ritual instruments, to touch an opponent and prove bravery without necessarily harming him. The pogamoggan had nothing to do with ceremony. No Indian picked one up unless he meant to maim or kill. To hit a man in the head with a pogamoggan without killing him took great skill. I proposed to see if I could do it, but I was ready to pardon myself if I swung too hard.

For nine days, I kept my mouth shut other than short answers when spoken to. Except for meals, I stayed away, sleeping in the woods. When we finished supper on the tenth day, I asked Win, "May I borrow the rifle that sack-head left behind?"

Surprised, he said, "Of course. It's yours anyway. You can have your handgun back too. Since they took your other one, I don't feel right about keeping it."

"No," I said. "I just want something temporary till I take back what's mine. I'll be riding on tonight. I want to borrow enough grub for a couple of weeks. It's a loan. I'll pay when I can. One more thing. I'd like to borrow a couple of scraps of paper to write on. If I could leave a pair of letters with you, I'd be obliged if you'd mail them for me next chance you have."

"Are you sure you're ready to travel, Milt? Louisiana is a long way from here." Win's voice sounded both sad and concerned.

"I still have things to do before heading for Louisiana. My thanks for looking after me all this time." I looked straight at Cris for the first time since she gave her opinion of me. "Thanks to both of you."

"You don't even have a hat," she said.

"Nothing to fuss about, ma'am. I'll be

70

doing all my riding at night anyway."

"Are you serious? Are you going back to Goliad to fight those men?" She sounded like she didn't believe it for a minute.

"I'm still not as strong as I'd like to be, so I'm going to take a few days to get to know the country around here first. Also, I need to let some time pass after I leave your place. Anybody comes looking for me, I don't want to leave behind any sign. If anybody asks, I got Win down from that rope, took him up to the house, untied you, and rode on. You haven't seen me before or since, and I didn't tell you my name. You two don't need to be involved in what's going to happen."

She sat leaning on the table with her chin on her fist, staring at me. "Nothing is going to happen. I don't believe you. You plan to ride bareback? I don't think you can lift your saddle by yourself."

Win cleared his throat, glanced at me, and said, "He already saddled the dun. I saw it waiting down in the woods."

"Then we'll never see him again if he goes to Goliad. It's nonsense. He knows those men will kill him this time. I still don't think he'll do it. He's neither that brave nor that foolish."

Win came to his feet and spoke sharply. "Cris . . . !"

I waved a hand to catch his attention and shook my head, stopping him. Then I winked at her.

"That's all right, Cris. I forgive you." I walked out to get the dun while she sat real still, strangely quiet. Win followed me out to give me writing paper, envelopes, and a pencil. When I rode up to the house half an hour later, Win handed up a heavy bag of food and the rifle I'd asked for. I shook his hand without dismounting.

Our handshake held for a long time. Neither of us said anything. Win never was all that much of a talker, and I had too much talent for saying the wrong thing. Finally, after our hands came apart, I gave him my letters, and rode on.

Cris stood in the door, but I took care not to look that direction. Whatever she gave me for food, I made up my mind to take it and gladly, but I'd heard enough of her voice to last a lifetime.

I took the whole two weeks and even a couple of days extra to explore the country around Goliad. Riding at night, I don't believe a soul saw or heard me. If I had to run, I felt content that I had found several routes to make good time and make any pursuer pay for the privilege if he came too close. If I had to hide, that country offered several isolated pockets where they'd have to hire an Indian tracker to trouble me. I stashed food in several places, living mostly on what I caught in snare traps.

The time had come for serious work, so

72

even though my ribs still gave a twinge once in a while, I decided to go to town and make my first call.

Dark shadows of dusk already hid the trunks of broad old oak trees as I rode into Goliad. I crossed a town square that lay empty and quiet, but light still spilled from the door and windows at the front of the saloon. I had lost track of the date, but it must have been August by then, so the hour was probably past nine o'clock.

Unnoticed in the near darkness, I passed by the saloon and saw my bearded friend, Sully, leaning on the bar talking to a grinning Charlie. Two men wearing cattlemen's garb, strangers to me, sat at one of the three tables playing cards, a bottle between them. Two horses stood hipshot at the hitching rail. I ground-reined the dun in the shadows beside the feed store next door and settled myself on a wooden box to wait.

The two cattlemen walked outside, mounted, and rode slowly away. I stood, stretched, cocked my borrowed rifle, and shifted it to my left hand, carrying it like a pistol. The pogamoggan slipped easily from my belt.

I eased up in the shadow beside the door just in time to hear, "Good night, Charlie. I got to go home and get some sleep. I hate this hot weather like poison. Even at night it don't get cool enough to sleep decent." My

73

timing approached perfection.

Charlie said, "Yeah and tomorrow always seems to come too early."

Footsteps approached the door, and I started the pogamoggan swinging in a slow circle, ready. I didn't intend to kill this man, so I had to hit with judicious, restrained force. Sully pushed aside the swinging door and met the stone with his forehead. His head jerked back sharply and stopped while his body kept moving forward. I had to grin at the way his feet walked out from under him. He made more noise when he hit the wooden boardwalk than a hundred pound potato sack dropped from the roof.

Charlie's hearty chuckle sounded right in the doorway. "What the hell, Sully, you walk out in the dark and bust your butt?"

I gambled and won. Charlie stuck his head out the door at almost exactly the spot I anticipated. The swinging stone met him squarely in the mouth, making a brittle crunch which raised gooseflesh on my neck. He toppled backward and his head bounced off the floor with a boom which seemed to echo from building to building.

After a quick glance around the deserted square, I dragged Sully inside, pulled his handgun from its holster and slipped it inside my belt, eased the solid door shut behind the swinging doors, latched it, and drew the shades over both front windows. A rapid check revealed that Charlie wore no gun.

Quickly, I laid my rifle and pogamoggan on the bar, stepped around it, flipped open the cash box, and upended the top drawer on the bar. Looked like less than a hundred dollars. I took the bills but left the coins, not wanting my pockets to jingle. A swift look along the open shelves, and there lay my Navy in my holster with my belt wrapped around it. That belt increased my enjoyment of the evening a thousandfold when it whipped around my waist. Habit took over and, first thing, I checked the loads in the Navy.

Sully lay like a dead man, but Charlie started to twitch. Keeping one eye on jerky Charlie, I scanned the area behind the bar one more time, and it was a good thing I did. In the bottom of the cash box, where it had been hidden by the top drawer, I spied my wallet. I slipped it into my pocket, not having time to check the contents because Charlie rolled over on his face.

I snatched the pogamoggan off the bar when I walked around it to tend to Charlie's needs. He rose unsteadily to his hands and knees. While he spat blood, saliva, and chunks of teeth on the floor, I dragged a chair off the top of a table where Charlie had upended it, evidently preparing to sweep the floor.

Seated, I asked, "Hey, Charlie, you awake?"

He looked up at me with glassy eyes and gave a vague, "Uh huh."

"That's good. You wouldn't want to miss this."

I stood up again to get a full swing. The stone struck his ribs on the right side with a gritty crunch. No fancy work went into that shot, no more holding back. I gave him full measure. He dropped face forward into his own blood and spit, twisting in agony. With no wind left in him, he could only make strained, wordless grunts.

"The way I figure it, Charlie, I should be able to break at least one rib per swing. What do you think?"

His face was toward me, cheek plastered to the floor, but he didn't raise his eyes to look at me. He wouldn't have seen me had his eyes been pointed my way. All his attention was focused inward, his body too filled with pain to leave room for any air.

Sully still lay unmoving. I bent over him and put an ear in front of his nose and mouth. I could hear his breath clearly.

Charlie began to gasp and moan, so I knew he was getting some air into tortured lungs at last. I jammed my foot in between his right arm and his body, kicked the arm up and out of the way, and struck the ribs of his right side again. An explosive grunt burst from him and he came to his knees, a frantic, unthinking burst of tormented energy.

The stone actually hummed on its way, this time to the ribs on the left. Charlie collapsed. His clenched fists fell open, wrists limp. I grabbed his arm and flipped him over onto his back.

"One more time on the left, Charlie."

The stone hummed again and struck with a crunching, sodden thud. I stepped over to take another look at Sully. He was sleeping through the whole party, and that didn't please me. The humming stone struck him once on the left, once on the right of his lower chest. He had to be truly unconscious. No conscious man, no creature of any kind, could take shots like those without giving some sign.

Satisfied that both men were unconscious, I trotted to the back door of the barroom and jerked it open. Darkness shrouded the narrow hallway, but I could make out two doorways obviously leading to other rooms and another that probably led outside. I hurried back behind the bar, grabbed a box of lucifers, and jogged down the dark hallway.

I jerked open the first door and struck a lucifer, revealing a small table with a coal-oil lamp on it standing beside a bed. Moving fast, I lighted the lamp and blew out the match. As soon as I straightened, my eye found a familiar shape. My rifle stood in the corner beside the bed. A quick grab and I ran back up the hall to the barroom.

Neither man had moved while I explored. Quickly, I checked my rifle. Charlie kept it clean, oiled, and loaded in my absence. Good old Charlie. I admired a man of good habits who looked after borrowed property just like it was his own.

I raced down the hall again, grabbed the lamp out of Charlie's bedroom, and jerked open the second door, a storeroom. Pogamoggan in my belt along with Sully's pistol, rifle in one hand, and lamp in the other, I began to feel cluttered up. A quick glance around the room revealed just what I needed. A coil of rope. I put the lamp on the floor, grabbed the rope, and got back to the barroom fast.

Charlie had curled up on his side, holding his arms around himself, eyes shut tight, his face a mask of pain. Blood and saliva rolled out of his slack mouth, past his crushed lips, and down into a spreading pool on the floor. Sully lay in the same place I'd left him, but he was stirring and trying to sit up, his eyes blinking stupidly.

When I kicked Charlie over onto his face and jerked his arms behind him, he came out with a weak, pitiful moan. Remembering my backward night ride with broken ribs, I knew how he felt and regretted I didn't have a horse to strap him onto. As soon as I had his hands and feet tied, I trussed the quiet, limp Sully too. Poor Sully couldn't stay awake; he'd passed out again.

Curious, I trotted back to the storeroom and looked around more carefully. Just when I reached for the lamp, a can caught my eye. Red paint. I stared at it for a few seconds before the idea took form. Paint can in hand, I took my time and walked back to the barroom.

Behind the bar again, I searched for something to pry the lid off that paint can. I couldn't see into the dark shelves very well, so I started sweeping the contents out on the floor. Among other things, out fell my Arkansas toothpick. Charlie had enjoyed my prior visit so much, he kept a bunch of souvenirs. My blade slipped into its old home just below my right knee, and I began to feel fully dressed again.

Among the other things which tumbled to the floor, I found a heavy spoon. I pried the lid off the paint can and walked over to Charlie. He closed his eyes and lay perfectly still while I poured paint into his hair, moving the can so as not to miss any spots. Sully, eyes open now but still blank, tossed his head and mumbled. Fearing I'd get paint in the man's eyes and blind him, I didn't get him covered as well as Charlie. Still, when that paint dried, they'd both have a hell of a good time trying to remove it. Half the paint remained in the can.

Another trip to the storeroom for a brush and I ended up staring at the big mirror behind the bar. After a bit of thought, I painted carefully, BAYNES COMEBACK. It pleased me to imagine people trying to figure if I meant to paint "comeback" or "come back" or even "came back." A little mystery would catch people's interest.

I searched through Sully's pockets, found a big key ring and a fat wallet. Both fit into my pockets nicely. The coal-oil lamps snuffed, I sat in darkness until my eyes adjusted before I opened the front door and surveyed the street. Goliad slept. I took the bucket outside and painted my little message across the front of the building twice, once on each side of the door. Painting began to grow tiresome, so I poured the remainder in Charlie's bed. Charlie gave pained grunts through his nose when I gagged him with a bar towel. Sully probably never felt it.

A short walk through the shadows brought me to Sully's general store. The third key I tried opened the lock on the back door. I found a big cloth bag, dropped in a smoked ham that smelled like heaven, a five- or six-pound chunk of cheese, a couple of tins of soda crackers, a few cans of beans, a few of peaches, a few of tomatoes, and two fresh boxes of .36 ammunition. Testing the weight of the bag, I flinched at the thought of what I almost forgot. I ground myself a couple of pounds of coffee.

I got almost to the back door before another thought hit me. I dropped the bag beside the door and turned back. I picked up a new Navy from a case with a glass top, tried several holsters and belts to get something that felt just exactly right. From the same case, I took a big, expensive-looking pair of binoculars along with a beautiful leather case and strap. After all, I didn't start any of this trouble, and I figured Sully and his friends owed me everything I'd lost or felt obliged to give away because of their meanness. A little bonus payment for my trouble seemed fair too.

While I was at it, I picked out a couple of wool blankets, new saddlebags, and a new wide-brimmed black hat. At the door, I paused to go over my mental shopping list one more time.

I went back yet again and picked up the broad, thick, square glass jar of hard candy. I just took the whole thing.

The mustang took one look at me staggering under the weight of that big old heavy, clanky bag full of stuff, carrying two rifles and wearing three pistols, and he bowed his neck. That damn horse spun around and got himself ready to kick my head off. He didn't take to the idea of carrying all that, but I bribed him. We left town at a dead-slow walk, both of us with a mouth full of hard candy.

SEVEN

I counted the money twice to make sure. My first call in Goliad restored a little over half the cash they had taken from me. The money left in my wallet, recovered from Charlie's cash box, came to exactly one quarter of what they had taken. That probably meant a four-way split. Sheriff Russ Mullins and Deputy Dutch Horton must have the rest of my cash, mine and my brother's.

My hope to draw the sheriff and his deputy out of town didn't pan out, even though I took pains to leave a clear trail. Probably, they hadn't paid attention to the dun's hoofprints, so they had no chance of picking out his sign among all the other tracks around town. Too bad. I guess I wanted things too easy. In town, they had advantages. In the countryside, they'd dance to my fiddler.

One bad thing — if they reasoned that I'd be back again, surprise wouldn't be so easy. They'd try to be ready next time. But that idea gave me a moment's pleasure. The thought of them jumping at every shadow put a grin on me. I enjoyed a good grin, now that my face had healed.

I ate good and slept the sleep of the virtuous for a couple of days, with one righteous eye open. The temptation to ride into town the very next night after my first visit plagued me for a while the first day out, but I had done some hard riding laying down a trail for them to follow, and I didn't want to go back to town on a tired horse. That line of thinking reminded me of the fine horses I'd seen on the Mill place.

Unlike most horsemen, I am a good walker and runner, always have been. A smart tracker can follow a horse trail almost anywhere, but a light-footed man wearing moccasins is the very devil to track over hard ground, especially if he's careful. If I couldn't approach the Mills's house on foot without leaving any sign, I deserved to have my toes shot off.

I decided to leave the dun at a safe distance and use a little of my recovered money to pay off my food debt to the Mills. If Win Mill agreed to leave a horse staked out every day where a man on the run could steal it, that'd be a convenience. He could easily pretend to be an injured party, victim of a horse thief.

Besides, I felt pretty good. My ribs hadn't given me a single twinge during my visit to Goliad. I had half my money back already, and my guns, plus a few extra. Hell, maybe I just wanted to spit in the red demon's eye one more time.

Windows lit like beacons surprised me, and the cluster of horses in front filled me with concern. Win had taken to my idea that sitting in the light was too dangerous, so I figured he must not be making the decisions in his own house. I circled cautiously, filled with dread at what might be going on inside.

Sure enough, a guard stood outside in the shadows, close to the horses. A real dimwit, the guard pulled hard on a cigar to make it easy for me to locate him, illuminating his face and all but blinding himself at the same time. As soon as I felt sure he was the sole guard, I watched him, waiting for a good chance. When his cigar went bright again, I stepped around the corner of the house, got behind him in about four steps, and tapped him lightly with the pogamoggan. I caught him before his knees hit the ground.

I pulled his pistol, stuck it under my belt, and ran my arm around his chest. Holding him in front of me, I pulled my Navy and stepped into the lighted doorway. Four men sat at the table with Win. Cris sat in her rocker beside the fireplace. All of them turned to look up at me, faces blank with surprise at the sound when I cocked my Navy.

"Are you all right, Win?" I asked.

"Why, yes, I . . ."

"Are these men friends?"

"Yes, they are."

I shoved. The guard, just regaining consciousness enough that I could feel him trying to straighten his legs, went tottering into the room. He reeled into one of the seated men, bounced against the table, and folded to a sitting position on the floor.

"Put out that damn light!" I snapped.

The lamp dimmed and died. The memory of the cocked weapon in my hand must have remained, though, because nobody spoke or moved.

"You must have killed all your enemies, Win," I said quietly.

His answer, a little slow coming, sounded sheepish. "They complained about sitting in the dark."

"I suggest, if these men are friends of yours, invite them outside."

Win spoke slowly and distinctly. "Gentlemen, may I suggest we step outside? Please step very carefully and make no foolish moves. This man will shoot, believe me."

One asked, "Are you all right, Wesley?"

"Yeah, I think I can make it. He sneaked up behind somehow and knocked the hell out of me. Got a knot on my head big as a turkey egg."

I stepped back into the dark shadows of the dogtrot, and the men walked out without further conversation. Once outside, Win asked, "Where are you?"

"Right in front of you. Nobody can see

85

anything at night after staring at a light. You silly bastards need a wet nurse."

"Gentlemen, I'd like to introduce Milton Baynes." Win sounded amused. He must have figured it was foolish to try to conceal his connection to me any longer.

A general sharp intake of breath told me the impact of my name on the group.

Then, one of them chuckled and asked, "You the Baynes that came back?"

"I am."

"I'm Bruce Cottingham. If you'll put that gun aside, I'd like to shake your hand." He took a step forward.

"You keep still, and I'll hold on to the gun, thank you. We can shake later, if we get to be friendly. Let's hear names for you other men." After a slight pause, the other men spoke in turn.

"Glenn Felix. Glad to meetcha."

"Jack Ross."

"Bill Lanmon. Howdy."

The last figure shifted his feet cautiously. "I'm Wesley Wilson. What did you hit me with?" He sounded like he was working up a good mad.

"Finger."

"How's that?"

"I thumped you with my finger."

A couple of the men snickered, and Cris, standing in the doorway, spoke for the first time. "Mr. Baynes has a rough sense of

86

humor, Mr. Wilson. That's his way of telling you that you're lucky, that he could just as easily have killed you."

I said gently, "You made it too easy, Wilson. You can't see much past a lighted cigar at night."

Cris asked, "Are you all right, Milt?"

"Yes, ma'am."

"Are you hungry or anything?"

"No, ma'am."

Win said, "These men are neighbors. I asked them to come here to see if we can figure out some way to protect ourselves."

"Some neighbors. I didn't see them when your barn burned."

Cottingham said, "I was trapped. A bunch of hooded men rode by my place that day. They said they'd sit watching with rifles in a grove of trees near my house. No way I could set foot outside without giving them a clear shot."

The others agreed, saying about the same thing happened to them.

Lanmon said, "We heard what happened to you. None of us was in town that day, but we heard several men wanted to help you. That damn sheriff warned them off, wouldn't let anybody get near you."

Wilson added, "Everybody in this part of the country has heard about Charlie and Sully by now too. That paint job you did on the front of the saloon attracted a lot of notice. One of the shades was pulled a little crooked, so the sheriff peeped through and saw Charlie lying on the floor." He stopped to snicker. "Made that damn sheriff turn pale as a ghost. He thought Charlie's head was blowed off."

Cottingham said solemnly, "Sheriff Mullins wants you, Baynes. That embarrassed him bad, you beating a couple of his friends half to death right in the middle of town."

Ross, a tall stooped figure in the darkness, asked bluntly, "Does you being here mean the Baynes clan has moved in?"

His tone sounded unfriendly, so I answered, "You find one Baynes, you're likely to find more." I didn't see how it would hurt anything if folks thought my whole family had taken a hand in local affairs.

Ross nodded. "Charlie said there was a bunch of you. Sully still ain't making good sense, last I heard. You ready to put that gun down yet? I'm tired of standing stiff as a post."

"Not yet. Win, I'd like a chance to talk to you and your sister. Let's just take a short walk."

"Why don't you stay?" Win asked. "We could use your help."

"None of my affair," I answered. Then I had another thought. "Two things you men need to understand. First, I was robbed and beat up in the middle of town. You know about that. I'd ride on right now except I have unfinished business with those who did it. The other thing is, the Mills helped me, so I owe a debt. If anybody bothers them, I'll make that my business too. You can tell whoever you think might be interested."

"We could work together," Win insisted.

"I won't deal with these men. I'm surprised you'd let them on your property," I said. "They all admitted they were afraid to step out their door while your barn burned. How will they act the next time something happens?"

A shocked silence fell for a second or two. I said, "Now, you men just step out in the moonlight."

They moved off the dogtrot into the open, and the lanky Ross said, "You talk rough when you're holding a gun on people, Baynes."

I eased down the hammer of the Navy, slipped it into the holster, and stepped out of the shadows. "Move away from the others and say that again."

Win called, "Stop! Don't you move, Jack Ross. He'll kill you and forget you before breakfast."

Cris ran out into the moonlight and stood between me and the group of men. Facing me, she said in a low voice, "Milt Baynes, behave yourself." She called over her shoulder, "Come along, Win. Mr. Baynes is leaving, and he wanted a word with us."

I walked the short distance to the woods, leading them in a direction away from my dun. Both stood silently while I listened for a couple of minutes. Then I whispered, "You do what you think best, Win. I been riding around looking things over. Draw out the same map you made in the dirt that day when we talked about the lay of the land. Take another look at it. All four of those men would give their right arm to have your place. One of them most likely tried to hang you."

When he didn't answer, I went on, "This is for feeding and looking after me."

Startled, he said, "This feels like money." He tried to hand it back to me and protested, "This is nonsense, absolute nonsense." He stopped, confused when he felt me press the heavy little box of ammunition against him.

"Those are to feed into the Navy I gave you. A man needs to keep plenty of extras handy if he's practicing like he ought."

I turned to Cris and said, "And this is for you."

"What? For me? What is it?" Curious as a chipmunk, she untied the string at the top and stuck her hand into the small bag.

"Win, could you stake out a horse on that little meadow with the white rock in it? I might need one someday, and I don't want to come too close to the house."

Without hesitation, he said, "I know the place. I'll put one out there every day, starting tomorrow morning."

I pulled the pistol from under my belt. "Give this back to Wilson. Tell him I'm sorry about the bump on his head."

Win chuckled. "That'll make him feel a lot better, I bet."

"Thanks. Adios." I moved away into the pitch-black shadows.

Cris called out softly in the darkness, "Be careful, Milt."

I like to move slow in the night, and I needed to circle back around them to get to my dun, so the comments they made came to me clearly, even though they spoke in whispers.

Win said, "I don't feel right about taking money from him, but what could I do?"

Cris laughed and said, "Wasn't it wonderful, the way he told off that stupid Jack Ross? Look at this, Win. He's the first man to bring me candy. Isn't that sweet?"

"I don't know. Let's see."

"Oh no you don't. That's mine." I heard a swat and a little scuffle. Then they walked back toward the house, laughing together.

EIGHT

The next day, shots brought me awake. Quiet and careful as a snake in a hogpen, I slid off my blanket, threw my saddle on the dun, and readied myself for fast travel. After the burst of firing which brought an end to my siesta, the hot, sticky afternoon settled into an ominous, brooding stillness.

The shooting hadn't been close. My guess was about a mile, but estimates aren't too good when you're jerked from a sound sleep. Clearly, somebody else was the target, but I had no doubt the target was people. Shots from a hunter don't come in clusters. Besides, even while only half awake and far away from the source, I felt pretty sure I'd recognized pistol shots.

Riding only at night and never sleeping in the same camp twice, I felt mighty exposed now, in the bright light of day. So, I stayed back from the edge of my stand of woods and settled down to watch. Sweat dripping from my chin although I sat in the shade, not moving except to breathe. The August sun in Texas can melt an iron bar.

If the sheriff or the vigilantes wanted me, they had no chance unless they figured out some kind of trap. I know how good I am on the trail, and I circled back many a time to make double sure. Nobody had tried to follow me. They didn't have a clue where I was. Their only hope was to draw me in somehow.

Thus I didn't really feel surprised when I saw skimpy traces of smoke. The sight of smoke brought me to the Mill place once. Maybe they figured it would bring me again. This time, it looked like it came from the Lanmon property. Lanmon had no barn, just a sod house, a corral, and a flimsy shed where he parked an old wagon and kept a few tools out of the weather. However, he'd been cutting wood and stacking it next to his shed. Still green, that woodpile would produce enough smoke to see from my distance.

Win told me about him when I asked about his neighbors. A wounded Confederate soldier who came home with empty pockets to find his wife and child half starved, he had started promptly to brand his wandering cattle and put his life back together. He was the only one to act friendly and pass the time of day with Win. All the others around Goliad saw Win as a damn Yankee, so they cut him dead or treated him with cold formality.

According to Win, Lanmon still couldn't afford hired help, but he held title to over ten thousand acres of prime pasture with good water and didn't owe anybody a dime.

Like almost every other Texas cattleman of the time, he had only a general idea how many cattle he owned.

The silence dragged on through the windless afternoon. Lanmon, I figured, needed no help or was beyond it. More shots might have got me curious enough to sneak closer, but the only thing making noise was grasshoppers.

I planned for Goliad to receive a visit from me again tomorrow night, and Lanmon's place was along my line of travel as I worked my way closer to town. At dusk, I decided to ride the dun about half the mile or so to Lanmon's, leaving him at a new place. My hopes rose at the thought they had laid a trap for me. I'd turn it back on them. If these Texans could trap me at night, with me on foot and alert, Milton Baynes would die from shame before they could kill him.

Heading straight toward his destination provides a clue a hunted man should never provide a tracker. So I had the dun walk in a direction well off to the left of a direct route toward Lanmon's place. After I slid from the saddle, I tied him on a long line so he'd have plenty of room to graze. That's another thing a hunted man does, keep his horse fed and rested whenever he can.

The smell of smoke lay heavy in the night air. I circled the place twice, gradually moving closer. A trap or ambush would, most likely, be laid for a man approaching directly toward the house. By making ever smaller circles and edging closer, I had a good chance to come at the trap from an unexpected direction. This cautious approach burns a lot of time and energy, but I had plenty of both. One more go-round and I stood on the edge of the clearing in which the sod house stood. It had to be past midnight.

My guesswork proved to be correct, but no pleasure came to me from it. The shed had vanished, leaving a bed of coals winking in the night through a cover of ashes. The woodpile, a mass of smoldering green wood, looked about half burned. The corral seemed like I remembered it from observing the place during my night rides around the country, but in the moonlight I could see the sod roof of the house had buckled in the center.

Part of the roof sagged while I watched, and a thin puff of smoke came out the doorless opening in front. Like many another poor settler, Lanmon made do with a cowhide hung across his doorway, waiting for more prosperous or leisurely times to get himself a wooden door.

I was fairly sure the woods around the house stood empty, but old age is often denied those who settle for being fairly sure. So, I took one more tour around the clearing. The crudest kind of trap that could be set would be to wait at the edge of the woods and shoot at anybody who walked out into the open. To my way of thinking, nothing could be cruder than these damned Texans.

They played it smart, so they almost got me. Luck saved me. Pure luck. I stopped when I heard a horse stamp and shake his head. Otherwise, I might have stepped right on top of them. In the deep shadows cast by the trees, the two of them must have taken turns on watch. The one backed against a tree leaned forward. Standing like a statue and looking exactly in the right direction, I saw the move.

My heart nearly stopped. I stood only about six feet away, frozen, knowing my next move might be my last. One lay wrapped in a blanket, half under a bush. The other sat with his back to a tree, rifle across his knees.

The one sitting by the tree touched the other and whispered, "Can you watch for a little bit? I caught myself dozing off." I knew that voice.

The other one threw back the blanket, stretched, and sat up. I used that bit of bustle to cover my move. Again, I was lucky. Only a half step put me behind a tree.

Peeping around it, I whispered, "Cris, don't shoot. It's Milt."

The figure against the tree wheeled toward

me, and it sounded like a cannon roaring in those quiet woods, but it was only Cris cocking that damned rifle.

"██████damn it, Cris, don't you shoot at me." My hat must have been six inches above my head, perched on hair standing straight up like porcupine quills. I drew myself up and tried to get skinny as a pencil behind my tree.

"Milt?"

"Yeah, it's Milt. Uncock the damn rifle, for God's sake. I'll not be shot by a nervy red-headed woman. Uncock that damn thing right now."

"How? How do you do that?"

"Oh Jesus. Win, are you awake yet?"

"Yeah."

"Get that rifle away from her before she blows my head off."

"All right. I have it." Win sounded amused.

"Milt, where are you?" Cris squeaked like a scared little girl.

I peeped around the tree again. Both of them knelt facing me, but I couldn't see the rifle.

"You got that damned rifle, Win?"

"Yeah."

"I'm behind a tree. If I step out and you let her shoot me, I'll whip your ass. I swear I will, Win. Word of honor."

Cris came out with a relieved giggle and whispered, "Oh Win, it really is him. Nobody

97

could fake his crazy talk." I heard the rustle of her skirt when she came to her feet. She ran past my tree and stopped, peering around. "Where are you?"

"Behind you."

She wheeled around, found me, and grabbed me with both arms. Her head against my chest, she hugged me with remarkable strength, giving me a flicker of worry about my ribs.

"Thank heaven you're here. This is the most horrible thing I've ever seen."

I stood there with my rifle in one hand, pogamoggan in the other, and Cris plastered to me, feeling as comfortable as a trapped rabbit.

She shuddered, face still against my chest, and asked, "Have you seen them yet?"

"Haven't been closer than this to the house. What's happened?"

Win came up behind Cris to stand so close I could have touched him. He whispered, "We saw smoke. Lanmon was the only one who agreed we ought to come to each other at any sign of trouble, so I came here as soon as we saw smoke. I brought Cris, unfortunately, since I was afraid to leave her at home by herself. We were too late. Someone set the place on fire and shot Lanmon, his wife, and their six-year-old daughter."

"All dead?"

"Oh Milt, they were shot to pieces," Cris said. "They even shot that little baby girl three or four times." She stepped away from me, pulled a handkerchief from somewhere, and dabbed at her eyes.

Win continued his whisper. "Looked like four horses to me, but I'm no tracker. The Lanmons were all lined up in front of the house, like they'd been shot by a firing squad. With the war over, I thought I'd never have to look at that kind of thing again."

"Where are they now?" I asked.

"I moved them into the shade of that old tree close to the house and covered them with one of our blankets. We just got here about an hour before dark. We didn't even take time to bring food with us."

"I have ham and cheese on my horse. He's close by. I'll go get you a bite to eat."

Cris shuddered and said, "I can't eat, not now, not here." Win said, "I'll ride to town tomorrow. Should be back with the sheriff before nightfall. Can you take Cris home and look after her until I get back?"

I nodded, realized he probably couldn't see that in the dark, and whispered, "Yes, I'll do that. You think going for the sheriff will do any good?"

He hesitated for a second before he answered bitterly, "If he does anything, it'll be the first time, but I don't know what else to do. This is the first time a whole family has been killed. Maybe he'll do something about this."

"All right. Cris, get your horse. I'll take you home now."

Cris asked, "Aren't you tired? It must be three o'clock in the morning."

"No, ma'am. I ride at night and sleep days. Wait a minute. I changed my mind." I turned to Win and said, "I want to take a look at those tracks in good light, so we'll wait for morning before we leave. I'll go get my horse. You can head for town as soon as I come back. If you do, you might get the sheriff back here by about noon with a burying party."

Win, his whisper dead serious, said, "That means I'll have to leave you alone with Cris. Will you be all right?"

NINE

Cris still lay curled asleep on her blanket when I started scouting around in the early morning light. Win called it right. Yesterday, four horsemen had ridden together to and from the Lanmon place. From the look of it, they rode up, called the family together, and shot them down in front of the house. Simple. Easy.

No way to tell for sure, but my bet was the whole family was caught so surprised none had even tried to run. They thought the killers were friends. Lanmon wore no weapon and none lay near where the family had fallen, so he'd either been caught outside unarmed when the riders arrived or they'd carried his guns away with them.

The riders left no clear boot prints on the hard-packed ground; they must have wasted no time, doing everything from the saddle except setting the sod house afire. The interior was still thick with trapped smoke, and the roof sagged pitifully, so I didn't try to go inside. Sod houses didn't look from the outside like fire would be a hazard, but every one I'd been inside had wooden corner posts, wooden slats supporting the sod roof, furniture, clothing, and other stuff that burned.

I spent an hour or so puzzling out the story as best it could be read from the ground. One set of prints matched those I'd seen after cutting Win Mill loose from a tree. This bunch must be the same, or at least connected, with the one which almost killed Win and later put out the word that got me a beating in town. If so, they were turning meaner.

They beat Win and let him hang from a rope. I couldn't say they weren't just trying to scare him. No telling what they planned before I ran them off. They might have intended to cut him down before he died. Charlie's remark in town indicated they'd put out the word to look for me. When they got me, like Win, they just beat me up. Maybe they stopped short of beating me to death on purpose, just intending to scare me and run me out of the country.

None of this made good clear sense. Could all this be the work of one gang, getting meaner by the day? Or, maybe two different gangs, one trying to scare people by treating them rough while the other was willing to kill. It's a big jump when a gang takes to killing. It's another big jump when they start killing women and children.

Lots of men talk tough about killing, but most of them wilt and back away when it comes to doing it. Most men would kill in self-defense. Only a few, hardened by the war perhaps, would kill in anger or to protect property. But it took a different kind of person to kill in cold blood. Most, even the most cold-blooded, would draw back from killing women and children. The killers of the Lanmon family were no better than mad dogs.

Cris had saddled her horse and had coffee ready when I came back from my scouting. Ham sizzled in my skillet over a tiny fire of dry twigs. Her little fire put out no smoke, none, and I caught her eyeing me when I took notice, expecting me to comment. I said nothing, not wanting to give her the satisfaction. My vicious mustang stood behind her like a sullen guard, giving me villainous looks while I poured myself some coffee.

She glanced at me, set the skillet off the fire, and asked, "Find anything?"

"One of the horses they rode was at your place when Win had his trouble."

Pointing at the cooling ham, she said, "This is yours. I went ahead and ate while I was waiting for you. That's the smallest skillet I ever used."

"No need for a big old heavy one, just cooking for one. Mostly, I cook on the end of a green stick. No need to wash a stick."

"Then why carry a skillet at all?"

"Sometimes I can't find a stick."

I stuffed the ham into my face, ignoring her wrinkled-nose expression of disgust, and after testing it with a finger to be sure it had cooled enough, jammed the unwashed skillet into my saddlebag. After scuffing out all clear prints the dun had left and swallowing my one-big-bite breakfast, I motioned toward her mount. Cris caught the signal and came right over, and I hoisted her into the sidesaddle.

"I never thought to ask before. What do you call this nice horse of yours?" she asked as I cautiously mounted.

"Judas."

"That's a terrible name for him."

"He's a mean, treacherous, tricky, stubborn, harebrained fool. It's a good name. Warns people what he's like."

"He's sweet as a lamb."

We had only moved about ten steps when I reined to a stop, looked her in the eye, and said flatly, "Look, I don't like to ride around these parts in the daylight. Half the damn Texans around here are meaner than Comanches. Not meaning to be rude, ma'am, but here's the way I want to do this. We don't say a thing to each other, not a thing, unless we see something dangerous. Anybody we see is dangerous. I like to see people first, and I don't like for them to see me at all. Hear me?"

She nodded, putting on a patient expression.

"If we ride into trouble, you do what I tell you, and you do it quick. I got neither the time nor the patience to argue with you while some damn bunch of Texans is trying to kill me. You understand that?"

She said quietly, "I agree."

All set for a big squabble, I sat looking at her, feeling like I'd stepped into a hole in the dark. I managed a lame, "You do? Uh, well, let's get along then."

Turned out, she did fine. Whenever I'd stop to look around, she'd stop too, without being told, and she didn't say a single word. We came in sight of her house about noon. I motioned her to stay hidden in some trees while I scouted the house, and she never moved till I waved her in.

When she rode up, I helped her dismount, and she said, "Come in. I'll fix something to eat."

"I don't think Win would take it kindly, me sitting around in the house alone with his spinster sister. I'll just stay out here, ma'am. I can see better."

She spun on me and snapped, "I'm no spinster. I'm not old enough."

I shrugged. "How old you need to be?"

"Seventy-five or eighty. I'm only nineteen."

"You get to be twenty, folks call you a spinster." I showed her a grin. She knew I had truth on my side.

"I'll be a married woman by then."

"Oh, you got somebody in mind?"

"Certainly."

"Who? I haven't seen anybody come around courting."

"Oh? I didn't realize you've been watching."

"Wait, now, I didn't say that."

"What did you say?"

"I said I better put the horses in that half-built new barn of yours."

Cris said, "You do that," and flounced into the house.

I went ahead and stripped the gear from her mount, stared at the dun for a moment, but decided to leave him saddled. After a while, she brought steaks out on the dogtrot and called me to eat. I carried my new binoculars with me.

She glanced at me about halfway through the meal and said, "Your manners have improved since this morning, thank goodness."

"House manners for the house," I answered, lifting one shoulder, "and trail manners for the trail."

She surprised me again when she nodded and said, "Makes sense." Pointing at my binoculars, she asked, "Will you show me how to use those?"

"Sure. Simple. First thing, the two telescopes have a hinge in the middle. Adjust that hinge until you have a single image. The telescope on the right adjusts. You turn the little wheel until the image is sharp. That's all there is to it."

"Let me see." She stuck out her hand for

the binoculars, so I passed them to her. She adjusted them and looked around for a while.

"Sometimes, if the sun is real bright, like it is now, you can see better if you block out the light by putting your thumbs up beside your eyes, like this." I showed her.

She looked around for quite a while before she glanced up at me. "This is fun, but what good do they do you?"

It seemed such a dumb question, I hesitated to answer, fearing she was about to spring something on me. But she waited me out, so I said, "You can see better from far away. They're a big help when you want to see but not be seen."

Impatiently, she waved off my answer. "No, no. I know that. That's obvious. But you ride mostly at night."

"Oh, I see. They help at night too. They magnify light. Say, it's a moonlit night, and I see something coming about a hundred yards away. If I use the binoculars, I can probably tell it's a man on a horse, what kind of hat he's wearing, if he's carrying a rifle, stuff like that."

"Really?"

"Sure."

"Milt." Her voice had gone tense. "I see dust. Maybe somebody's coming." She handed the binoculars back. "Look a little above that bunch of bushes and a little to the right. People ride that trail when they come from town."

I looked, but saw nothing. Handing the binoculars back to her, I said, "Keep looking." I trotted to the barn, pulled my rifle off the dun, and hurried back. "See anything more?"

Cris said, "I'm not sure. Maybe Win didn't go back to the Lanmon place with the sheriff. Maybe he's coming straight home."

"Maybe. Whoever it is, if they come up to the house, you stand out here and call them by name when you say hello. Act as natural as you can. If you don't know them, ask who they are so I'll know they're strangers. I'll stay inside by the window. You stay on the dogtrot real close to the door. If it's trouble, you jump inside quick as a rabbit and get down flat on the floor."

She had her eyes glued to the binoculars and didn't answer.

"You hear me?"

A wave of the hand as if to tell me to shut up and she said, "Yes, yes, I'll do it. I can see two men now. You look."

I shook my head. "You're doing fine. Tell me how they act and how close they come. I got to watch all around to make sure others don't come at us from another direction."

She looked up at me with the sweetest smile a man ever saw and said, "I'm sorry, Milt."

"What? What're you talking about?"

"I'm sorry I said you weren't an outlaw.

You really are, aren't you? Gosh, I'm glad you rode to my house that day." Before I could move, she stretched up and kissed me on the cheek. Then she went back to looking through the binoculars.

I stood there blinking for a moment, like a duck that's been hit on the head with a spoon. Then I sputtered, "You aren't scared at all, are you?"

She shook her head. "No, not while you're here. Can I have a gun too?"

"Hell no. This is no game. This is serious business."

"Men have all the fun."

"Fun? Are you all right, Cris?"

"Did you look at Mrs. Lanmon's body?" She never glanced at me, keeping her attention on the approaching men, but her voice had gone hard.

"No."

"If you had, Milt, this would be fun for you too. They shot that sweet little woman four times. Go inside now and get by your window. They're only about three hundred yards off, but the trees are in the way. I still can't tell who they are."

I stepped into the front room, pulled the little cushion from Cris's rocker, and settled myself on one knee beside the open window. No need to be uncomfortable if it can be avoided.

Cris's voice was crisp, hard. "One hundred

yards. One is Dutch Horton, that awful Sheriff Mullins's deputy. I've never seen the other before. You ready?"

"Yes, ma'am."

As long as I took care, I felt sure the slanting sun on the flimsy curtains allowed me to look outside without being seen against the shadowy background in the room. Cris stepped inside, gently placed the binoculars on the floor by the door, and ducked outside again.

"Good afternoon, gentlemen," she said, cool as a deep well.

Horton never answered, just swung off his horse and stood with his hands on his hips, grinning under his mustache. The other man swung off too, showing tobacco-stained teeth in a big smile. He said, "This is gonna be more fun than that Lanmon job."

Cris said, "Did you see my brother? He rode to town to see the sheriff."

"Yeah, we got him in jail," Horton answered.

"In jail? What for?"

"For murderin' the Lanmons. And while he's there, somebody's gonna burn this place, and you're gonna disappear. We'll just say folks was mad at your brother for what he done, and you probably ran off somewhere."

"Ran off?"

"Yep. After we're through with you." The man with brown teeth chortled and walked forward.

Cris, her voice suddenly tremulous, jumped through the door, crouched down, and said, "Milt?" She sounded like she was afraid I wasn't still there.

I rapped the windowsill with my rifle barrel and said, "Howdy, boys."

Horton went for his gun, and Tobacco Teeth went for his horse. That made everything work out nice. Horton was so slow I couldn't believe it. He was so sure he was just dealing with a helpless woman he hadn't even loosened the thong over his handgun. I took my time, aiming at the tag hanging from his shirt pocket. The force of the bullet knocked him back a step. His handgun, just clearing leather, spun out of his hand to fall about six feet away in the dust. He took another step back and leaned against the hitching rail.

Tobacco Teeth hit the saddle with one jump and spurred around the corner of the house. I walked out to the dogtrot, stepped down to the ground, walked to the corner, leaned against the wall to steady myself, and took careful aim. Sure enough, leaning far forward and urging his horse to greater speed, he swung his head to the side and looked back. I shot him in the face. He hit the ground hard and slid quite a distance, made a big cloud of dust.

"Why did you wait so long?" Cris asked. I looked down to find her standing beside me.

"Didn't I tell you to stay in the house?"

"I asked you first. Why did you wait?"

"Didn't want him shooting at the house with you in it. He only had a handgun, no rifle. So I let him get out of handgun range. He was going pretty fast. A hundred yards wasn't such a long wait."

"Did you really think about all that with things happening so fast?"

"Once Dutch Horton was out of it, there was no hurry. That other fellow was a runner, could tell by looking at him."

"How?"

"Eyes. Did you see his eyes when I rapped the windowsill?"

"You know I couldn't see anything. You made me hide on the floor."

"Oh yeah, that's right. Well, anyhow, his eyes told me. Once Horton got his, the fight was over. That other fellow was so dumb he rode straight away. A ten-year-old ought to know to dodge around."

"You walked right in front of Horton. Weren't you afraid he'd pick up his gun and shoot you?"

"Men shot where he got his don't pick up anything. They just fall down and contemplate."

"How could you be so sure?"

"I aimed at that tag hanging from his shirt pocket."

She walked to Horton's body. He'd fallen

on his back. She leaned over, plucked the tobacco sack from his pocket, and brought it to me. The rounded nick at one end of the tag told the story.

"He stood real still, and I had lots of time," I said modestly.

"None of this bothers you, does it, Milt?"

"No, ma'am. I feel right good about it."

"You know what?"

"No, ma'am. What?"

"If you had told me this just one day ago, I'd have felt insulted and would've thought you were crazy."

"Told you what?"

"That this wouldn't bother me either. I feel good about it too. You hear me, Milt? I feel good! They beat you and Win up, but men beat each other up from time to time. I've seen how men act. But when they killed that poor Mrs. Lanmon, it did something to me. I think I understand now about hate and vengeance."

"Slow down, Cris. Those feelings can get you into a lot of trouble."

"Really?"

"Yes, ma'am, the Bible is full of it."

"You warn me about revenge? You? Why are you still here? And why were you going to Louisiana in the first place?"

TEN

I let it pass. Some things a man has coming to him when he starts giving others advice.

She didn't pursue it either. "Let's go get Win out of jail."

"Just like that?"

"Of course. We can do it. We need to move fast. No telling what they may be doing to him."

To tell the truth, I felt a bit droopy. The sun blazed from a cloudless sky, making everything in the distance wobble and waver behind heat waves. I had to stop and think about when I slept last. The ache behind my eyes told me I needed rest. Out of habit I rubbed a hand across my ribs. That part of me felt sound, but the rest of me felt tired.

I said, "What do you mean 'we'? If I took on such a job, I'd do it alone."

"You going to leave me here all by myself?"

I dodged the question. "Where can Win go if I get him loose?"

"We can hide out with you till this gets straightened out."

"Look, Cris, none of this is going to get straightened out. That dead fellow roasting in the sun in front of your house was a deputy sheriff. You and I know he was crooked and rotten, but that won't help."

She nodded and stood quietly for a moment before she said, "They'll kill my brother. We've got to take him and go away from here, go somewhere else to live."

I said, "You think on it. I'm going to clean things up."

Tobacco Teeth's horse took me a little time to round up, since he'd trotted on quite a distance after his rider fell off. I had to trail him for about two miles before I found him standing under a shade tree. Having seen his sign twice before, once at Win's hanging and once at the Lanmon place, tracking him presented no problem. After I brought the horse back and tied the dead man across the saddle, I led him over to Horton's body.

Horton's mount dozed peacefully, still standing at the hitching rail in front of the house. While I stood over Horton's body and counted the money from his pockets, I noticed Cris's questioning expression.

"This brings me up to a little over three quarters of the money taken from me. Maybe I'll find the rest if I see the sheriff tonight. I need writing paper and a pencil."

She went in the house and brought them to me.

I wrote, "Crooked lawman. Baynes is still here," on one sheet, folded it carefully, and put it in the dead deputy's shirt pocket. I did the same thing for the unknown man, except I left off the part about crooked lawman and wrote "woman killer" instead.

Cris shaded her eyes so she could look up at me. "You sure you want to put your name on those?"

"Fits my public reputation around here, ma'am."

"What good does it do?"

"What harm?"

"I thought you were trying to clear your name."

"That seems like a long time ago, Cris. Besides, maybe this is the best way to do it. The good folks in a small town like Goliad probably know who the bad ones are. I might be making a few friends and not even know it yet."

While I gathered up dead bodies, Cris packed what she wanted for herself and Win. I had to catch two more of Win's horses, one for him to ride and one to serve as a packhorse for the stuff I knew she'd insist on bringing. For once, I got a lucky break. When I checked to see if Win had staked out a mount for me, I found he had, and a friend had joined him, so I picked up the two horses I needed with one trip.

She was ready to go before I was. By the time I got back with the horses for Win, she'd already been to the barn, put the saddle back on her mount, turned the milk

116

cow loose, and opened the door to let out the chickens.

I waited quietly while she looked at the house. Her expression took me back a few years. As a boy, I'd had to ride away from the home where I was born, leaving my mother in a freshly dug grave, putting my boyhood behind forever. We'd left dead men in the front yard of my home, men who had come to force me and my brothers into a war we didn't want to fight. At least, she hadn't been obliged to kill anybody. I'd done that part for her.

I tried to think of something, anything, to say, but I finally decided to leave her alone while she took a last look. There comes a time when the only comfort a person can seek must come from within. Finally, she lifted her reins and turned her horse toward me, sitting small but straight in the saddle. She didn't speak, but I knew she was ready to go.

We rode slowly to save the horses in the heat, taking the long way to town through the woods both to stay out of the sun and to try to avoid being seen.

Cris spoke in almost a whisper. "I know you don't like to talk, but do you have a plan? Will you tell me how to help?"

"I been pondering it. Maybe we can draw the sheriff away from the jail. Suppose we slipped up to the saloon with those two

117

bodies and tied the horses in front. As soon as somebody comes out of the saloon or walks by and sees those two dead men, he's bound to run for the sheriff. We can hide near the jail, get Win out, and run for it before the sheriff knows we're up to anything."

"Good. I wouldn't have thought of that, but what if we can't find the keys? What if he's hired somebody else to watch the jail while his deputy's out?"

"We'll hang a rope on a door or window or whatever and pull the place apart. If somebody else is there, we'll give him a choice."

"What choice?"

"Stand aside or fall aside."

"Oh."

"Oh, what?"

"Oh, that seems simple enough. What do you want me to do?"

"Stay out of the way. Don't give me any trouble. Let me forget you're even there. You shouldn't be."

"Wouldn't it be better to try to catch the sheriff by surprise? Hold him up? Then you could make him give you the keys. You could tie and gag him. Maybe nobody would know the difference till in the morning. That would give us all night to ride and get a lead on him if he comes after us."

"Great idea," I said sarcastically. "How do you think we can surprise him so easy? If I knock on that jail door, he'll open the door

118

and stick a gun in my face."

"Suppose I knocked and pleaded to see my brother. I think he might be surprised to hear my voice. I bet he'd open the door and not be so cautious as with a man."

"Maybe, but that puts you right in the line of fire if anything goes wrong." I thought awhile. "I still have the keys to the store. Suppose they haven't changed the locks. I might find some blasting powder in the store and use it on the jail to blow the front door in. Then I might get the drop on him while he's still shocked from the blast."

"Oh Milt," she chortled, "that's priceless! Let's do it that way. Please. That's a real Baynes breakout. People will be telling the story for years. That's wonderful."

"Woman, you're crazy. What happened to your idea of getting a big head start before anybody found out?"

"I wasn't thinking about it being night. They can't trail us in the dark anyway, can they?"

"Blowing that door open will wake the whole town. Somebody might shoot at us when we ride out."

Cris's eyes were dancing and she squirmed in the saddle with excitement. "It's worth it. It's wonderful. Please, let's do it that way."

I found myself grinning at her in spite of myself. "It does have a certain, uh, elegance."

She laughed until she swayed in the saddle.

"Perfect. The invisible Milton Baynes. Then, boom! And he's gone again. It fits you, Milt."

We rode into town about ten o'clock, walking the horses quietly through the dust. I asked Cris to stand at the back door of the store and hold the horses. When I tried the key, the lock opened without even a click. The way it turned out, I took half an hour fumbling around in the dark finding the powder and another ten minutes locating the fuses and punk sticks.

Then I had to turn up proper containers, which nearly wore me out until I settled on some nice big tobacco tins. By the time I walked out of that store, I must have lost ten pounds of nervous sweat. Luckily, I'd watched powder charges set when my family did some mining in Montana Territory, so I knew how to do it.

I figured one container would take the front door right off that jail, but Cris suggested that I prepare six, just in case. I was so nervy at the long delay, I did it without protest, sitting on the back step of the store, knowing damn well she'd start an argument right in the middle of everything if I didn't.

While I did my work preparing powder, Cris "went shopping" in the building and came out with a big sack of God knows what. I tried to stop her, but she skipped around me quick as a squirrel, and I couldn't afford to chase her around all over the damn place. That crazed woman scampered around making a lark out of the whole thing and a nervous jelly out of me.

When I stepped back inside to hide the flare of a lucifer to light a punk stick, she whispered from the door, "Light me one too."

"What for?"

"In case yours goes out."

Once again, the quick way was to avoid an argument. She was perfectly capable of starting a nattering contest on the spot, so I lit two and handed her the second when I walked out to the horses. She waited stubbornly beside her horse when I jumped into the saddle. I had to dismount to give her a boost. Shaking my head, I climbed on again. What a hell of a time to insist on dumb little courtesies. She could mount unassisted easy as pie. I'd seen her do it, the little red devil.

Once again, Goliad slept in darkness except for the light spilling from the saloon door and windows. Half a dozen horses dozed at the hitching rail in front. I dismounted and, holding cans of powder in each hand and the smoking punk stick in my mouth, examined the jail door. It was solid wood, made to swing inward, and had no knob or handle on the outside. Probably, a heavy bar secured that door on the inside.

I couldn't afford a failure, so I carefully

held both fuses to the punk stick to light them at the same time, wedged a can into each corner at the bottom of the door, and ran around the corner of the building.

The double blast shook Goliad, with the sound of shattering glass following the explosions. I hesitated a second or two, not being absolutely sure if both cans of powder had blown, and having no taste for running up to the second when it went. Then I darted around the corner and felt my way through a hanging cloud of dust and smoke to a doorless entrance. I jumped through the empty doorway and stepped to the side. The interior was dark as the devil's ambition and smelled like he'd just visited.

Crouched against the wall, desperately trying to see in the darkness and smoke, I heard gritty boot soles scuff on the floor and a half-strangled cough. A shadow appeared so close in the doorway I could have touched it with my fingertips. As quick as I ever moved in my life, I shifted my Navy to my left hand, slid the pogamoggan from my belt, and tapped the shadow. The stone didn't land solidly, but the shadow dropped, falling half through the door into the moonlight. The sheriff lay still, his thin blond hair shining in the pale light.

"Win?" I stepped aside quickly, half expecting a shot to answer my voice.

"Yeah." His voice sounded far away.

"Anybody here but the sheriff?"

"No."

"Good." I stepped into the doorway and snatched the sheriff's gun from where I'd heard it hit the floor. "Where are you?"

"Come straight in from the door to a flight of stairs. I'm in a cellar."

"Where are the keys?"

A flash of light flickered through the door and another blast from down the street shook the building. Men shouted frantically and horses screamed and plunged. I could only hope and pray crazy Cris didn't blow herself to kingdom come.

Win yelled, "I don't know. Look for a desk. I think I heard them drop the keys into a drawer and slam it shut."

A few cautious steps in the thick darkness brought me up against something. I felt around, knocking a tin cup rattling to the floor. A glass lamp toppled to the floor with a splintering crash, but I had to be fast, not quiet. Groping, I found a knob on the other side, pulled open a drawer, and heard a metallic clink. My hand fell on a key ring as if I'd been able to see it. I walked toward the sound of Win's voice, sliding my moccasins through broken glass until I found the top step.

I felt my way down the stairs. Darkness this thick scared me. A man can always see when he's outside, but inside a windowless cellar, there's no light at all. He kept talking to guide me. He extended his arms through the bars, and I walked blindly right into them. He guided my hands to the lock on the barred door, and I had him out with the second key I tried.

"Hang on to my belt and stay behind me, Win. If I have to shoot, I got to know where you are."

He answered, "Let me guide you by pulling you around with me then, as soon as we get back up the stairs. I know where Mullins put my guns, and I want 'em back."

The open doorway let in enough light to let me breathe better when we reached the top of the stairs. Win jerked me around while he collected his rifle, found the Navy I had given him, and even located his hat.

He chuckled. "Your blast woke me up, and I had a suspicion. I rolled out and pulled my boots on."

As if he'd called for it, another blast rocked the street outside.

"Here we go," I said. "Cris is with me, holding the horses, I hope, if she's not too busy blowing up the town."

We stepped past the sheriff. Since he was up on his hands and knees, I gave him another friendly tap with the stone, just to rest his mind. Quicker than an honest man might think possible, I patted his pockets and came up with what felt like a money clip.

Then I muttered, "What the hell," kicked him over onto his back, and whacked him a couple of humming good shots to the chest with the pogamoggan. "Sorry you slept through that, you bastard."

As soon as we stepped out into the street, Cris came riding up leading our animals, and I thought I saw a trail of sparks flitter through the jail door. Sure enough, we'd hardly ridden thirty yards before the jail rocked and glass tinkled again. I looked back and noticed the saloon front had collapsed. The roof of the porch had fallen, blocking the front door and windows.

Another trail of sparks went over my head and bounced a couple of times in the middle of the street. I looked straight ahead and heeled the dun into a gallop. A moment later, another lightning-like flash came. The heavy boom rocked Goliad again, but I heard no glass falling after the blast. Maybe all the windows in town had already been shattered. When I glanced back the last time, the whole town had vanished, lost in a pall of dust and powder smoke.

We moved along at a gallop for a while before I reined the mustang back to a calm walk. Win and Cris slowed when I did. We rocked along without saying anything for a while.

Win finally asked, "Who's your partner, Milt?"

I took my first look at Cris in the moonlight. Her face hidden in the shadow of a man's hat, she rode along wearing a man's shirt over her blouse, a gun belt around her waist. The handgun dwarfed her, hanging down about knee level from a belt she could wrap around herself twice. On her, the revolver looked so big it needed wheels. She rode along, looking straight forward, but I'd have bet my last cup of coffee she had her eyes cut over at me and that she was grinning like a possum.

I shrugged and said, "That's Red Plague, general store thief, powder monkey, and jailbreak expert."

Win leaned in the saddle and stuck out his hand. "Glad to meet you, Mr. Plague."

Cris gave a muffled titter and shook his hand.

"No offense, Mr. Plague, but you giggle like my little sister."

Win turned back to me and said, "Thanks, Milt. Mullins sat down and told me he'd made a mistake. He said he should have shot me right away, but he put it off because too many people were around. Cool as you please, he said I was going to try to escape as soon as his deputy got back, and they were going to have to shoot me in the back."

Cris said, "Milt shot Dutch and another man in front of our house. He tied them on their saddles, and we led their horses into

126

town with us. I imagine someone's found them by now."

"Killed them both?" Win sounded like he'd been offered a surprise dessert after a good meal.

"Graveyard dead," I said flatly. "They were rude to Plague there. I hate rudeness. I hate it almost as bad as talking too much when riding through dangerous country at night."

That killed the conversation for a goodly spell.

ELEVEN

I finally broke the silence in the coolness of predawn. "You did some quick thinking last night, Win. You were mighty steady in a tight spot."

He shrugged and balled a fist in frustration. "I've been puzzling on it all night. What's an innocent man supposed to do when a crooked sheriff accuses him of murder, throws him into a cell, and threatens to kill him?"

I answered, "Break jail, wallop the sheriff, and blow up half the town."

He chuckled, tipped back his hat, and ran a hand across his forehead. Win and the red demon both looked hollow-eyed and bleak in the early morning light, but they perked up now and put on grins. Some people find it depressing to ride most of the night in complete silence, even without having murder and jailbreaking charges to weigh down the spirit.

Win said grimly, "I didn't do anything. You and Cris did all that stuff. It seemed a good idea last night, especially after Sheriff Mullins told me exactly how and when he intended to shoot me. I didn't expect to live out the night. But now what? I can't just go home and forget it. They'll be after me."

"Who?" I asked. "The sheriff won't feel like forking a horse for a while, and he's lost his deputy. Who else thinks you're guilty or even gives a damn?"

Cris said, "It's not fair. There ought to be someone we could go to, a judge or somebody."

I said, "Maybe that's something we ought to consider. From what Win says, the sheriff wasn't planning to fool with a trial. He figured to shoot your brother, ma'am. He also figured his deputy would put you out of the way, and that would be the end of it."

She shuddered. "Before you shot him, that man with Dutch said something. I forget exactly what it was, but he said he'd enjoy this more than the Lanmon job, or something like that. He as much as said he was there when they were killed."

"His horse was, ma'am."

"What?"

"His horse came to Win's hanging and to the killing of the Lanmon family. That was the first thing I noticed when I had to run the animal down after shooting that fellow. You ought to pay more attention to tracks, ma'am."

"I leave that to tall skinny men who look and smell like wild Indians. Besides, my name is Cris. You ma'am me to death. I know you do it to irritate me. Will you please stop that?"

Win slowed his horse and swung behind her to the other side. She now rode in the middle. He stretched and yawned before saying in a relieved tone, "Ah, that's better. I hate getting between you two when you fight, and you fight all the time. Let's see, now, where were you? Oh yeah, Cris, you just fired a good shot." Then he grinned and squeaked in a high voice, "I know you do it to irritate me. Will you please stop that?" He scratched his belly contentedly and said, "It's your turn, I think, Milt."

I didn't hesitate. "I'll never say ma'am to you again, never, never, never. I promise."

"Thank you."

"Now that's just plain mean."

"What?"

"If a man said thank you to me in that tone of voice, I'd thump his head."

Cris drew a deep breath and said, "I'll never say thank you to you again, never, never, never. I promise."

I threw up my hands. "Hopeless. You're all thorns and poison, a spinster gone sour."

"Win, make him stop that. That's the second time he's called me that awful name. I'm not a spinster, am I?"

"When was the first time?" he asked, slick as a lawyer, dodging her question.

"He wouldn't even come in the house yesterday for lunch. He said you wouldn't like his being alone with your spinster sister."

Win nodded slowly. "Yep. He was right. I'd have to shoot him unless he married you."

I said, "You'd have to shoot me."

She turned to look squarely at me, eyes wide in a tired little face, and I swear she looked hurt, but she turned away quickly. Her voice brought Montana winter to Texas when she said, "We better talk about what we're going to do next, don't you think?"

"Not yet," I said. "I want to talk about something else first."

Both of them gave me a questioning look.

"I want to talk about jokes that go sour. I was joking a minute ago, just making fun. Now I think I need to ask a brave little lady to remember I was just teasing."

"I do believe you're trying to apologize." Her face softened just a bit, it seemed to me, but she rode looking straight down the road.

"Yes, ma'am. Uh oh, that one slipped out."

"I'll just bet it did. So much for your promises."

"Ease up, Cris. I know you don't think much of me, but there's no need to keep grinding it in."

"You don't know anything about my likes and dislikes, nothing at all."

"Of course not. You call everybody names like blockhead and coward, right?"

I couldn't tell whether her face flushed or it was a trick of the brightening dawn light.

"I didn't know you then. I know better now."

"Is that an apology?"

"Yes."

"Oh." My throat stuck. I couldn't think of a single damn thing to say.

Win said, "Time out. I judge this round to be even, so it's a good time to quit. Let's have a truce. I'm tired near to death of both of you. We got all the enemies we need without fighting amongst ourselves. Shake hands on it, you two."

I stuck out my hand, but Cris reined her horse close, grabbed a fistful of my shirt, and pulled me toward her. Again, I found myself surprised at how strong she was. I got tugged halfway off my saddle.

She kissed me on the cheek and said, "God bless you for breaking my brother out of jail. I think you're brave and wonderful." Then, catching me still surprised and off balance, she pushed me away so hard I nearly went off the other side of my mustang.

Blinking, I shot a glance at Win, but he was rubbing the back of his neck and staring off in the opposite direction.

Cris straightened in the saddle, stretched, and yawned out loud before she said in a smug voice, "I'm not about to shake hands with a big, dusty, sweaty man who stinks of gunpowder."

I said, "No need. We got us a truce. No doubt about it." We made camp in the best place I'd found during my nights of wandering around Goliad. Trees gave protection from the withering Texas sun, and we had water. Most important, nobody could come up on us without being seen. If a posse did come at us, we had a choice of two good covered routes to get away.

Win claimed he was the most rested of the three of us, so he took the first watch. Cris took over from him and didn't wake me, so I slept like a dead man for over eight hours. The afternoon heat baked me dry or I might have slept till dark. It was a toss-up whether a parched throat or the smell of coffee brought me awake.

I rolled out, buckled on both Navies, took a slow, careful look around, dug into my saddlebags for a piece of hard candy, cautiously approached the dun, fed him the sweet, backed off quickly before he could kick at me, marched off into the trees to pee, went to the creek, washed my shirt and shaved, and put the shirt back on without wringing the water from it.

When I approached the tiny fire, I lifted a hand in wordless greeting to Win. He replied the same way. Cris poured coffee and handed me the cup. She sat staring at me until I got irritated and asked, "What's it now? I didn't say a single word yet, so I couldn't have said anything to make you mad. What did I do? Whatever it was, I'm sorry."

"I'm not mad. Are you all right? No head-ache?"

I sat cross-legged to sip my coffee and considered.

"No headache, thanks, not for several days now. How did you know about that?"

"The book said you'd probably have them, and they might be terribly painful. I didn't want you to ride away when you did. You have the awful habit of sneaking off to hide when you're in pain. You nearly drove me crazy when you insisted on going back to Goliad, and I knew you weren't well yet."

Solemnly, I nodded. "I got the impression you weren't happy with me. Just a feeling, I suppose." I allowed the sharp edge of annoyance to creep into my voice. "Surely, it couldn't have been anything you said."

She spooned grits from a small pot onto a tin plate, added ham from the skillet beside the fire, and handed it to me.

"Milt, I don't have the feeling anything I say makes any difference to you. You just ignore me, so I end up saying mean things, hoping to get you to pay attention. Do you think all women are stupid, or is it just me?"

I sat there chewing ham and grits. Win squatted on his heels, watching me with a challenging little half smile. I took a deep breath, swallowed, and put my plate aside, so angry my hands shook. "My mother came from a rich, aristocratic family in New Orleans. She taught me and my brothers everything except how to handle guns and horses. Pa did that. She taught us to read, write, and speak Spanish and French as well as English. She taught us to read the best books in all three of her languages. She taught us mathematics, science, proper dress and manners, everything. No, Cris, I'm not the man to think of women as stupid creatures, not with the mother I had. I was reared to respect women. I did not realize my conduct had fallen so low as to allow doubt about that."

I knew damned well Cris and Win could see my hands shaking, and a muscle near my eye went crazy and started twitching. Any fool knows better than to blurt out that kind of long speech at people. Few things can be as embarrassing as knowing you have made a perfect dolt of yourself, bleating out things best kept private.

Quickly coming to my feet, I muttered, "Pardon me. I seem to have been taken by a babbling seizure. I guess I'm not awake yet. Please excuse me."

Cris came to her feet with me, again surprising me with her quickness. "Let's walk together. Excuse us, Win." She latched on to my arm before I could avoid it. I would have given a hundred dollars to jerk loose and walk away, but she'd hang on like a tick, and trying to shake her loose would only make a maddening situation worse.

We walked about twenty steps into the trees, and I said grimly, "There's no place to walk out here except through thorny black-berry bushes. I just wanted to get away a minute to get myself collected and stop chat-tering like an idiot."

"You never sound like an idiot, never. I'm the one with that problem. I never meant to imply you aren't a gentleman." She pulled me to a stop. "You must believe that."

I shrugged and looked away.

"You started out filling me with such terror I couldn't think. The first time I ever saw you, you crept into the house holding a gun, looking like walking death. I thought you'd come to kill me. Then, before I could catch my breath, you brought Win up from the woods. He looked like he was dying, and that scared me out of my wits again. Be-sides, I've never been around a really hand-some man before. You made me feel so awkward and homely, it caused me to act mean and foolish. I knew if I tried to be nice to you, you'd laugh at me. You laugh at everything."

I looked down at her and found myself staring into strangely compelling and attrac-tive gray eyes which bored into mine with a blazing intensity.

"Are you saying you like me, Cris?"

Her face rigid, she said, "Don't you dare laugh at me. Please don't." Her gaze dropped. "Try not to."

"I'm not about to laugh. I'm trying to get myself adjusted. I thought you washed the floor every place I set foot, like I was a mangy dog."

"That's nonsense," she snapped. "You . . ."

I put a warning finger about an inch from her nose. She stopped speaking at once.

"Don't bark at me or I'll go right to the top of the closest tree."

She gave a little grin and looked away.

"And no more cursing me. I hate that."

"I do not curse," she said, fiery hot, looking like I'd slapped her.

"Blockhead, bonehead, coward — those are pretty good curse words, enough to cause a shooting if you were a man."

"I already said I was sorry about that."

"An 'I'm sorry' never stopped any bleeding nor raised any dead."

"I'm not inclined to use such language," she said loftily. Then she poked an accusing finger at me like a small caliber, pink gun barrel. "It's your manner that sets me off. It's your fault, the way you look past me when I'm talking, like I'm not even there, or you look smugly amused, insufferably patient, like I'm a braying jackass. I hate that."

"I never did any such thing, but I won't do

it anymore." She chuckled and shook her head. "Nobody else could twist a denial and a confession into such a tidy mess."

I stuck out my hand. "Truce?"

Cris looked disgusted.

"What then, armistice?"

She struck my hand aside and stepped close, her face uplifted. "Alliance."

A few moments later, side by side, we walked back toward our tiny fire. I whispered, "No man would ever laugh at you."

Her answer came back with a squeeze on my arm. "As long as you don't, that's all that matters."

Win looked me straight in the eye, and I figured it best to lay out my cards in plain sight. I said bluntly, "Cris and I have come to an understanding."

He nodded. "I guessed that."

"You did?"

He shrugged. "Two walked away, one dry, one with a wet shirt. Two came back, both wet, one pink as a rose."

I started to speak, but he held up a hand to stop me, his left one. He went on, "You been honest with me, just like I expected, so I'll be honest with you."

"Honest about what?"

"I was watching. She's my little sister, you know."

"Well, I'll be damned."

He nodded again. "Yeah, that's probably

so." He came to his feet, shook my hand, kissed Cris on the nose, and continued, "Let's get saddled. I want to take Mr. Plague farther away from Goliad. Let's head over toward Victoria where it's safer."

TWELVE

Win led, circling and backtracking so much I soon lost a sense of our primary direction. Since I didn't particularly care where we went as long as we put a goodly distance between us and Goliad, I just relaxed and followed along. We traveled slowly in the darkness and stopped before dawn. Again, we found shade trees and water.

Cris rode mighty well, but few women are hardened to sleeping on the ground and spending whole nights on horseback. After we made camp and ate, she said, "I'm going to wash up," and walked stiffly to the creek bank. Win and I shifted our seats without comment to face the other direction while she splashed around in the water.

"You sleepy?" Win asked.

"Not yet."

"Let's do some talking."

I nodded.

"What do you plan to do next, Milt?"

"My money's back in my pocket, plus a little extra. I got my guns back, plus a few more. The men who set upon me have been repaid in kind. I'm even with everybody. Seems to me my business around Goliad is finished."

"You fixing to ride to Louisiana?"

140

His question hung in the air while I took my time thinking about it. "Can't seem to decide."

He nodded and rubbed his finger along the side of his nose, saying nothing.

"You've been a friend to me," I said. "Seems lowdown and shiftless to ride away when things are going so bad for a friend."

He shook his head, a barely noticeable movement. "You aren't obliged to me. It's the other way around."

"Maybe, but it's troublesome to me. I've taken an interest in that water bug splashing around behind us. That's a new problem that kind of jumped up all of a sudden. I don't know what it means yet, and I haven't got myself used to it."

Cris, in the water only about a dozen feet behind us, spoke sharply, "So I'm a problem to you, am I?"

Without turning my head, I said quietly, "Three things, Cris. First, if you use that tone of voice to me again, I promise to ride off and never come back. Second, my mama taught me it was rude if I didn't look at people when they spoke to me. If you open your mouth again, you better have clothes on. Third, this here is a tough problem for me. Don't say another word, just hush up and keep quiet unless you can say something helpful."

Win cut his eyes at me without moving his head. We both sat through a long silence. Even the splashing stopped. Then he widened his eyes into a look of astonishment, winked at me, and put on a crooked grin.

After a good long wait, I went on as if she couldn't hear. "My thinking about everything is all tangled up. This little understanding between me and Cris may not come to much, but I take it serious. That means this trouble of yours is almost a family matter. Up to now, I figured things were either family connected or not, but this falls somewhere in between."

Win said quietly, "Looking ahead, no matter what you and Cris decide to do, you can't take me to raise just because of my sister. I got to plow my own field."

"Agreed. Seems to me you have no chance back in Goliad. You willing to ride away? There are lots of pretty places in this country, places where a man can make a living and not worry about lawmen. Maybe you ought to come to Louisiana with me."

"I already let them run me out of Kansas. Running can get to be a bad habit. Seems to me you're headed straight at big trouble in Louisiana yourself, so we might not gain a thing by riding in that direction. Besides, I sank everything I had into buying my place."

"If you liked it enough to buy it, somebody else might too."

"I don't want to sell out, and I don't want to run. I want to clear my name and be left alone."

"You think there's a chance to beat that sheriff?"

"Not if I don't try."

Cris joined us, combing water out of her hair. I felt drops hit me, but it happened two or three times before I caught on she was flipping them from her comb at me on purpose.

Win continued. "Cullen Baker, Bob Lee, and some other men in east Texas have been trying to fight back. Some folks say those boys are just plain outlaws. Others say they're good men and would settle down quiet as foxes if they got an honest shake. They have to live on the dodge for now, hoping for a decent chance when the Reb-hating military leaves. But none of them has to take a little sister along."

I shook my head. "No future in it. Besides, those boys have advantages. They're all ex-Rebs. East Texas is full of their friends. They grew up there. I hear Bob Lee comes from a well-known and respected family. The same folks who help them would take pleasure shooting at you. You're just another damn Yankee."

Win cocked an eye at me. "What are you?"

"I'm even worse. I'm a southern-born nigger lover. My family helped slaves escape before the war. My pa is a Unionist and an abolitionist. But we rode west to stay out of the fighting, so even the Yankees see us as yellow-bellied traitors."

Win spoke cautiously. "Yeah, with those beliefs, seems you would have been comfortable wearing the blue with me during the war."

I nodded. "Except my pa didn't believe a war was the way to settle the question. He figured both sides were in the wrong, and being on the wrong side in a shooting war is a hell of a place to be."

He shook his head gravely. "Sons and fathers argued bitterly about it all over the country. Brother fought brother. Lots of families split over that war."

"Not mine," I said shortly. "My mama won't allow it."

He lifted his head and blinked. "That's a surprise. I thought your mother had passed on."

"Makes no difference. She left a mark that can't be rubbed out." I flipped a hand impatiently to dismiss the subject.

Win caught the signal and moved on to other matters. "We're out of Goliad County, so Sheriff Mullins has no authority here. We crossed into Victoria County last night. Our uncle lives close to Victoria town, the county seat. He was married to our mother's sister."

"Was?"

"Yeah, she died eight or ten years ago. Anyway, he's got property north of Victoria. We stayed with him when I was looking for a place of my own. Maybe he might have some

144

ideas. At least I think Cris will be safe there for a while."

"Is he another Yankee?"

Win grinned sardonically. "No, he's a special kind of Reb, I guess, but he wasn't in the fight. He liked the Republic of Texas best. I think he lost interest in politics when Texas joined the Union in the first place. He's an old-timer, served under General Sam Houston. That's how he got his start, from a land grant to veterans of the Army of Texas."

"Does anybody back in Goliad know he's kin to you?"

"Don't remember mentioning it. Folks around Goliad don't invite ex-Yankee soldiers to talk much."

"How much farther to his place?"

"Maybe ten or fifteen miles. We've gone the most roundabout route I could figure, Goliad to Victoria through Canada." Win rubbed sweat from his face and gave me a sarcastic grin. "I figured that would please you."

I glanced at Cris. "We'd best rest the horses today. We can start after midnight and get there in the morning."

"I saw that look," Cris said. "You're trying to say I need rest, not the horses. I feel fine, Milt. We can be there before the hot part of the day if you want to ride on in."

She'd caught me fair and square, so I

145

nodded. "Yeah, you got me. I figured to use you as an excuse to stop here for a while. Fact is, crossing a county line doesn't make me feel safe. I have my own way of doing things when I think somebody's after me. Most of the time it's easier to outsmart people than outrun them. It's foolish to run the horses ragged, and I'd rather have time to scout our back trail. Besides, we don't want to bring trouble to your uncle's front door."

"Win lets me talk to him when he's deciding what we ought to do. You plan to threaten to ride off every time I open my mouth?"

"Seemed to me you were trying to start an argument over nothing. I find it hard to think when folks bite at me. I got irritated and made a dumb remark. I take it back."

"I didn't feel like a problem to you when I fed you water from a spoon."

"All right, I made two dumb remarks. I take back both of them."

"No more threats?"

"No more threats."

Win asked quietly, "Does that mean you decided to stick with us, Milt?"

I reached down and started tightening my leggings. Both of them waited in silence for my answer. Finally, I looked up and said, "Let's let it ride a while longer. If we can come up with a plan that offers a good chance to clear things up, I'll stick with you. If we don't, then you need to stick with me. We'll leave Texas behind and find another place. I got no stomach for suicide. Nobody wins if they fight the law, even crooked law."

Neither said anything more, so I finished my leggings and jogged away, circling through the trees. I picked a comfortable spot with a nice view and watched our back trail till midday. When I came back, Win rose from his blanket to go on watch. Cris was sound asleep. Ten seconds later, I was too.

The sharp snap of a rifle cocking woke me in near darkness. I was reaching for my Navy when Win called softly, "Cris, it's me." Then I realized she'd awakened me by cocking my Spencer.

"Come on in, Win," she answered. "I wasn't sure it was you."

"Keep your hands off my rifle," I grunted.

She snickered, handed my Spencer to me still cocked, and said, "If I had toys of my own, I wouldn't play with yours."

When her brother came close, I eased the Spencer off cock and said, "Let's get ready to move."

Cris said smugly, "The horses are saddled. Your food is warm beside the coals of our last fire. We can go as soon as you eat."

I hardly noticed what I ate because it bothered me so much that she'd been able to sneak around and work without waking me.

When we'd finished, she washed the plates in the creek without making a sound. When I moved in her direction to help, Win put up a hand to stop me and shook his head. Later, standing beside her horse to give her a boost, I took the opportunity to say, "You're handy."

She didn't answer.

A little later, Win stopped by a little stream to water the horses. When Cris walked through the woods to get out of sight for a few minutes privacy, he said quietly, "Only two little words, but you said enough. You're learning."

We pulled up on a wooded knoll and looked across a shallow valley at a cluster of rock structures about a half mile away. Houses sprawled comfortably under huge old oak trees, surrounded by corrals, outbuildings, work sheds, and vegetable gardens. Thin smoke rose from chimneys.

"Is that your uncle's ranch?" I asked, finding it hard to believe. I'd seen towns that were a lot smaller.

Win nodded. "Big operation. Uncle Caleb has his own blacksmith, his own horse trainer, just about his own everything. He has eight or ten regular hands, a cook, a housekeeper, and I don't know what-all. All the help lives on the place with their families."

I handed the binoculars to him. "Maybe

you ought to take a good look before we ride in. I hate to walk into surprises."

He watched for a while, but he finally handed them back to me and shook his head. "Most of the men must be off working somewhere. I didn't see my uncle or his foreman either."

"What do you think?"

"Let's ride in. The women act normal. If they were afraid, or if anything was wrong, I think I could tell."

I turned to Cris. "What do you say, Plague?"

"Your decision. You're the outlaws."

It seemed to me her voice was still a wee bit crabby, so I pushed a little. "Quit dodging. What do you think?"

"What do you care what I think?"

"Cared enough to ask twice. You want to give an opinion, or you just want to sulk?"

She lifted her chin and narrowed her eyes, but she spoke in a civil tone. "I think we ought to wait. What's the difference? We can sit here all day just as easy as not. When we're more sure, we can ride on in. Why take chances?"

I swung off the saddle and shrugged at Win. "Makes sense to me." His feet hit the ground in about two seconds.

Cris looked down at me and asked, "Are you trying to coddle me?"

I froze. Standing perfectly still, I darted a

narrow-eyed, suspicious glance at Win. "If I coddle her, is that a marrying offense?"

He rubbed his chin and said cautiously, "Let me ponder on it for a minute. Let's see, coddling don't sound too serious, but cuddling, now, that's plainly a shotgun matter."

She held her hands out to me and said, "Get me down."

As soon as I helped her from the saddle, she turned on Win and said sternly, "Don't let him turn you into a clown too. One is more than enough." Then she turned to me. "Fetch me some fire sticks. I want some hot coffee."

I gathered dry wood while Win tended the horses. Then, when I put on my staggering, dying-from-hunger-waiting-for-breakfast act, she threw one of my own sticks at me. I fell to the ground moaning, but she ignored me.

We kept watch and waited until late afternoon when six riders came into sight, riding slowly in the hottest part of the day. Win announced quietly after a long look through my binoculars, "That's Uncle Caleb and some of his men. Let's ride to meet them."

We went to the horses, tightened cinches, and mounted. As soon as we rode out of the woods, the other riders spotted us, turned toward us immediately, and began to spread out.

I commented quietly, "Not a trusting

bunch. In fact, those boys don't look the least bit friendly."

Win answered in the same tone, "Uncle Caleb doesn't encourage trespassing. Be careful with him, Milt. He's a hard old man. He's been boss over everything for a long time, and he doesn't like to say anything twice."

"I'm careful with anybody who has five armed men with him." I pulled my mustang to a halt when the men in front of us pulled rifles from saddle boots. "To hell with this."

"Don't turn. Don't do anything, Milt. Sit still." Win's voice had gone tight. He pulled up too.

Cris jerked off her hat and shook out her hair. Every man in the group converging on us straightened in the saddle. We weren't close enough to see the expressions on their faces, but two of them were so surprised they pulled rein. She waved her hat and kicked her horse into a gallop, heading straight at them. I doubt if any man in Texas could mistake Cris, small as a child in her side-saddle and with that mane of red hair streaming behind her in the glaring sun. Rifles started disappearing into saddle scabbards.

She reined in beside one of the men, and he dismounted at once to help her to the ground. Win said, "Let's go," and started his horse forward at a walk. Our horses hadn't gone two steps before Cris was hugging somebody's neck. Arm in arm, they turned to watch us ride up.

Win dropped to the ground at once and shook hands with a tall, gray-bearded, smiling man. I stayed in the saddle, remembering my manners, until the big man bellowed, "Get down, son, get down. Who might this be, Win?"

"Uncle Caleb, this is Milton Baynes. Milt, this is my uncle, Caleb Cowan."

Cowan gripped my hand firmly, his smile fading. "Baynes? Your name's Milton Baynes?" I felt my face tighten. Once again, it looked like my name had traveled ahead of me, poisoning wells before I could taste the water.

"Yes, sir," I said.

"You'd be Milton Silvana Baynes, middle son of Darnell, brother to Luke and Ward?"

I dropped his hand and stepped back. The old man sounded like a law officer about to make an arrest. A glance around showed me his men wore neutral expressions. They simply looked ready. Still, I never dodged my name or denied my family in my life, and if it was going to cause trouble here, so be it. "Yes, sir, I'm proud to say that's right."

Cowan said, "You sure took your time. I been about to give up on you. You've finally come to look things over, have you?"

THIRTEEN

Cowan stared straight at me, sizing me up while I blinked and tried to figure out what his odd comment meant. Finally, I said, "Beg pardon, sir? You were expecting me?"

He said gruffly, "I haven't talked it around. That was the deal, but it's no secret, boy. The sale is registered at the courthouse. Anybody can find out who wants to take the trouble to check. I've told all my hands. Wouldn't have been square not to let them know. But my men don't talk about ranch business off the place."

I rubbed my forehead and couldn't help but notice the flicker in his eyes when I did it with my left hand. "You have the better of me, Mr. Cowan. I don't know what you're talking about."

"You mean you don't even know about it?" he asked, grinning as if at some huge joke.

"What is it I should know, sir? Have we met before? Few people know my full name. I don't even use my middle initial in my signature. Should I remember you?"

"No, son, you don't know me, but I feel like I know you." He motioned toward my mustang. "Mount up. Let's go to the house. We have things to talk about."

After we took the short ride to the cluster of rock buildings, Cowan rode directly to the largest of the dwellings. A Mexican boy ran to take our horses, but I spoke quickly. "I better tend to this mustang myself. He's a bad horse."

Cowan nodded. "Suit yourself, but I'll bet that boy has handled worse. Just walk in the front door of the house here when you're finished with your animal. We'll be expecting you, so there's no need to knock."

He dismissed his men with a wave of his arm and turned back to Cris and Win. "Let's go find a cool place." They went into the house.

The boy led the way to an enormous barn with rock walls three feet thick. He went straight to work looking after the other horses. Without comment, he simply waved toward a stall for Judas and pointed out the grain bins. He watched me out of the corners of his eyes while I cautiously groomed and fed my sullen mustang. I got so used to his silence, it startled me when he burst out laughing and spoke in Spanish.

"I see, it is a game."

"What, little brother?"

"You play a game. My father did that too, sometimes, when he was very fond of a particular horse. He said a good horse should be taught to be mean in useful ways for everybody to see. That way, enemies think twice

154

before trying to steal him, and friends never want to borrow him."

I brushed my hands together and faced his smile. "You must not tell everything you know, little brother."

"Your trick is safe with me, *patrón*." The little fellow bowed like a Spanish cavalier. "We *caballeros* have our secrets."

"I'm Milt Baynes," I said, extending my hand.

"Ricardo Gonzales, *patrón*. I'm honored."

"A pleasure to meet a man of discretion."

We solemnly shook hands on our pact of secrecy, and I headed for the big stone house, wondering who the boy's father could be to have taught that child so much. That little boy had a sharp and knowing eye. He'd also made a clever play on words. The Spanish word for gentleman, *caballero,* also meant horseman. The child had paid me a double-edged compliment in a part of the country where skill with horses was much admired.

I felt like a fake. Fact was, Judas came by his meanness naturally, but I had let it become a game. It made life more interesting, and nobody ever tried to borrow Judas, not ever.

Cowan rose when he saw me come into the huge room. Few places make a man feel at home the moment he enters, but the immense room with its spacious, polished floor and impeccable cleanliness greeted a visitor with a sense of ease and cool comfort. Walking out of the Texas sun into such a place was like stepping out of a forest fire into a shady woods. All the sturdy furnishings, made of leather, massive wood, and wool, seemed built to last for generations.

"Come in, Mr. Baynes. Come over here and join us." Cowan waved me toward the long table where he, Cris, and Win were grouped at one end. "Welcome to my home. This is the part I didn't let you buy, this house and the homes of my men and their families."

A Mexican woman appeared as soon as I took a chair. She slipped noiselessly to my side to pour coffee into a delicate china cup she placed in front of me.

"Mr. Cowan, there must be some mistake. I've never bought nor owned a piece of property in my life."

He leaned forward, obviously watching my face to catch my reaction when he asked, "You really don't know about it, do you?"

I lifted both hands to show my puzzlement and waited for him to speak again.

He sat back and grinned at Win. "Your friend here owns this ranch, or at least a big part of it." He shifted his attention back to me and asked, "How long has it been since you've been in touch with your family?"

"Nearly a year, I guess."

Cowan dropped his grin and spoke solemnly. "Okay, son, here's the story. I ended the war with a shipping crate full of Confederate money and requisition slips. Soldiers give you requisition slips when they don't even have worthless money to offer. That's how they steal your property legally, by giving you one kind or another of no-account paper.

"All this is a fancy way of saying I was dead broke, and there's not a bank in the state of Texas in shape to lend anybody any real money. Besides, I never trusted banks much anyway. I was about to lose everything I owned to the auction block for not being able to pay taxes when your uncle rode up."

"What's my uncle got to do with me? Which uncle, by the way?"

"Rodrigo Silvana, he calls himself. At least, that's two of his names. Seems he has about six in a row, like most Spanish folk. You do know the man, don't you?" he asked with an edge of sarcasm.

"Yes, sir, I've known him all my life. He's one of my mother's brothers. He's also one of my pa's closest friends."

"You left Louisiana in a hurry, didn't you?"

I stared into his grin and hesitated, not wanting to speak with anger. Cris put her hand on my arm and spoke sharply. "He was riding back to Louisiana to clear his name when he stopped to help us."

Both Cowan's grin and his eyes widened

into an exaggerated expression of astonished amusement as he stroked his beard and slowly swung his gaze to Cris. "Well, now, what have we here? You've found a defender in my family, I see, Mr. Baynes. My niece has put on her angry face. She looks ready to fight."

Cris jerked her hand away from my arm and blinked for a couple of seconds, her color rising. She put her hand back and said quietly, "I guess that's right."

Cowan glanced at Win, who was wearing a trace of a smile. The old man cleared his throat and said gruffly, "I'm not sure I believe what's happening. I've never been much for fairy tales."

Win leaned forward to rest his elbows on either side of his coffee cup. "I've never been much for fairy tales or for mysteries either, Uncle Caleb. I don't know what you're talking about. By the way he looks, Milt can't figure it out either. You know something we don't. Maybe we could all make sense of this and share your enjoyment if you'd tell us what's going on."

Cowan nodded and said, "Rod Silvana offered to buy this place on terms I could accept. My home and the homes of my men stay ours. He bought the land and cattle in the name of this young man and his father and brothers. I stay to run the place for a percentage of the profits until the Baynes family comes to take over."

Win and Cris both turned questioning looks at me. I shrugged and said, "This is news to me. When we were on the way out of Louisiana, my father made out an unlimited power of attorney and mailed it to Uncle Rod so he could look after my family's property. I haven't seen or heard from my uncle in over five years."

Cowan chuckled and sipped his coffee. "My only sadness about selling the place was that I couldn't leave it to Win and Cris. They're all the family I have. The way it turned out though, Win's already got himself a fine little place of his own, and I had to sell mine or lose everything. At least, I got me a nice little piece of money out of it for my old age. Now, it looks like the land is gonna stay in the family after all, if Cris has anything to say about it."

He gave her a broad wink. "That's the fairy tale part. A thing like this couldn't happen again in a thousand years."

He leaned forward and directed a huge grin at Cris. "Ain't you the smart one, Crissy? Me, now, I'd look at Milton Baynes, and I wouldn't think he'd have two dollars to rub together."

For once, Cris didn't seem to be able to answer. She sat with her hand on my arm and didn't say a word.

"You'd be right, Mr. Cowan. My uncle may

have bought this place, but he didn't do it with my money. My pa is the man you need to talk to."

Cowan shook his head. "You listen to me, young man. I know what I'm talking about. You can go to the courthouse in Victoria and see for yourself. This property is recorded in four names. Each man in your family is on record as owning an equal share. That's how I came to know your full name."

He turned to Win and said, "Darnell Baynes gave all his sons the same middle name, Silvana, his wife's maiden name." His eyes came back to me and he continued, "Me and Rod Silvana had plenty of time to talk. He said your family would honor any agreement he made in your name. Rod talked a lot about honor when discussing your family. He also said you can come back to Louisiana any time you take the notion. The trouble you had there ended with the Confederacy."

Cris asked, "What trouble?"

Win said, "If he wants to, that's something for Milt to tell you in private, Cris. It's not a thing to ask him in front of other people."

But her question hung in the air like a foul demon that followed me everywhere. I sat through a short silence, doing some fast thinking. Everybody seemed to pause, waiting for me to speak. The ticking of a tall clock against the wall behind me was the only sound for a few moments.

Her question wasn't out of line, considering everything. After all, I'd planned to go to Louisiana to bring out the truth. I should welcome any chance to tell the true story to anybody willing to listen. Win shifted uncomfortably, like he intended to rise.

I lifted a hand to hold him in his seat and said quietly, "Five drunks and a stupid deputy sheriff rode out to our place one day, intending to force me and my brothers to fight in the Confederate Army. That was the grimmest day in my life. My mother had died that morning. We'd hardly finished burying her when those men rode up to our front door. They couldn't have come at a worse time. When my pa warned them off, told them of our sadness, they wouldn't listen. They pulled guns. All six of them died in about half as many seconds."

The Mexican woman appeared as if by magic, and moving silently on bare feet, poured coffee in my cup and leaned toward Cowan's. I stopped talking. The quiet in the room made the clock sound as loud as a hammer striking an anvil.

Cowan looked up at her for a moment before his gaze came back to me. "Christina grew up on this place. Apache torture couldn't make her talk about what she hears in this room. You can speak your piece and not worry, son."

I nodded, but my throat closed up on me, and my eyes started to water. I cleared my throat and rubbed my face. For some reason, telling the story after all these years was getting to me, bringing everything back like it happened just yesterday. I figured, now I'd told part of it, I had best try to tell it all.

"My little brother killed three of them. He's almighty fast and sure with a pistol. I don't know if there's another in the world who can match him with a handgun. Anyhow, that day did something awful to him . . . and to me. He was sick to his stomach right after the shooting. That didn't worry us at the time, him being such a young boy and all. We didn't notice the change in him until later. Doing that killing seemed to destroy part of him. From then on he didn't care about anybody but us, the family."

I glanced around the table. Christina had left the room, and everyone sat perfectly motionless, watching me.

"In Montana Territory, he met a sweet little girl from Virginia. A couple of men made threats against the family, and they mentioned her too. Ward killed them on the spot. I was with him when he did it. Twenty witnesses called it a fair fight. There was nothing fair about it. It was more like an execution. Those men were mean, and they were tough, but they wanted to live. They had no more chance against Ward than a

162

mouse against a fox. It's a terrible thing to watch a man who doesn't give a damn kill somebody. Ward wasn't mad, wasn't scared, wasn't anything. Ward was just sweeping trash off his front porch."

Cris's hand tightened on my arm. I took a deep breath, determined to finish it.

"Ward set store by that little girl the minute he saw her, and I saw him change into a proper man again, with feelings. He's still dangerous if he's pushed, but at least you have to make him mad before he kills you. Now, he might even think about it later and be a little sorry.

"What I'm . . . what I'm trying to say . . . the good thing is, Ward changed. He got better. The bad thing is, I haven't." I raised my head to look squarely at Win.

"You remember that fellow named Ross? You told him I'd kill him and forget him before breakfast. I thought about that later. You were right, Win. I was ready to shoot him, and I would have if he'd taken a single wrong step or said a careless word. It didn't make a particle of difference to me either way."

Caleb Cowan tapped his spoon lightly against his saucer. Christina appeared instantly. He said, "I let my coffee get cold." Quickly, she brought clean cups for each of us, filled them, and carried the cold ones away.

Cowan spoke again. "You notice that she always fills your cup first, Baynes?"

I jerked a hand, palm up, indicating my surprise, and maybe, a little irritation. Of course, I had noticed, but it seemed a matter of chance, a trivial thing. I asked, "Why should I pay attention to an accident like that?"

He said, "Christina don't do nothin' by accident. You're the *patrón* on this ranch now and an honored guest in my house. These people are very loyal, very respectful of tradition. If you violate their simple trust, I'll chop enough wood to burn you in hell forever."

The sudden change of subject left me blinking.

Cowan chuckled. "Son, all you've told us today makes me believe you'll make a fine Texan. I figured I'd start getting you acquainted with the way we do things. It ain't healthy to worry about shooting stray skunks. A proper man worries about his land and the folks who depend on him. I think I'd like your little brother. These are hard times. Hard times call for hard men. Let's give your voice a rest and get Win to talk awhile."

With a simple shift of his eyes, Cowan turned all our attention to Win. "This sudden visit is a pleasure, Nephew, but I don't think you came just to visit an old man. I smell trouble all over you. Want to tell me about it?"

FOURTEEN

Win told Cowan all that had happened since the sack-heads taught him to dance at the end of a rope. When he came to the jail-break, Cris interrupted and told that part. She so obviously enjoyed the telling of it that Cowan winked at me and Win.

Cris snapped, "I saw that, Uncle Caleb. I don't care. You can grin behind your hand if you like, but I had a wonderful time. Those awful people . . . if Milt would make me some more bombs, I'd ride back to Goliad by myself and do it again."

Cowan solemnly nodded at me and said, "She's a bad influence on you, son. Born outlaw. Bloodthirsty. Runs in the family. I know what I'm talking about. I married one of them redheaded women my own self. You got a fast horse, boy?"

Cris smiled like an angel and said sweetly, "You heard the story, Uncle Caleb. He tried to ride away from me once. His friends in Goliad sent him right back home."

I nodded. "Yep, well chewed, swallowed, and spit up."

Her smile turned into a disgusted grimace, and she wrinkled her nose at me. "Milt, don't talk ugly. That's awful."

The old man leaned back in his chair and said, "The short of it is that you, Win, are probably charged with murdering a whole family and with breaking jail. You, Milt, are probably charged with a couple of killings, one of them a deputy sheriff, plus battering three men to a bloody pulp, one of them a sheriff, helping with a jailbreak, robbing a store, and blowing up about half of Goliad. Have I left anything out?"

Win said, "I think that's all of it."

Cris smirked at me. "Maybe they could charge Milt with being a public nuisance. He slept out in the middle of a Goliad street one whole afternoon."

Win scowled. "Cris, don't accuse Milt of talking ugly. That was a mean thing to say."

Cowan said quietly, "My advice is, head for Mexico. You ain't got a chance. I ain't heard a thing from Goliad but trouble since the war ended. We can't hold a proper election in Texas. As long as they insist on the iron oath where they make a man swear he never served the Confederacy, there ain't hardly a man qualified to vote.

"Hell — excuse me, Cris — they can't even fill a jury box in some counties. If a man even kept cemetery records during the war, he can't take that oath. So all the lawmen are appointed by the military or elected by damned — excuse me, Cris — Republicans. Our so-called governor don't

166

amount to nothing. Nobody voted for him. But even that poor devil gets overruled by the Army if he tries to do anything right.

"Shootings, vigilante hangings, horse stealing, cattle rustling, they got it all over there at Goliad. They're still trying to fight two wars, the one with Mexico and the one between the states. Those silly bastards damned near — excuse me, Cris — starved San Antonio by shooting Mexican cart drivers who were carrying flour and stuff up from Indianola on the Gulf coast."

I asked, "Don't you have the same thing up here?"

He swung his head slowly to look directly at me. "Son, I'm about a day's ride from town. Every trail into this place is marked real plain with signs to keep out. Nobody comes here unless it's on business or to visit my people. Even then, everybody who comes here knows to stay on my roads. It's mighty unsafe to wander around on my property. My hands are mostly Mexican *vaqueros,* and they didn't leave me to go to war, so my stock is tallied and branded and looked after. My men carry the best weapons I can find for them. I buy ammunition for them to practice with, and they use it."

While Cowan spoke, I recalled the way his riders, apparently without command, spread out and pulled rifles when they saw us.

Cowan's eyes rose to meet those of the

167

Mexican woman standing silently in a doorway. "Supper's near about ready. Christina frets if I don't eat at regular times. Maybe you folks want to clean up a little first?"

Cris and Win evidently knew where they were to stay, having visited with him before, so Cowan and I were alone when he led me to a second-story room. When I walked over to a long narrow opening in the wall, he spoke from the doorway. "Yeah, it's just an old firing slit. Maybe I ought to make the windows bigger since we ain't had no Indian fights in these parts in quite a spell."

I turned back to face him and said, "I wouldn't be in a hurry to do that. The Comanches and Apaches have just about driven every settler west of San Antonio off their land."

"Ain't no surprise in that, son. The Army is more concerned with protecting freed slaves than settlers. Win said you came this way from Mexico."

I nodded.

"Dangerous country. The freighters have had pure hell on the run to Chihuahua since the war. I hear the Indians have stripped the haciendas down there clean of horses and cattle both. You make that ride alone?"

I nodded again. "I always ride alone unless I'm with my family."

"Except for Win and Cris?"

"Uh, well, they told you the story. Win and I sort of fell into the habit of helping each other, not having much choice in the matter."

"Have you spoken for that girl?"

"No, sir. I've just got to the point she doesn't shoot on sight."

He winked and lifted a hand as he stepped toward the door. "She acted spoken for. Look to your hole card when they start acting like that, son. See you at supper."

After that first day, I started riding in the daytime again. Since Cowan insisted I owned part of this land, it seemed like I should get myself acquainted with the place. Cowan rode with me, and Ricardo tagged along as if he always followed the old man everywhere.

The first day out, Cowan said flatly, "Ricardo's daddy was my foreman. A couple years back, I took a little herd to Indianola to ship to New Orleans. A thief who happened to be a deputy sheriff tried to cut out a steer for himself. When Gonzales tried to stop him, that deputy turned right around and shot him."

We rode for several minutes in silence before Cowan spoke again. "Somebody went and hung that deputy a few days later, and they burned his house down too. Nobody ever found out who done it. Ain't that a shame? Texas is sure enough a lawless country these days." The old man sounded like a distressed citizen worried about the reputation of his community.

Following another long period of silence, he said, "Ricardo used to ride along behind his daddy. He did that ever since he was a little feller. Now, he rides with me except when I have something special for him to do. He'll be leaving in a couple of days with some more of my Mexican folks to visit relatives in Goliad. When he gets back, we'll find out everything that's going on over there."

When we topped a low rise, a rider came into sight, riding at a pounding gallop toward a single oak. As soon as he came almost abreast of it, he drew and fired at the tree. He went through the sequence twice more while we rode closer. By the time we joined him, he had dismounted to examine the target.

Cowan spoke. "Bill Longley, meet Milt Baynes."

A youngster, surely not over seventeen, Longley did the same thing everyone else did when they heard my name. He paused and threw a sharp glance at me. "Milt Baynes? Are you the Milt Baynes from Louisiana?"

I nodded.

He stepped forward with a friendly grin and stuck out a heavily callused hand. "I done heard of you." Tall, painfully thin and narrow-shouldered, he showed the awkwardness of a young man still unaccustomed to his height. His close-set black eyes glinted with humor when he added, "Yes, sir, I surely heard of you. I heard about you whipping that sheriff down at Goliad and taking Mr. Mill out of jail. That was a fine thing."

"How'd you hear about that so quick?" I asked.

He shifted his feet and glanced quickly at Cowan, looking like a schoolboy caught talking out of turn.

Cowan spoke in a matter-of-fact tone. "Every now and then, I send my people to the towns close to my property. They just look around and listen. It sort of keeps us country folks up to date on what's going on."

"You were doing some fancy riding there, Mr. Longley," I said.

He shrugged and answered, "Thank you, sir, but everybody can ride. The shooting's the thing."

Cowan said, "Bill had him a little trouble back home, so he came here to get away for a while. His daddy is an old friend of mine from the Army of Texas, lives up at Evergreen these days. Bill is trying to use up all the powder and lead on the place. This boy loves to shoot those Dance pistols of his."

Longley's grin faded. "I surely do, Mr. Cowan, but I don't mean to take advantage. I'm used to spending most of my money for ammunition. If I'm shooting too much, sir, I'd be pleased to pay for what I use."

Cowan ignored the suggestion and asked, "How many hits today?"

Longley ducked his head and looked uncomfortable. "I fired ten shots and hit the tree nine times." With the sincerity of youth, he added, "I think I had a bad load, sir. My pistol didn't sound nor feel right one of the times I fired."

I commented, "It's easy to get a drop or two of sweat in the powder when it's as hot as it is today. You willing to take a suggestion, Mr. Longley?"

"Yes, sir. I'd be obliged."

"You shot five times. My daddy taught me to save one, not ever to shoot a gun empty when practicing."

Longley nodded. "That's good thinking. That's why I carry a second pistol." He touched the coat he wore even in the Texas heat. Sure enough, he had a second pistol shoved under his belt.

Cowan, overly casual, asked, "Want to try it, Mr. Baynes?" Instantly, Longley said, "I'll plug the holes," and turned away to press twigs into the tree, marking where his shots had drilled into the trunk.

I trotted my mustang far enough away to bring him to a nice gallop by the time I came back past the oak. I fired twice on each pass, shooting once on the approach and swinging around to fire once again after passing the target. After two passes, I circled back and slid from the saddle beside the tree to reload.

"Four hits, easy to find, 'cause I can cover 'em with one hand," Longley announced, flashing a friendly grin my way again. "That's pretty shooting. You been practicing too, haven't you?"

I shook my head, returning his grin. "My pa made me practice with a pistol ever since I was a little boy, but we never shot at a tree from a galloping horse. You're right, Mr. Longley, that's fun."

Again the picture of boyish sincerity, Longley said, "I never saw anybody shoot any better than you, once you get your pistol out. No offense, Mr. Baynes, but I'd like to suggest you take too much time with your draw. If I were you, I'd try to get my gun out quicker."

"That would be an advantage, but I don't know how I could do it any faster."

"If you'd allow me, Mr. Baynes, I'd be proud to show you some things my friend, Cullen Baker, showed me. You might want to try them to see if they help."

"I'd be obliged." I glanced quickly at Cowan. "Man gets powder and shot free, seems sinful not to have some fun with it."

As we rode off, leaving Longley to his practice, Cowan said, "That kid is a good hand, works hard for his pay. But he's got a terrible chip on his shoulder. Near as I can piece together, two white men talked disrespectful about his daddy. Bill heard about it and went looking for them. Those men were up on a house, mending the roof. Bill rode up, the way I heard it, and shot them right off the roof without saying a word. They were both only wounded, so they recovered, but his not killing them was kind of an accident."

Cowan pulled a big handkerchief and wiped his face and the sweatband of his hat before he went on.

"Later, he killed a Negro for the same offense. The man was drunk, riding up and down the street with a shotgun, insulting everybody he saw. He cussed Bill's daddy, Bill stepped out in the street, the man swung the shotgun toward him, and Bill shot him down. Again, the story goes, he didn't say a word. He's a good boy, but when he gets mad, he shoots people. Bill ain't unfriendly, exactly, but he rides alone just like you do. Be careful with him."

After that, Bill Longley and I practiced together in the last light of every evening. Bill was no careless kid just having fun with a weapon.

FIFTEEN

Five days later, Ricardo returned with news from Goliad.

"Emilio, one of my cousins, said he thinks he knows you," he said in Spanish, smiling at me. "He said he was taking his goat home when you spoke with him on the road. Emilio thinks you are a very pleasant gentleman. He sent you a map he drew." The boy handed me a roll of leather.

Cowan said gently, "Speak English, boy. My niece and nephew don't speak Spanish."

Ricardo turned at once toward the Mills, seated with Cowan and me at the long table in the spacious dining room. The youngster twisted his sombrero uneasily, bowed, and said, "Pardon me, I forgot."

In Spanish, I said quietly, "Don't be nervous, little brother. These are gracious members of Señor Cowan's family, even if they aren't refined enough to speak the language of cultured people."

Cowan burst out laughing, and Ricardo's broad surprised grin almost closed his eyes.

Cris looked sharply at me and asked, "Did you say something insulting again?"

"Again?" I raised my eyebrows.

"What did he say, Uncle Caleb?" she asked.

175

Cowan said, straight-faced, "He said you cut out the tongues of Mexican boys if they speak Spanish to you. He said that's what turned your hair red, eating little boys' raw tongues."

She shuddered and turned a twisted face to me. "That's horrible! But it sounds just like you. Did you say that? Answer me. Did you?"

"Your uncle's just joking. I told Ricardo . . ."

Cris snapped, "Stop. You're fixing to tell another lie. I can tell. You get a revolting smug look when you're about to lie."

"Hey, now, who's being horrible?" I crossed my arms and looked at the ceiling. "This conversation is simply too crude for a sensitive man like me."

Cris whipped around to face Ricardo. "What did he say to you, young man?"

Without a trace of hesitation, Ricardo answered, "He said not to be afraid, señorita. He said the lady's great beauty is only a small thing next to her kindness."

Cris froze for a second, then glanced from Cowan to me and back again. Eyes narrowed, she said, "I don't think you two are good for each other, and both of you are bad for this little boy." She took a long look at Ricardo, who wore the expression of an altar boy awaiting the priest's blessing.

"Can we let the kid tell us about Goliad now?" I asked, afraid Ricardo would collapse under the red demon's stare.

"Is this boy truthful, Uncle Caleb?" Cris asked, finally shifting her attention away from the boy.

"He's mighty dependable," Cowan said.

"You didn't answer my question."

"You got the best answer you're gonna get, young lady. That's an insulting question."

I asked, "Did you find out anything interesting, Ricardo?"

"I think so, *patrón*. My uncle, a carpenter, helped put a new door on the jail and to repair the saloon. He says most of the Anglos are laughing at the sheriff when he can't hear them."

Ricardo glanced at Win.

"The Anglo men say the little quiet Yankee somehow made friends with Milt Baynes. Everybody say that Milt Baynes gave a warning not to bother the little Yankee, so the sheriff make a big mistake. They say everybody should know the Baynes clan is very bad."

The boy's gaze shifted to Cris.

"Some of the Anglos saw you that night at the jail, señorita, or they think so. They talk about a very small rider they think was you, but nobody saw Señor Baynes. Everybody is laugh very hard. Even many Anglo women laugh very much. The women say maybe you knock down the sheriff and take your brother out of jail and throw bombs by yourself. The

Anglos make many jokes about women with red hair."

Finally, the boy looked at me.

"Some others say it is easy not to see Milt Baynes . . . or to see him too late."

I asked, "Are we wanted? Does the sheriff still claim we are killers?"

Ricardo nodded and hesitated. "Yes, *patrón*, but nobody thinks he is right. Many Anglos say there is no proof. Many others talk about how bad they need a new sheriff."

He shuffled his feet and fought against a grin. "The sheriff, he stay in bed for four days. His head is hurt very bad, and his ribs are broken. He try to collect money to put a reward on you, but everybody refuse."

I asked, "Has the sheriff got a new deputy?"

Ricardo shook his head. "No, *patrón*, I don't think so. He would not ask a Mexican, and all the Anglos say they don't need the money bad enough to fight the Baynes clan. They say only a fool would take that job, even at ten times the money."

The boy's eyes widened, "Oh, *patrón*, I almost forgot. The Anglos say the *juez*, the judge, wrote for soldiers to come to Goliad."

I glanced at Cowan, and he shook his head. "The county judge might've wrote for help, but I bet none comes." He shifted his gaze to Ricardo. "I think your mama has something good for you in the kitchen."

Ricardo bowed with exquisite formality to each of us, asked to be excused, looked me in the eye, and said in Spanish, "If I may be of further help, *patrón*, I am at your service."

I answered in Spanish, "A new friend discovered among strangers is better than gold found in the pocket."

After the boy backed away, bowing, and left the room, Cris asked, "Please tell me what you two said to each other." Since she asked so nicely, with no sharp edge on her voice, I told her as exactly as I could. I even told her how Spanish sometimes sounds odd when translated, sometimes sounding more flowery and other times more formal than English.

Then she asked, "How long did it take you to learn to speak Spanish so well?"

"I don't remember learning anything. My mother spoke as much Spanish as English to me when I was little. It was the same with French. She was easy with all three languages."

Cowan growled, "Well, what's it to be? You boys decided what you're going to do?"

Win said slowly, "I was a captain of cavalry in the United States Army. I think the best thing to do is to take our case straight to the Army. They seem to make the final decisions on everything anyway, Uncle Caleb. I think I can talk sense with those officers. At least they're honest."

Cris said, "You may be right, Win, but they're far away, and it would take a lot of effort for them to get the facts. They're just as likely to arrest you and send you back to Sheriff Mullins. It seems to me we ought to take our case to the county judge in Goliad. If there's no proof against us, and we haven't heard of any, it seems the judge ought to be able to make that awful sheriff leave us alone."

I shrugged and thought for a moment while they waited for me to speak. "Looks like all our trouble comes from one man, the sheriff. Maybe I'm dumb, but it seems to me, if we persuaded him to back off, or if we ran him out of Goliad, our problem would be solved."

After a brief silence, I glanced at Win. "The Army probably can't be bothered. I think that shapes up to be a waste of time."

Then I shifted my gaze to Cris. "The county judge in Goliad probably got his job the same way the sheriff did, and he's probably just as crooked. If he wanted to do anything, seems to me, he's had plenty of chances already. I think fooling around with him is probably a waste of time too."

Win shook his head. "Sheriff Mullins is quick to use a gun. He'd probably shoot both of us on sight, Milt. Trying to persuade him is a lost cause. He was ready to kill me when you took me out of his jail. The man's ruthless. We need help from higher up to get him put out of office."

Cowan said, "There's a chance all three of you are right. Ever think of that? Why don't you try all three ways? If any one of you is right, the problem gets solved."

Cris said calmly, "It won't do. Suppose Win and I both succeed. What if Win gets the Army to take a hand, and I persuade the county judge to intervene? What good does that do if Milt gets himself killed messing around with that sheriff?"

Win said, "Timing. Maybe good timing is the answer. Will you wait, Milt? Will you stay right here and let us try? If we fail, then you can take a hand."

We talked for a long time after that, but Win and Cris talked me into it, with Cowan sitting like a statue and not saying a word. I let them talk me into waiting until they had their try.

So I waited. I waited till the autumn rains started falling. I waited, listening to Cowan say he'd never seen such rains. I waited till the trails and roads turned into spongy slop, until cart traffic from the coast up through Goliad and Victoria to San Antonio halted to wait for things to dry out.

I waited until Bill Longley rode in one day

and told me there were soldiers in Goliad, that Win was in jail down there, and that Cris was being held in the hotel, under guard.

I rode out of the huge barn just in time to meet Cowan, stalking through the mud, rain dripping from the wide brim of his hat. He took a final drag from the tobacco wrapped in paper, a habit he'd picked up from his *vaqueros*, dropped the smoke, and spoke slowly.

"Three things, son. I wrote some letters. There was a time in Texas when a letter from me might help a man, but times have changed. Anyway, I done it. Next, Bill Longley told me you were saddling up and getting ready to cut loose your dogs. Bill said if that sheriff gets you, he's gonna ride down there and kill him a lawman. Last, this rain is an awful trial for a fighting man. Son, always think of your powder. Whatever you do, don't never forget to keep your powder dry."

Cowan reached up, shook my hand, and quickly stepped back to avoid Judas's attempt to stamp on his feet.

I rode a little way before I turned in the saddle. When I looked back through the rain, the old man had gone back in the house. Ricardo waved from the barn, wiped a sleeve across his eyes, and crossed himself.

One man had no chance against a crooked sheriff with the U.S. Army behind him.

That's the way anybody with good sense would figure it, and that had to be my advantage. Nobody would figure I'd bet everything straight into the face of a stacked deck. What I planned to do would seem so crazy, nobody would be ready for it.

Judas pointed his nose straight at Goliad.

SIXTEEN

I'd used up the better part of four beautifully tanned sheepskins to cut, fit, and sew boots for three horses. Made so they'd lace tight with the wool facing out, I planned to make it hard for a tracker to follow us. Ordinarily, our horses' hooves would sink deep into the soaked ground, even in heavy grass. The wool boots would stop most of that.

Unless they put a real tracker on my trail, I hoped to confuse anybody who tried to come after me. A fine woodsman wouldn't be fooled, but he might lose some time puzzling out the trick. Even after that, his job would be harder, and it would take only a light rain to wipe out the smudges we left.

For the last time, just to be sure, I studied Emilio's drawing Ricardo had brought back from Goliad. A work of art rather than a map, the boy's pen-and-ink picture drawn on smooth leather showed every feature of the town. Each little square indicating a house was marked with its owner's name. Even the huge oaks, one of which was called the hanging tree, were carefully inked in around the courthouse at the center of town. Cowan had admitted he didn't know for sure if anybody had ever been hanged there, but the stout widespread branches were perfect for the job.

An arrow drawn at the edge of the map showed the direction to the old Spanish *presidio* and the crumbling mission which still stood a few miles from town. The boy's tiny but clear script named each fully, PRESIDIO LA BAHÍA DEL ESPÍRITU SANTO DE ZÚÑIGA and MISÍON DE NUESTRA SEÑORA DE LA BAHÍA DEL ESPÍRITU SANTO. Another arrow indicated the direction and distance to the spot where General Santa Anna disgraced his name forever by executing over three hundred prisoners. The cry, "Remember the Alamo! Remember Goliad!" brought fire to every Texan's eye. Many innocent Mexicans lived to curse Santa Anna. They faced hatred and contempt because of his cruelty and dishonor.

I came into town in the gray light of late afternoon. Hat pulled low and collar pulled up, I hunched over just like any tired man in a slicker on a wet day. If ever a man needed an extra pair of eyes, this was the time. But maybe there's truth in the old saying that God protects fools and drunks. I happened to ride in on a day when rain and wind cleared the muddy streets of onlookers and smeared the windows to hinder casual watchers. When I rode into the livery stable and dismounted, I felt sure nobody had given me so much as a curious glance.

The hostler hadn't lit a lantern yet, so the inside of the stable was dark as a cave, but Judas told me where the man stood. I had my Navy aimed at him before he spoke.

"Señor Baynes?"

"Who's asking?"

In Spanish, barely above a whisper, he answered, "It matters not. I will get the horses for you. The saddles hang right there. See them? I will help you saddle up. Take these blankets. I have food here. Please, if they catch you, tell them the stable was empty. I'm not here."

"You were expecting me?"

The shadowy figure paused at a stall gate. "It is a good thing the sheriff has no Mexican deputy. You have come back to Goliad twice already, no?" He chuckled and opened the stall. "You are a man who goes away and comes back as he pleases, señor. I think Mexicans understand such men better than Anglos."

He led Win's and Cris's horses from their stalls, handed me the reins, and darted to the door. After a quick scan up and down the street, he returned to help with the saddling. When he had both horses ready to travel, I pressed a bill into his hand and cut short his effort to return it by turning to Judas. Mounted, I leaned down to shake hands.

"A thousand thanks. I like to know the people I owe a favor. Tell me your name."

"Another time, señor. For now, I was a friend of Ricardo's father. That is enough."

"As you wish. Adios."

"*Vaya con Dios, patrón.*"

The heavy clouds and falling rain brought darkness early. Freshening wind and grumbling in the heavens sounded a forecast for a real Texas gully washer. Judas took me along a narrow alley, across a wide road that was fast turning into a flowing stream, and up beside a shed behind a two-story white house.

My nose told me I'd found where the judge kept his horses. I leaned down and pulled a wooden pin from the hasp. The wide door swung open quietly at my touch, and I rode inside without dismounting.

Black as a pit inside, the meager light coming through the open door revealed a fancy polished buggy pushed against the back wall. Two horses stood watching us from roomy stalls.

I whispered, "Judas, you might as well be dry while I plead my case." Another thought struck me when I slid from the saddle, so I did some looking around. Five minutes later, Judas and his two friends from the Mill ranch were munching corn and feeling at home. I stood and watched them for a minute or two, even though there was little enough to see in the darkness. Actually, it was the soothing sound of chewing from the horses that held me for a moment.

More than anything else, the famous outlaw, Milt Baynes, paused a minute to consider his prospects. Hiding and feeding his horses in a judge's barn while he trees a town makes a good story to tell later, if a man lives to do the talking. I'd already used up a lot of good luck. The hard part still lay before me.

Hidden and safe with friendly animals in the warm darkness, I just stood around for a while. It's a comfortable thing to do when a man is scared to death. The calm sounds of horses and the soothing patter of rain on a shingle roof can be homely reminders that there are a lot of simple pleasures in life. I took a deep breath or two, straightened, and squared my shoulders.

No other moment offers such a test as the last opportunity to turn back. At such a time, it always seems only a fool would press forward, and only a coward would back away.

The time had come to start moving or face a spell of shudders and shakes.

I stepped out into the rain and followed a series of flat stones through the bedraggled remnants of a vegetable garden. The white house seemed to glow in the increasing darkness. A wide porch circled the whole building. Rain rolling from the porch roof shrouded the first floor of the place like a thin windblown curtain.

As I came closer I could see a spacious empty kitchen through the back windows. Easing my feet down slowly, I went up the steps, crossed the porch, and tried the back door. Locked. I crept off the porch to avoid boards which might creak and moved along the side of the house. Light spilled through wide glass windows, and I could clearly see a man and woman at the table in a small breakfast room adjoining the kitchen. I backed away and went around the house on the other side where it was darker.

The front door opened under my hand and closed quietly. The narrow foyer opened to stairs directly ahead and into a luxurious parlor on one side and a formal dining room on the other. Hearing laughter, I moved into the parlor and away from the light filtering into the dining room. I had to make sure, as best I could, that no one else was in the house. Five minutes of listening convinced me that either nobody was in the darkened upstairs or else they were already in bed. At the back of the spacious parlor, a doorway led into the pantry. I passed through into the kitchen and eased across to the lighted doorway of the breakfast room.

Both of them were still chuckling when I edged up to the door. The man had his back to me, and I could almost hear my mother's voice saying, "The master of the house should always sit with his back to the kitchen." The woman didn't notice me, so I cocked the Navy. At the sound, she looked up, saw me, and froze. Her fork clattered off her plate to the floor. The man turned and started to his feet. I shifted the Navy just a fraction to catch his attention. He stopped.

"Since you're halfway up anyway, Judge, step over there and draw the shades."

"Who are you? How dare you break into my home."

When he spoke, I felt assured I had found the right man. Physically, he was built more like a miner than a judge, with broad shoulders and a thick neck. He looked about my age, far younger than I expected. But his manner of speech showed both schooling and arrogance.

"I didn't come here to argue with you. A gent smart enough to be a judge should know better than to argue with a man holding a gun. I'm going to tell you one more time before I get mad. Cover those windows."

He stalked across the small room and drew the shades. When he turned back to me, I nodded toward his chair. He caught the signal and sat down. When he grasped the arms of his chair to turn it toward me, I said, "Don't." His hands relaxed slowly.

"I'm Milton Baynes." The judge was obviously a young and active man, capable of moving fast. I didn't want to tempt him into making a mistake. I kept my eyes on him while speaking to the woman. "I apologize for the intrusion, ma'am, but I need to ask the judge for some help. If I came here openly, I'm afraid the sheriff in this town would try to shoot me."

"What help could I give you?" The arms of his chair prevented him from turning to face me. Few things bother a man more than turning his back on danger. Still, his voice offered nothing, and his tone had more go-to-hell in it than question.

"By the way, Judge, I've never heard your name."

"I'm Reid Bilbrey."

"A pleasure, sir. The help I need is to get Mr. Win Mill out of jail."

"I can't do that, Mr. Baynes. He's accused of murdering a whole family. I wouldn't even set bail for him. Clearly, he'd flee to avoid prosecution if given the opportunity."

"Yes, sir, he's mighty eager to run away and leave his ranch and his stock. He's eager to leave his sister behind too, so she can be treated like a lost stray. Is this your wife, Judge?"

"Of course."

"Mrs. Bilbrey, I hate to inconvenience you, but your husband has already convinced me he's taking sides, and he's on the wrong one. I'm going to have to tie you up."

Mrs. Bilbrey looked me straight in the eye

and asked bluntly, "Why?"

"The judge is going to take a walk with me. If things stay simple, he'll be right back home in a few minutes. If problems arise, there's likely to be shooting, and he might get hurt. I wouldn't want you to cause a problem and then feel bad about it later."

Her gaze never wavered. I began to feel edgy. She was over the first shock and now showed no trace of fear. A young woman, wearing an expensive dress, she showed the distinctive and often misleading softness of aristocracy. Her next comment didn't make me feel any better.

"Suppose I refuse to allow it?"

"Mrs. Bilbrey, where are you from?"

"Philadelphia. Why?"

"Well, ma'am, let me explain the local customs. In Texas, everybody does what a man holding a gun tells them to do. You break that rule and all the society people down here will be scandalized. You'll never hear the end of it."

She came to her feet and stood watching me. I'd seen that expression before. Little schoolmarms wore that look when facing overgrown boys half again their size. "I'm going to walk into my kitchen, Mr. Baynes."

Judge Bilbrey extended a hand toward her and spoke sharply. "Susan, please! What are you doing?"

"I'm going to the kitchen to bring in another plate. I don't believe Mr. Baynes has had any supper.

I stood like a post, with my tongue stuck to the roof of my mouth, and thought fast. She was going to do it, no question. The idea the woman would flatly refuse to do what she was told hadn't occurred to me. She was going to gamble that I wouldn't shoot her, and she'd win, and she already knew it. I had better find something to do, and I'd better do it fast.

"I may not want to hurt you, but I can shoot your husband. Yes, ma'am, I can do that."

She started around the table. Bilbrey spoke harshly. "Susan, stop this. The man's from an outlaw family. No telling what he might do."

She stopped and turned slowly to him. "Reid, I have the advantage of you. I went to the hotel this afternoon to take a few things to that young woman they're holding. She's lonely enough to die, poor thing. We talked for almost two hours. Also, you're seated so that it's awkward for you to watch him closely. You can't see how he holds that pistol."

The lady turned to face me again, and I could tell she made each move at about half speed so as not to upset me. "You have yet to point that pistol directly at either of us. You're being very careful. I don't think you'll shoot. I think you're bluffing. Am I correct, Mr. Baynes?"

She walked right at me, one careful step after another, watching my eyes. When I stepped aside, she walked past, opened a cabinet and a drawer, and came back with a plate and silverware. I thought I might breathe for a minute, but she came at me again. When she forced me to step aside a second time, she laughed and explained, "I have hot bread on top of the stove."

She returned to the table, and for a moment, things simply seemed to stop. The judge and his wife sat waiting. The clean plate, napkin, and silverware waited. Bread and a big serving bowl full of stew sat there cooling. That soft little woman had turned me from an armed intruder into a dirty-faced kid with a toy pistol. I stood in the doorway, feeling ridiculous and wondering what to do. My bluff had been called, and I had no hole card.

"All right, ma'am, you made me look like an ass, and I guess I had it coming, but I came here on serious business. I have to get my friend and his sister loose. They're innocent. And I can't take food from somebody at gunpoint. I don't care what you think or what lies you've heard. No Baynes has ever done such a thing."

Bilbrey said, "My wife has already proved you don't want to use that gun, Baynes. At least, she's proved it to my satisfaction. No offense intended, but now that we know that, you look a bit foolish waving it around."

I eased down the hammer of the Navy, dropped it into my holster, hung my dripping slicker on the kitchen door, dropped my hat on the floor, and sat down. Assuming my best hangdog expression, I spread butter on a piece of hot bread and said, "This is going to ruin my reputation if it gets out."

SEVENTEEN

Susan Bilbrey chuckled. "That little Cris Mill is the one you have to watch out for. She insists you're not an outlaw and never have been. I think she's determined to ruin your reputation."

I swallowed a mouthful of buttered bread and said, "Yes, ma'am, I can believe that. I'm afraid she's not impressed with my abilities. She thinks I'm not up to outlaw standards."

Still smiling, she answered, "I didn't receive that impression from what she told me. In fact, she said you have amazing talents, and it's a good thing you aren't an outlaw. She also said you'd be devastatingly handsome if you'd cut your hair and wear decent clothes."

"No offense, ma'am. Miss Mill is a lovely little lady, but she's got a twisted sense of humor. You have to watch out for her little jokes."

"Precisely what she said about you," she said, ladling stew onto my plate.

I blinked and put on an astonished expression. "She said I was a lovely little lady?"

Both of them laughed. Judge Bilbrey said, "It seems that we have two descriptions of you, Mr. Baynes. One from the little lady and another from everyone else around here. My wife seems to like Miss Mill's version best." He added quietly, with a pointed glance at Susan, "I'm sorry we have no coffee."

Susan rose and lifted an eyebrow at me.

"Ma'am, I've already failed at ordering you around in your own house, but would you promise not to make trouble, just to quiet my nervous stomach?"

"If you'll promise not to take that gun out again."

"Ma'am, I can't do that. Your husband would pounce on me and beat me up. Look how big he is."

She spoke over her shoulder as she went through the kitchen door. "In that case, I'm going to sneak out and scream for help."

Listening to her footsteps in the kitchen, I lowered my voice and asked the judge, "She wouldn't do that, would she?"

Bilbrey, poker-faced, matched my low tone and said, "Only God knows what that woman might decide. Now that you've found out that I can't help you, what are you going to do?"

Susan demanded from the kitchen, "Talk louder, please. Whispering is rude."

Lifting my voice, I said, "Excuse us, ma'am. We thought you'd already run outside in the rain and were getting yourself ready to start screaming."

Speaking normally again I said, "I've got to get Win away from the sheriff. Mullins threatened to kill him when he had him before. He'll surely do it the first chance he gets."

The tap of hurried footsteps announced Susan's approach. She brought in a coffeepot and cups on a tray and poured for each of us.

Bilbrey shook his head. "There are soldiers in town. Did you know that? Soldiers are standing guard over Mill at the jail and over his sister at the hotel. I don't see how Mullins could kill a prisoner with them watching."

I answered, "I don't see how he could accuse Win in the first place. I saw smoke at Lanmon's and rode in several hours after it happened. Win and Cris were both there. For heaven's sake, Win wouldn't take his sister with him if he was going to kill somebody, and he wouldn't hang around afterward, covering the bodies with one of his own blankets. I looked at the tracks. Four men did those murders and burned the place."

Bilbrey said, "Mullins claims he had two eyewitnesses, two men who saw you and Mill do the killing, but you killed one of his witnesses and the deputy he sent out to investigate. He said you put notes on the bodies to brag about what you'd done. Then you brought the bodies back to town and broke Mill out of jail."

I answered, "Look, Judge, if he claimed he had two witnesses, that just means he'd lined up two liars. From what the one I shot said to Cris when he rode up to her house with the deputy, he was a witness all right, because he was one of the men who did the killings. I don't think he was just talking big. His horse was one of the four ridden by the killers."

Bilbrey's face revealed nothing, gave no hint whether he believed me or not. He said flatly, "Watch what you say. You just admitted killing a man."

I decided to give him my side of the story. He could believe what he damn pleased.

"This is what happened. I'll start with the first day I rode into this part of Texas." I told the story from the beginning, leaving out our stay with Cowan. I finished with the question, "Suppose this is all true. What would you do if you were me?"

He answered promptly. "I'd turn myself in. I'm trying to get Mullins removed. I wrote to the military district commanding officer, explaining that we were nearly in a state of rebellion in Goliad County. How else could I describe an armed attack on the county seat, complete with the use of explosives? A military officer is here to investigate, and the soldiers are here to enforce his decisions."

Susan said quietly, "After I left the hotel today, I saw no soldier posted at the jail. Do

199

you suppose Sheriff Mullins persuaded the lieutenant to remove the guard on Mr. Mill? Maybe the sentry just moved inside to get out of the rain."

I said, "That clinches it. Judge, I can't depend on the Army to keep Mullins from killing Win. They wouldn't expect that from a sheriff, wouldn't be watching for it. Here's what I'm going to do. I'm going to force you at gunpoint to knock on the jail door and get us inside. After I take Win out of there, we're going over to that hotel and get Cris. Then we'll let you come home, and the Mills and I will ride clear out of this crazy state. You can feed Goliad to the chickens if you like. We'll be gone."

Bilbrey said sternly, "Now you're talking like an outlaw. Your plan is extremely unwise and dangerous. In fact, it's crazy. You'll never get away with it. Those soldiers are black Seminole scouts. Even if you get out of town alive, which I doubt, they'll track you down."

That bit of news made me flinch inside. So far, my big edge had been that I didn't think highly of Texans as trackers. That advantage vanished if the judge was right. Scouts recruited from among escaped slaves living with the Seminoles were likely to be tough and trailwise. Besides, the Army didn't care a flip about county lines. They'd get on my trail and keep coming.

I nodded and answered, my tone of voice

just as grim as the judge's, "I can't sit around and be wise and safe while Win's the one about to be murdered by a vicious sheriff. And I'm not going to let Cris stay locked up in a hotel or anywhere else. As far as I'm concerned, Mullins has no evidence, and he knows it. He sent two men to kill Cris, and he expected to kill Win. He even told Win exactly when and how he planned to kill him. You don't tell a man something like that if you expect him to be able to talk about it later."

I put my fork down carefully beside my dinner knife on the plate and shoved it forward.

Susan asked, "Is that all you're going to eat?"

"I'm not a big eater, ma'am, but that was mighty good. I'm obliged."

She persisted. "You hardly ate anything. Have some more. There's plenty." When I grinned and shook my head, she looked intently at me and said, "You're scared, aren't you?"

"I'm feeling jumpy as a hot flea, ma'am. How'd you know? Am I turning green?"

Susan said, "I'll make you feel better. You don't need to tie me up. I'll stay right here. I'm convinced you'll shoot my husband if I don't keep quiet."

Judge Bilbrey took a long hard look at his wife, but she avoided his gaze by staring at me. Finally he said, "All right, but there's one last thing. There are less than fifty men in the whole county who are qualified to vote. I think that army lieutenant might be impressed if you brought in a recall petition against Mullins signed by a bunch of registered voters. I have a copy of the voter list in my study upstairs. Shall I go get it?"

"Word of honor you won't come back down the stairs packing a gun?"

"Word of honor."

"I'd be obliged."

Bilbrey came to his feet without hesitation and left the room.

Susan said in a low voice, "I know you're going to try to be careful, but if shooting starts, knock him down. He so despises to soil his clothes or lose his dignity. It would be just like him to stand there and be shot rather than get himself muddy."

"Mrs. Bilbrey, you're looking straight at the most careful man you ever met in your life. Considering the size and shape of him, trying to knock your husband down wouldn't be a cautious thing to do. But don't worry about him. With a little luck, he'll be back home in less than an hour. Ma'am, did you see how many guards were at the hotel and where they were posted?"

"One. He sat in a chair right beside Crissy's door. She's in room 203 on the second floor. The guard is relieved at four-hour intervals, and there was a change at noon, so I expect they'll change again at eight o'clock tonight. That's only twenty minutes from now."

I straightened in surprise, but before I could say anything, Susan added, speaking rapidly, "Crissy told me about all that. She watches everything. She was very sure you were coming, by the way. She said she didn't mind talking about it, because she didn't expect anyone to believe her. She was right. I thought it was a wild idea. I was amused.

"Her things were packed and ready to go. She seemed so refined and sensible otherwise that I thought her sitting there waiting for you was incredible. She didn't seem to be the kind of young woman to indulge in girlish fantasies."

Susan Bilbrey smiled, eyeing me. "Are you really that predictable?"

"It's just that breaking people out of jail is a basic outlaw frolic, ma'am. It's the first thing we have to learn."

Judge Bilbrey walked in, handed me a list of names, and said, "We should have this timed pretty well. By the time we get to the jail, it'll be after eight. The guard there is probably relieved about the same time as the one at the hotel."

When I cast a questioning glance at Susan, she said, "We were talking about that, Mr. Baynes, when you appeared like a ghost in the doorway. We were laughing at a silly young woman timing the guards and such foolishness. It seemed pathetically funny. Who would have thought her hero was really coming?"

Bilbrey nodded. "Oddly, you may surprise them even more because you've done this sort of thing in Goliad twice before. I, for one, didn't think you'd dare try to do the same thing over again. The military always checks guards and sentries once before and once after midnight. I hope you don't plan to harm a soldier?" He acted as if the thought had just come to him.

"I got no quarrel with soldiers. By walking in behind you, Judge, I should get the drop on them. Nobody should get hurt." I picked up my hat.

Bilbrey shrugged into his slicker and said, "Let's go. It's time." He leaned down to kiss his wife.

While they were occupied with each other, I slipped a dollar under my plate. The way things had worked out, I felt I had been invited to eat, but my horses hadn't. A Baynes pays his way.

When I moved to follow the judge to the front door, Susan said, "I hope you are very, very good at basic outlaw frolics, Mr. Baynes."

I said, "Thank you, ma'am. We'll know in less than an hour, won't we?"

Reid Bilbrey stopped and turned to face me when he opened the gate to the white picket fence in front of the house. His voice was a whisper, but he spoke like he was giving instructions from the bench. "I must walk in front in order for you to keep a gun on me properly. You understand that everything I'm doing is under duress?"

"Yes, sir."

"I'm in fear for my life, and tortured with concern for my wife's safety."

I nodded like a simpleton in the darkness, but I guess he saw it.

"Very well. Where's your damn gun?"

"I got it under my slicker, Judge. I don't want it to get wet."

"Can you get it out quickly?"

"Yes, sir. You might be surprised how quick."

"Good. Follow me, and let me do the talking if we meet anyone."

"Yes, sir."

He stalked off without looking back, a straight-backed and dignified young man of authority, his highly polished boots squishing in the mud.

EIGHTEEN

Judge Bilbrey had no notion of going anywhere quietly. He walked down the streets of
Goliad like he was leading a band, every step
firm and confident. He seemed completely
unaware that his parade-ground manner of
walking plastered me to the knees with mud.
Twice, he slowed. The first time he sent me
a questioning look.

I whispered, "Seemed more natural looking
if I walked beside you, sir."

He nodded curtly, but a few steps later, he
slowed again and asked in a low tone, "Good
heavens, it just occurred to me. You need a
horse. Where's your horse? In fact, you'll
need three. Did you think of that?"

"Yes, sir."

"You have horses?"

"Yes, sir."

"Where are they?"

"Hid."

"Oh. Of course. You have food?"

"Yes, sir."

"Have you thought about the hardship
you're taking that young woman into? Ten
minutes into this weather and she'll be
soaking wet. Suppose you make her ill?"

"I'll find ways to look after her, Judge. Her

brother's a caring man too. She'll be fine. Besides, it's got to stop raining sometime."

I flinched, but I couldn't claim to be surprised when Bilbrey struck the jail door three times, much like a man would do if testing to find the best spot for a battering ram. At the same time, he growled irritably, "Open the door! This is Judge Bilbrey, and it's raining out here."

After a moment, when the bar lifted inside and the door opened a cautious crack, Bilbrey stepped forward, blocking the view with his tall broad body. He said impatiently, "Open the door. Hurry up."

The door swung wide, the judge stepped in and aside, and I put my Navy against the sheriff's stomach just when he holstered his own weapon. I knocked his hand away, lifted his pistol from its holster, stuck it under my belt, and heeled the door shut. Mullins stood like an idiot, hand still groping at his empty holster, his mind about two steps behind what had already happened.

I shoved Mullins, he staggered back into a Negro trooper, and I had my Navy leveled at the scrambling soldier, all in less than three seconds from the time the sheriff first opened the door. The soldier was alert and fast as a scalded cat, but I had him cold. His rifle in hand and ready, he needed a split second more to cock and bring his weapon to bear, time he didn't have because the stumbling sheriff had gotten in his way.

I spoke as calmly as I could. "You might get me, but I got the edge. You decide. Do we both die today, or do you put it down?"

My luck was holding. Bilbrey, Mullins, and the soldier were all clustered so I could watch all three without shifting my eyes. Otherwise, I'd have had no choice. I'd have had to shoot him, and the sound of a shot would have set Goliad to humming like a swarm of bees.

The eyes tell everything in a situation like that, and this man had no fear. He sized me up, calculated his chances coldly, and found he had none. Once that was decided, this kind of man instantly started thinking about the next time. "I put it down, you shoot me anyway?"

"I won't do a thing like that."

"I put it in the corner? That satisfy? This floor dirty."

"Just so you put it down."

He looked me right in the eye while he thought it over. "White man's word no good. You look Indian. Indian's word means somethin'."

"I'm not Indian. Common mistake."

Without taking his eyes from mine, he moved with painful slowness but leaned his rifle in a corner. "Don't blame you, chief. If'n I was white, I'd try to look like somethin' else too."

I took a deep breath and let it out slowly, knowing with absolute confidence that facing this man had brought me as close to death as I'd ever been.

"What's your name?" I asked.

"Private Jonas."

"Jonas, you got some rope here?"

"Yonder." He motioned with his head.

"Get it. Tie the sheriff's hands and gag him with something. Gag him tight."

Jonas bound Mullins's hands so tight he grimaced and groaned in protest. He stuffed a swatch of dirty cloth into the sheriff's mouth and whipped a short length of rope across his face to secure the gag. When the rope jerked tight in the soldier's powerful hands, Mullins's jaw sank back and down under the brutal pressure, bowing his neck and cruelly distorting his face.

I asked, "Is it tight enough, Sheriff?"

Mullins, his head frozen in place by the crushing pressure, moaned frantically through his nose.

"Good job, Jonas. Now we go downstairs, gentlemen." I jerked open the same drawer I remembered from my prior visit and picked up the same ring of keys. The sheriff was evidently a man of habit. I plucked Win's gun belt from a peg on the wall. "Bring the lantern, Judge."

Win waited in the same cell, leaning against the bars. He said, "You took your

209

time, for heaven's sake. I thought I heard your voice, but with all the chitchat, I thought maybe it was just the sheriff's friends dropping by for a drink and a poker game."

Showing him my saintly-long-suffering-sad-grin, I answered, "Gripe, gripe, grumble, nag. You sound like your sister."

I unlocked the barred door and shoved Mullins inside as soon as Win stepped out. Win grabbed his gun belt, moving so fast he fumbled with the buckle when he strapped it on. Still, he had it fastened before I turned the key to lock Mullins safely away.

"Private Jonas," I said, "we need to tie and gag you too. We need to keep things quiet here for a while yet."

"No chief. Private Jonas ain't never wearin' chains or ropes again."

"Jonas, I don't have time to argue with you."

"No chains. No ropes, chief. Not never. You gonna have to shoot me after all."

Judge Bilbrey said quietly, "You could give your parole, Private Jonas."

"What that be?"

"It's usually a solemn promise from a prisoner that, if released, he'll not again take up arms against his captors. Normally, the promise is given in writing, but I don't think Mr. Baynes would demand that. You could give your limited parole that you won't make any noise or cause any trouble until the guards are inspected or changed. Then you'd be free to do any duty you are assigned."

"That git me in trouble? The lieutenant be mad at me?"

Bilbrey answered, "My wife did it with my approval. Mr. Baynes trusted her word. I don't know whether he would take yours, and I can't tell you what the lieutenant would think."

"You speak up fer me, Judge?"

"Yes, I'll try to explain that you've done a fine job here under difficult circumstances. These men are desperate. If they have to shoot you, they'll probably go ahead and shoot me and the sheriff too. Seems to me you have to try to prevent bloodshed if you can."

Jonas turned to me and said, "I give you my parole, like the judge said."

I glanced at Win. He shrugged and said flatly, "I'm not going to shoot him. You're not going to shoot him. He'll put up a howling fight if we try to tie him up. What the hell choice is there?"

I stuck out my hand. Private Jonas stared at it for a long moment before he raised his own. When he grasped my hand, he grinned and said, "Look at me. Shaking hands with a white man. Ain't nobody gonna believe this. I ain't sure I believes it neither."

Win asked, "You going to invite him to

step into that other cell?"

"No. I either take his word or I don't. It's either good or it's bad. There's nothing in between."

Win and Bilbrey moved toward the stairs. When I turned to follow, Private Jonas spoke softly. "Mistah Baynes, if the lieutenant put me on your tail and tell me to shoot you, I gonna do it."

I walked back to look him square in the eye. "If you come shooting at me, Private Jonas, you're a dead man. I'll piss on your grave."

His delighted belly laugh followed me all the way up the stairs and across the sheriff's office. It boomed in my ears while I shouldered the coil of rope left over from binding Mullins. The sound of it echoed in my head even after I shut the front door and followed Win and Judge Bilbrey down the muddy street.

If Private Jonas was an example of the kind of men the Army sent to bring quiet to Goliad, the whole game had changed. He wanted the contest taken out of town, wanted me to know his satisfaction and anticipation. Looking forward to it gave him intense pleasure.

My days of running circles around citified men and owning the nights had ended.

Jonas looked forward to running me down the same way I used to love raccoon hunts.

No, it would be more like tracking a mountain lion. The hunt offered more flavor if the quarry could circle back and strike with fang and claw. Thus he'd given me fair warning, not out of courtesy but to enhance the chase.

I'd seen many like Private Jonas when I was a boy in Louisiana. Some broke under the weight of chains. Some made the best of it and rose above their condition. Others developed a malignant patience, feeding their consuming hatred coal by glowing coal, until nothing remained of them but a deadly savage awaiting an opening.

Jonas had found his heaven. Blessed is the man who does his purely honest duty and settles old scores at the same time.

A chill came into the night.

NINETEEN

Win said sincerely, "Thanks, Judge. Cris and I had about given up hope that there was any honest law left in Texas."

I spoke quickly. "I got to tell you, partner, Judge Bilbrey is with us at the point of a gun. His story is he's under duress, in fear for his life, and tortured with concern for his wife's safety."

Win slid to a stop in the mud and snapped, "What the hell's going on? Who threatened anybody's wife? You accusing me or Milt of threatening your family, you lying son of a bitch?"

"Hey! Wait a minute. Don't say another word. Just keep walking toward that hotel, Win." I put a hand on his shoulder and gently urged him forward. "Don't go red-headed on me right in the middle of everything. Let me finish what I was saying. I sneaked into his house and pulled a gun on him. Not knowing me, the judge naturally felt a concern for his wife. That's just a regular, ordinary way to act, don't you think?"

"Oh. That makes sense. Sorry, Judge, I spoke too quick. Jail doesn't sweeten a man's disposition. I apologize."

"Accepted. Spoken like a gentleman,"

Judge Bilbrey answered stiffly.

Win glanced at me. "We going to the hotel to get Cris, or do you just plan to take a room and spend the night?"

"We're going after Cris."

"You got a plan?"

"Yeah. I figured, if a clerk gets in the way, you can hold a gun up his nose and ask him politely to keep quiet. I'll go upstairs behind the judge and pull a gun on the soldier they got up there for a guard. He won't want to shoot through the judge at me, so that should be easy."

Win nodded. "Then we just walk away to Montana Territory or someplace? I don't see a horse anywhere."

"The horses are saddled and eating his corn while they wait in Judge Bilbrey's barn."

The judge gasped, and it was his turn to slide to a halt in the mud. "Is there no end to your impertinence? Baynes, you're the damndest . . ." He stopped, dragged in a deep breath, sighed, and started forward again. "It'll probably work. It just might. It reaches yet another and higher level of insanity."

Win asked, "What happens to the poor terrified judge after all this running around at gunpoint?"

"We walk him home and ride away. When I borrowed him, I promised his wife I'd look after him. Soon as she inspects him and says he's fit, we can go."

Judge Bilbrey said sharply, "That's enough of that. I'll not be talked about by a couple of fugitives from justice as if I were a basket of peaches. Mind your tongues, gentlemen."

We walked a few steps in silence before Win asked with exaggerated courtesy, "Judge Bilbrey, sir?"

"Yes?"

"No offense, but would you put your feet down a little easier? Walking beside you gets a man muddied clear up to his ears."

"Oh. Of course. I beg your pardon."

When we approached the hotel, Win asked, "We just going to walk right in?"

"Yup. The nice big judge will walk in front, in case anybody starts shooting, then me, then you. You sweet-talk the clerk; the judge and I go upstairs and gather up Cris. Simple. It either works or it doesn't. Here we go."

We started up the stairs to the front porch, and Judge Bilbrey stopped suddenly. Half crouched, Navy in my hand under my slicker, I looked all around, nearly frantic, wondering what had brought him to a halt. I heard scraping. He swayed back and forth, calmly cleaning his boots on the mud scraper attached to the porch floor. I sincerely wanted to holster my Navy and tap him a couple of times with my pogamoggan to show him how much I enjoyed the delay.

On second thought though, if we were being watched, what could look more natural and ordinary than the way he was acting? Finally, he stepped toward the front door, stomping the rest of the mud off his feet, stomping hard enough to loosen every nail in the planks underfoot.

The lobby lay empty and silent before us, a small coal-oil lamp dimly lighting the sparse room. Judge Bilbrey headed for the stairs, his heels thumping the floor loud enough to send echoes through the building. He tramped up the stairs, and I wondered if the whole hotel swayed and creaked under his heavy footsteps or if my imagination was getting to me.

The sentry was on his feet, wide-eyed, when we came to the second floor. From the racket, the poor soldier probably expected to see a drunk on horseback coming up the steps. Bilbrey strode right at the guard like an inspecting officer in a hurry and said, "I'm Judge Bilbrey. Where's that Mill woman? Which room?"

Flustered, the guard answered, "It's this one, suh." I don't think the man even saw me approaching behind the judge until I stepped around and jammed my cocked Navy into his stomach. Holding his rifle across his chest, he froze. With my left hand, I gently lifted his rifle from his hands and tapped the door with it. When Cris opened the door, the guard backed in, moving in response to the pressure of the Navy against his middle.

Cris whispered, "Don't you dare hurt him. He's a nice man."

Ignoring her, I said quietly, "Shut the door, Judge."

As soon as I heard the latch click, I motioned with the sentry's rifle toward the four-poster. He didn't move.

I said, "Stretch out on the bed. We're not going to hurt anybody. I just want to tie you up, so you won't give the alarm till after we're gone." He still didn't move.

"Look, soldier, I'm offering to tie you up and leave you in a comfortable place. I'd just as soon bend your own rifle barrel over your head, tie you up, and hang you out the window. It's up to you. It doesn't make a damn to me."

When he moved slowly to obey, I propped his rifle in the corner and pitched the coil of rope to Cris. "Tie and gag that nice man." She tied one of his hands to a bedpost and pointed at my leg. I pulled my knife from my legging and handed it to her. She cut pieces from the rope, so she could tie him spread-eagled. A pillowslip served as a gag.

I leaned over him to check the knots. "Wait till the guard is changed or inspected, nice man. By then, we'll be gone. Don't make a fuss. Your lieutenant doesn't want a gunfight in town. We don't either. Understand?"

He nodded, black eyes calm and indifferent. He wore the expression of a man taking a good look at me, so he could add me to his private list of wanted men. That's all I needed, yet another Jonas.

Cris stepped up close to the bed and spoke to him. "I hope you don't get in trouble because of this. None of it's your fault."

He shrugged, shook his head, and shifted his gaze to me. The gag kept him from answering, but his eyes sent a clear message saying who he thought was in for trouble.

We filed out of the room, closed the door, went down the stairs, found Win waiting in the lobby, and walked out into the muddy street.

I said in a low tone, "Judge, can you pick a way to get back to your house without us having to say hello to the Army?"

When he nodded curtly and led the way without comment, Cris said, "We're walking? Don't you have horses?"

I said accusingly, "Judge Bilbrey didn't offer his buggy." Win snickered, and Bilbrey said severely, "Miss Mill, I am an officer of the court. I was forced from my home at gunpoint to walk through cold rain and mud. My clothing has been soiled, probably beyond repair. I have been subjected to great danger and forced to stand by helplessly while an officer of the law was humiliated, soldiers were threatened, and criminal suspects liberated from detention.

"Nevertheless, had the thought crossed my mind that this adventure had the slightest prospect of success, I would gladly have hitched my buggy and had it ready for your comfort. I apologize. The idea never entered my head."

"You didn't think I'd succeed? That wounds me, Judge Bilbrey."

"You're a brave and clever man, Baynes, but you have a lack of reverence for the law, a criminal irreverence in fact. Still, having accompanied you on this escapade, I'm convinced you and Mr. Mill are both falsely accused. You had ample opportunity to take lives this evening and went to great risk to avoid doing so. This outing has been most informative."

I answered, "Judge, I had to keep things quiet or the Army would have been all over me. One gunshot and they'd be nailing my hide to a wall right now."

"You have no respect for other people's intelligence, Baynes. I thought silence was the reason for your restraint at first. I hadn't noticed that vicious-looking knife of yours until we were in Miss Mill's hotel room. You could easily and quite silently have killed the sheriff and both those soldiers had you chosen to do so. The temptation to kill that stubborn Private Jonas must have been great."

We trudged on in silence until Cris spoke.

"You deserve a round of applause. Congratulations, Judge Bilbrey."

"For what, Miss Mill?"

"You're the first one I've ever seen who could make Milt Baynes hush without knocking him unconscious." Everybody but me seemed to find that remark the best joke of the evening.

We'd come through the front gate and were walking toward the house when I saw movement on the front porch. I whispered, "Watch it, Win," and jerked Cris behind me.

"Reid?" Mrs. Bilbrey walked to the edge of the porch and called again in a low voice. "Reid, is that you?"

"Yes, Susan. It's me," he answered softly.

We gathered at the steps, and Mrs. Bilbrey asked, "Are you coming inside, Mr. Baynes?"

"No, ma'am. We'd track half of Goliad into your house. You'd be mopping up mud all day tomorrow. What time is it?"

She said, "It's about ten till nine, I think. I'd have to go inside to look at the clock again to be sure. Why?"

"Because I told you he'd be back in less than an hour, didn't I, ma'am?"

She laughed like a conspirator and said, "I'm glad you're good at basic outlaw frolics, Mr. Baynes. Good luck, Crissy." She extended her hand.

Cris reached up until the two women's hands touched briefly. "Thank you, Susan."

Judge Bilbrey said, "I'll be giving the alarm soon. You'd better be going."

I said, "Judge, I know you give more advice than you receive, and rightly so, but can I give you one little suggestion?"

"You can try."

"Sit tight. Let somebody else stir up trouble. If you walk away from your house and somebody else gives the alarm, no telling how many people might shoot at anything moving." I turned to Mrs. Bilbrey. "I brought him home safe. He's smart, ma'am, but he's a bit arrogant. It makes him too brave. It's up to you to keep him home. If he gets shot by mistake in the dark, the sheriff will come up with ten witnesses who'll swear I did it."

I started around the house toward the barn, hearing Cris's and Win's soft goodbyes as they followed me away from the Bilbreys. At the dark side of the house, I paused a moment to let her catch up before I hissed sharply at the small shadow following me, "Cris!"

Her tense answer came quickly. "What is it?"

"Come here. Quick!"

She darted forward to stand beside me. "What's wrong?"

"Take my arm. Walk real slow. Get close to me. Closer!" We walked very slowly toward the barn. I shortened my stride to match hers.

"What is it?" she whispered. "What's wrong?"

After a couple more steps, I said, "Nothing."

"Nothing's wrong?"

"No, I don't think so."

"When why are we walking like this?"

"I like it. It's cozy."

TWENTY

Win and I talked briefly in the barn before we climbed into our saddles. We agreed to save the wool boots for later. I led the way out of town, following the exact route I'd used on the way into Goliad and holding Judas to a slow walk. Since I didn't know where the lieutenant had camped his troops, that was the only direction I knew for a certainty I'd not blunder into the army bivouac.

The way I read the weather, the rain had set in for the night. We changed directions a couple of times a few miles from town and finally angled over to take the cart road toward Victoria. It was like riding a road covered with a couple or three inches of soup mixed with sand and rocks. I stopped twice and circled back on foot to strike a couple of matches and examine our trail. Our tracks filled with thin mud and vanished a few minutes after we passed.

The rain stopped about an hour before dawn, but no break showed in the heavy clouds. I led the way into a thick clump of woods and slid from the saddle.

Cris stopped her horse beside me and asked, "Can we talk now?"

"No. You can listen. Proper women keep quiet and listen to the men."

She snickered, let me help her from the saddle, and said, "Just for that, you can build the fire and brew your own coffee."

"Who says we're going to build a fire and have coffee?"

Win spoke for the first time since we left Goliad. "I say we are.

I said, "No. You two are. I'm going to scout around. Hardest thing in the world after a good rain is to build a fire without sending a smoke signal. Can you handle it?"

Win answered, "It's not even light enough to see smoke, for heaven's sake. Does it really make any difference, Milt? No fooling?"

"Probably not. How about giving me a few minutes to look around before you do anything? Keep quiet until I get back. There are almost always places to find dry wood if a man takes the trouble to look. Besides, I always like to wander around and check a place where I plan to sleep."

Cris asked, "We're going to stop here and sleep on the wet ground? Why don't we ride on to Uncle Caleb's? Couldn't we get there by noon?"

I said, "The law couldn't track us after all that rain if they had a tribe of Indians and a pack of dogs. That means it's even more important that nobody see us in the daylight. We're dealing with the Army now. That lieutenant might send patrols out in all directions to ask questions. A woman riding on horseback in this sloppy weather would attract attention, don't you think? Most women prefer to ride in buggies or on wagons."

When nobody answered, I said, "Give me thirty minutes to look around. Then we can make ourselves at home."

They both nodded, so I moved deeper into the woods. I made good time, not feeling I needed to be too careful. As soon as I circled our campsite at a distance of about a hundred yards, I began to relax. I found no sign of old fire sites or trails, nothing to indicate that this was anybody's favorite stopping place. Only a short distance from where Cris and Win waited, I found a clearing in the trees, a little spot offering good grass for the horses. On the way back, I got lucky. A deep pile of windblown leaves had stacked up beside a huge downed oak. I brushed off the closely packed top layer and allowed myself a smug grin.

When I came back to them, I found Win squatted on his heels while Cris paced aimlessly back and forth. One look at her face in the early dawn light told me that she was walking to fight off sleep. I said, "A perfect place for us is only about fifty steps away. We'll even have graze for the stock. Let's go."

They followed me without a word, leading the horses. When we got to the downed oak, I turned to Cris and said, "Leaves often pack down so the top sheds water just like you see here. There are probably enough dry branches mixed in that pile for me to put together a skimpy fire. I'll fix you a nice cup of coffee, Mr. Plague. Then I'll spread you a bed of leaves to keep you off the wet ground. You'll be so comfortable you'll feel sinful."

Win loosened the girth on his horse and said, "I'll unsaddle and picket the horses."

"What do you want me to do?" asked Cris.

"You just look pretty and talk to me."

"I thought you said women are just supposed to listen."

"Yeah, I did, but I lie a lot. You know that."

Win grinned over his shoulder at me as he led the horses toward their patch of grass.

I found a nice strong branch and started probing the leaf bed. Sure enough, it was full of brittle, dry sticks. I pulled several from the pile, watching carefully. "You can go ahead and start a fire, Cris, and I'll put together a place for you to sleep."

She knelt and started nesting small branches, hardly larger than matchsticks, to start the fire, but she finally stopped and stared curiously at me. "What are you doing that for?"

I stopped too. I was in the middle of carrying batches of leaves away from the big pile and sifting them through my fingers into another heap. Her question puzzled me. "I'm doing what I just told you I'd do. I'm making you a place to sleep."

"Why don't you just brush the wet ones off the top? I can bed down right there. Why carry them to a different place?"

"I can do that, Cris. It'd be a lot easier, but I thought you might be particular who you sleep with."

Her eyes widened, and she lost her sleepy expression in an instant. "I beg your pardon. What do you mean by that crude remark, Milt Baynes?"

"I mean that I'm moving these and sifting through them as carefully as I can for you. Everybody picks their own friends, I guess, but maybe I forgot for a minute how mean you are. Still, I figured you wouldn't want to lie down and sleep with a family of snakes or a nest of scorpions."

She made a face at me and shuddered. "I shouldn't have asked. I knew I shouldn't. Why can't I learn not to ask you anything? Now all I'll think about is spiders, scorpions, and snakes. I won't sleep a wink."

"Wrong. You'll sleep like a princess, because you know I'm looking out for you."

She tried to cover a smile and asked, "Do you have any matches?"

I groaned. "You mean you don't have any matches? Do I have to think of everything for you?"

Cris took a deep breath and closed her

eyes. I went ahead and dug out my matches, untied the knot, and unrolled the waxed canvas cover. When I walked over to her and extended the cluster of matches, I said, "Take all you want. Take all of them. I can't deny a beautiful woman nothing."

The breath she was holding surged out of her with an explosive little gasp of laughter. She shook her head in pretended disgust, took a match, and started the fire. After watching carefully to be sure she had a healthy flame going, she turned to me and asked, "Milt, why are you pestering me this morning?"

"To make you a little bit mad."

"You succeeded. Why?"

"Look, Plague, you were acting half dead a minute ago. How do you feel now?"

Her head jerked up in surprise, and her eyes narrowed.

"You feel great now, don't you?" I pursued. "All my numerous women enjoy a bit of before-breakfast cheerful repartee. It quickens the blood, sharpens the wit, and stimulates the appetite. Nothing like a little joust." I assumed a fencing stance, danced toward her, and pretended to run her through.

"What the hell are you doing?" Win asked. He'd returned quietly from picketing the horses.

"Entertaining the cook," I said quickly,

dropping the pose. "She was about to go to sleep and fall in the fire."

"Well, she looks perky enough now."

"Sure, Win, all my women . . ."

Cris cut me off with, "Oh hush up, Milt."

I shrugged and gave Win my best exasperated look.

Win smirked and said, "Coffee's going to be good, but I wish we had something to eat. You bring any food, Milt?"

I nodded and pointed at my saddlebags.

He asked, "What you got in there?"

I said, "How would you like tortillas, hot tamales, and stuff like that?"

Win said, "Wonderful, I guess. Cris and I never have gotten around to eating any of the Mexican food here in Texas. Let's get at it."

Later, Cris swallowed a big bite of tamale and said, "Milt, this is absolutely delicious. Where did you get this kind of food?"

"Got it from a Mexican fellow in Goliad."

"Do you know how they make these wonderful things, these tamales?"

"Well, yeah, I do, Cris, but I don't think you could do it."

"Why not? I'm a good cook. All I need is the recipe."

"True, but I don't think you could even get past the first step."

"What's that?"

"Killing the dog."

Both of them froze and sat staring at me.

Win had a mouthful of tamale. His jaw stopped working, his eyes grew big and round, and he glanced around like a tobacco chewer looking for a place to unload.

Cris asked in a tiny voice, "Dog?"

I grinned at Win and said, "Go ahead and swallow. They always scrape the hair off before they cook it."

Win looked stricken, and Cris brought a hand up to her mouth. Behind her hand, she asked with a strained voice, "Joke, Milt? Is it a joke?"

I chuckled. "Yeah, everybody thinks it's funny." Win took a long trembly breath and swallowed. Cris shuddered and relaxed.

Then I added, "Except the poor dogs."

"Damn you, Milt Baynes!" Win sprang up and crouched over me. Cris came to her feet too. She stood half bent over, her hand still over her mouth.

Win's voice shook. "That's meaner'n hell. How can you do something like that?"

I grinned up at him. "About as easy as you two watched a helpless, sick man with broken ribs nearly choke to death on milk and raw eggs."

Cris said sharply, "Oh, that's ridiculous. That's not the same thing at all. Everybody knows milk and raw eggs is good for you."

"Is that so? Then everybody knows that tamales are good for you, right?"

Win put a hand on his stomach and gave

me a suspicious glance before he swung his head to stare at Cris. "He got both of us because of your little trick," he said accusingly. His gaze came back to me. "I thought it was funny at the time, Milt. I could have told you right off that milk and eggs taste good, especially with honey mixed in the way Cris fixes it. I guess we're even."

"Why don't you two get some sleep? I'll stand first watch," I said.

A moment later, Win spoke from his blankets. "Milt?"

"Yeah?"

"You don't suppose a man would get worms from eating a dog, do you?"

I took my time answering, pretending to give the question grave thought. "Not unless the dog had worms."

He sat up and gasped.

"Forget it, Win. It was just a joke."

"You wouldn't lie to a friend, would you, Milt? Tell the truth."

"Joke."

He took a deep breath and sank back.

"Milt?" This time it was Cris.

"Now what do you want? I thought you were sleepy."

"I'm sinfully comfortable, just like you said I'd be. Thank you."

I went to stand beside her and dropped the ring of keys on her blanket. "Why don't you hang on to those for me? The way your brother keeps going back to the Goliad jail, we might as well have our own set."

She pulled the ring under her blanket and said quietly, "Thank you for coming after us. I knew you would."

"That so? You forgot something, though. You promised you wouldn't say thank you to me, not ever again."

She smiled at me, looking like a ten year old with a new ribbon.

"I lied, Milt."

She was still smiling when sleep closed her eyes.

TWENTY-ONE

The next evening we saddled and put the wool boots on the horses. Although all three of us were anxious to be moving, we sat around and talked for a while, waiting for the last light of day to pass.

Win said, "I don't mind doing it, but putting boots on the horses seems a lot of trouble for nothing."

"Probably. I always found being extra careful is a cheaper price to pay than putting up with bad surprises."

He nodded and raised both hands, indicating he had no wish to argue.

I went on, "Jonas scares me, Win. That's a tough man, and he's no tenderfoot. Another thing, I didn't like the way he talked about his lieutenant."

Win straightened and blinked. "Why? I didn't hear him say anything bad."

"That's what worries me. He spoke with respect, honest respect, no fake stuff. He made it clear, if that lieutenant told him to do something, that ended the matter. I don't like that. An officer who can command that kind of an attitude from a man like Jonas must be damn good. A smart officer can run us flat into the ground if he decides to do it.

Those Negro scouts are used to tracking hostile Indians. Like I said this morning, he's liable to send patrols all over the place looking for us. The only way to keep them from catching us is to ride clear out of the country."

Talking about it made me nervous. I took a few steps and scanned the road. Nobody had passed all day, and that didn't surprise me. It would be futile to try to move freight through that deep mud, and anybody going visiting would wait for better weather. When I turned back to Win, I went on, "We'd have a better chance with Indians chasing us. At least an Indian would probably lose interest after a while. A man like Private Jonas would track us clear to Georgia and love every minute of it."

Win shrugged. "So what? They won't patrol at night. They can't try to follow every trail laid down by three horses either."

"You're right, Win, they'll rest easy at night and patrol nice and relaxed in the daylight till they cross our trail. My bet is they found out our horses were kept in Judge Bilbrey's barn. We left prints in there. If he has a bunch of real trackers, and I'll bet he does, they'll know our trail at a glance. That's why I want the wool boots on our horses."

He glanced at me and frowned. "You think Bilbrey will tell about the horses?"

"I'd bet on it. He'd feel a duty."

Win shook his head. "He was stiff-necked,

but he didn't seem unfriendly."

"He's a judge. I don't think he's inclined to harbor fugitives or whatever the law might call it here in Texas. One good thing about Bilbrey though, he wants Mullins out of the sheriff's office too. He suggested we try to get signatures on a petition to recall him. He gave me a list of all the registered voters in Goliad County."

Win said, "That makes sense. We might get rid of him that way. I never thought of that."

I spat in disgust and got a frown from Cris. I had almost forgotten she was watching and listening. "Win, that makes no sense at all. It's the worst thing we could do. We'd need to ride all over the county to get those signatures. Haven't you been listening? They'd run us down. No doubt about it. I got you out of jail twice, Win. There won't be a third time, not with them. Those soldiers probably wouldn't even bring us in across our saddles. They'd be more likely to leave us where we fell. Private Jonas and his kind don't take many prisoners."

Cris asked, "What do you think we should do, Milt?"

"Ride to your uncle's house, rest up and say goodbye to him, and get out of Texas as fast as good horses can run."

Win acted like he hadn't heard me. He asked, "What do you think would be the best way to get those signatures Judge Bilbrey wanted?"

I couldn't keep an edge of sarcasm out of my voice. "One of us could sit in the saloon and the other could hang out in the general store. I imagine most everybody comes to town every month or so. We could sit around, pass the time of day with the sheriff, and let him introduce us to the voters when they come to town."

Win gave me a disgusted glance. "I'm serious."

I sat for a while, thinking hard. "Look, why not just hold off and see if the judge can skin this cat for us? Maybe we could hide out at your uncle's place and wait. The judge could get together a recall petition easier than we can. As far as that goes, he might talk the lieutenant into getting rid of Mullins without a petition. The lieutenant could do it with no fuss and bother. He represents the Army, and the Army still calls the tune in Texas."

Win asked, "How long can I stay away and still expect to find any of my stock when I go home? I spent the best part of a whole year building a house and barn. They burned the barn and maybe, by now, the house too. That place is all I have, Milt. Without it, I'm dead broke. I can't just ride away."

Cris asked, "Where could we go?"

I rubbed my hands together and wished I was headed for Canada. As far as that goes, I wanted to visit most anywhere that was a long way from Texas. Sometimes a man cares little where he's going as long as he's putting distance between him and a bad situation.

Win waited patiently for me to speak. I had to say something, so I walked toward the horses and said, "Let's go to Cowan's. He might have some ideas. If we decide to dodge the Army all over Goliad County while we try to collect signatures, at least we'll have a place for Cris to stay while we're at it."

We rode slowly. Neither of the Mills said another word, having learned by now that talking on the trail made me edgy. Even so, we arrived at Cowan's place two or three hours before dawn. Dogs started barking while we were still two hundred yards away. When we came near the first building, I heard the sound of a weapon cocking. A man asked sharply, "*¿Quién es?*"

I answered in Spanish.

The figure in the shadows responded in English, "Welcome home, *patrón*. I will wake Señor Cowan."

We rode slowly to the big house and waited in the saddle for the old man to invite us in. I asked, "Win, did you notice guards at night when we stayed here?"

His answer came quietly out of the darkness. "I wouldn't have noticed if Uncle Caleb hadn't mentioned it. He keeps two men on watch every night. All his hands sleep with guns close at hand. He's not a trusting man.

He runs this ranch like a military post in the middle of hostile Indian country."

I remember Cowan mentioning a bunch of renegades trying to ride in and take over his place. Those bandits must have had no warning, no suspicion about what they were riding into. I'd bet they thought they were riding into a typical little village full of un-armed Mexicans.

With thick walls, narrow firing slits, and heavy shutters ready to cover all windows, each of the buildings in Cowan's little settle-ment was like a small fort. Horsebackers had no chance, and the idea of riding unwelcome into this place gave me a shudder. Anybody who attacked Cowan would probably need disciplined troops and a lot of patience or a few cannons.

Cowan appeared in the front door, carrying a lantern. He laughed and said, "By damn, you didn't waste time, did you, Milt? I fig-ured you'd get 'em loose. Come in the house. Come in here and tell me how you done it."

Settled at the huge dining table, sipping coffee again served promptly by the silent, ever-present Christina, I told the story.

"Sounds like it was easy enough," Cowan said when I finished. "You're the luckiest man I ever did see, Milt Baynes. I've heard of jailbreaks from time to time, but I never heard of any salty son of a bitch — excuse me, Cris — breaking somebody out of the same jail twice. That sheriff can't even hold a prisoner with the Army helping him."

He switched his gaze to Cris. "You don't look hard-used, button. You must take to night riding."

She nodded and flashed a big smile at me. "It was fun, Uncle Caleb. Milt loves to talk while we ride. He kept us entertained every minute."

Cowan gave me a surprised glance.

I shrugged and said, "She's learning to lie. Still needs lots of practice."

The old man leaned forward, eyeing her, and asked, "Think she shows promise?"

I rubbed my chin as if considering carefully before I answered. "She's got more meanness than she needs, but I'm not sure she's got enough smarts."

Win blurted, "Uncle Caleb, you ever eat tamales?"

"Sure, lots of times."

"What do you use to make them?"

"Cornmeal and ground meat, hot peppers, stuff like that. I ain't sure I remember too good. I ain't made any tamales my own self for years now."

"What kind of meat?"

I caught Cowan's eye and winked. He paused for a moment, then said slowly, "Most anything we can catch. Why, Nephew?"

Win looked half sick, half disgusted.

Cris said spitefully, "Milt winked. I saw it.

They're both lying, Win."

I sat up straight and put on my wounded expression. "How could I be lying? I didn't say a word."

"I saw you wink," she insisted.

"So I blink once in a while. Everybody blinks. Isn't that so, Caleb?"

Win leaned forward. "Uncle Caleb, I'm serious. What kind of meat do you use in those things?"

Cowan shifted under Win's intense gaze. "Well, folks use different kinds. You know how that goes."

Win wasn't going to turn loose. "What kind do you use? You. Never mind other people."

Cowan shifted uncomfortably and shrugged. "Aren't you going to tell me?" asked Win. "Why you so curious about a little thing like that?" Cowan avoided looking directly at Win.

Cris asked suspiciously, "What's the big secret?"

Win demanded, "You don't use dog meat, do you?"

"No, never, not on my place," Cowan said sharply.

Cris cried, "Milt has been making a horrid, disgusting joke. He said tamales were made from dogs. What are they really made of, Uncle Caleb?"

Cowan darted a quick glance at me, and I

241

looked at the ceiling, keeping a poker face. When I sneaked a peek at him again, he'd put on a tense expression, his eyes darting around the room like he was searching for a way to escape. He shuffled his hands and feet awkwardly for a moment, shrugged, and cleared his throat. "Well, we don't talk about that much."

Cris and Win stared hard at him. Win asked, "Why not?" Cowan flipped a hand as if giving up. "We don't want to waste 'em. It's good meat."

"Waste what?" Win demanded.

"We got to kill 'em off now and then. The barn gets full of 'em."

"Full of what?" Win grated.

"Rats, of course. What else?"

Win sat back, his mouth working.

Cowan protested, "These are good clean country rats. They ain't nothin' like those nasty, flea-bit city varmints. I wouldn't have a city rat on my table, and that's the truth. These are good grain-fed stock, raised right here on my own property."

Christina appeared in the doorway and caught Cowan's eye. As if delighted to change the subject, he smiled broadly and asked, "It's a mite early, but ya'll ready for a bite of breakfast? I'm hungry. You hungry, Milt?"

"Yeah, I could eat a bite or two," I said, rubbing my hands together like I couldn't wait.

Win turned away, his face gray, looking like he smelled something long dead.

"Christina?" Cris's question caught the Mexican woman still framed in the doorway.

She paused there, smiling. "Yes, señorita?"

"What meat do you use in tamales?"

"Beef, señorita, only beef."

TWENTY-TWO

I slept a few hours but soon woke feeling restless. I enjoyed the rare pleasure of shaving with hot water, but the sound of a blacksmith's hammer brought an idea to me, so I wandered over to watch him work. He stopped when he saw me walk into his shop, rolled a cigarette, and sat down to pass the time of day. When I asked him to shoe our three horses, he shrugged and agreed to do it. The idea of shoeing our animals to confuse army trackers had been slow coming to me, but having a blacksmith handy wasn't a thing I was used to.

Late that afternoon, the dogs went to barking, so I stepped out of the shop to see Bill Longley ride in. He waved and dismounted in front of Cowan's big house. About a half hour later I looked up to see him riding over to the shop. A born Texan, he'd climb into the saddle to travel twenty feet. He arrived just in time to watch me and the blacksmith finish putting the last new shoe on the meanest mustang in the world. He tied his mount in front of the shop and waited quietly till we'd finished. Then he said, "I don't think I ever saw that many ropes on one horse."

I walked over to shake hands. "You probably never saw a horse this mean, Bill. You know how to cuss in Spanish?"

He blinked and nodded. "Yeah, a little bit."

"Stick around and learn some new words. This smith is an expert. Judas always brings out the best in people."

The blacksmith, his shirt drenched with sweat, said in Spanish, "You untie him, *patrón*. As a favor, wait until I am safely at home with my wife." With a polite nod to Longley, he walked off.

Bill laughed, and I enjoyed hearing it; the boy was far too solemn for his age. He stepped inside and leaned against the wall. "The blacksmith in Goliad does pretty well at blistering the air too, or so I heard."

"You been to Goliad?"

"Yep. Just got back. Mr. Cowan told me to go down there and watch the goings-on. He's mighty good at telling people to do things he knows they want to do anyhow. We didn't figure you'd get back before I did, weren't sure you'd even come back. I just finished talking to him over at the big house."

"Find out anything interesting?"

Longley squirmed back and forth, scratching his back on the rock wall like a long, bony black-eyed cat. In that moment, it came to me that Bill's eyes were the feature I would remember most about him. Intense, serious, watchful, they seemed out of place in a face so young.

He said, "They called the blacksmith to get Sheriff Mullins out of his own jail. Mullins cussed him for being too slow. The smith cussed back and walked off."

I grinned and snapped my fingers. "That's right. That slipped my mind. I got excited and carried off the keys."

Longley stepped away from the wall, straightened his galluses, and sat on the bench just inside the door. "That Goliad blacksmith, he wouldn't even let anybody else use his tools. Several town men fought those bars and fussed around without doing any good. They finally saw it was going to take them a week to get that door open, so they gave up and sent to Victoria to get somebody to do the job. Sheriff Mullins sure got popular all of a sudden. Everybody in town dropped by to take a look to see how he was doing."

He chuckled and stretched his long legs. "I figured Mr. Cowan would like to hear about what was going on, so I left early this morning and worked my horse half to death coming back. Mullins was still in jail when I left."

"Good place for him."

"Yeah, didn't see anybody in Goliad show overmuch misery about it. Everybody but Mullins seemed to be having a right good time."

"What's the Army doing?"

"The lieutenant sent out a bunch of patrols. It looked like four men to a bunch. It looked like they went out in five or six directions, but I ain't sure. In fact, I'm not even sure they went out after you, but I saw 'em leave and figured that was what they was doing."

He rocked idly back and forth on the bench for a moment. "Those black soldiers are different. They aren't what I expected."

"How's that, Bill?"

"They act right, don't go swaggering around, speak civil. I went to Houston once. They took some freed slaves and used them for policemen down there. You never saw the like. Heaven help the poor white man they decided to take down. I was only fifteen, but I vowed then and there I'd never get caught without a gun again. I heard they got so ruthless and out of control the Army took their guns away from them. But you know what they gave them instead? They gave them a piece of chain with a wicked steel ball on the end of it. Can you imagine what it would do to a man to get hit with a thing like that?"

I wondered what Bill would think of the pogamoggan hidden inside my leather shirt. This wasn't the first time Bill had made it plain he hated and feared ex-slaves, even though he'd told me earlier that his daddy was against slavery. In fact, Cowan said Bill's daddy had spoken his mind on that issue when such talk could get a man shot.

I asked, "Judge Bilbrey all right?"

Bill said, "I don't know him. Heard talk that maybe he and Sheriff Mullins don't cotton to each other. Heard lots of folks say the judge got off light. Seems that feller Baynes had a bad habit of knocking people in the head."

"You want to step outside, Bill?"

"Why? You fixing to untie that mustang?"

"Yeah."

He watched me take off the ropes which probably had saved the blacksmith's life. "Why don't you shoot that vicious devil and get yourself a good horse? He's gonna kill you someday."

"No, he probably won't. We have an understanding."

I reached for the blindfold, and Bill stepped outside the door. "Mr. Cowan said you had an understanding with Miss Mill too."

"Yeah, she and Judas are about the same.

I heard Cris's mean harpy voice. "What? What did you say?"

Bill hadn't given a hint to warn me she was nearby. I had just removed the blindfold from Judas when she popped into the doorway out of nowhere. I turned toward her, and Judas got another chance at my backside. Out of the corners of my eyes, I saw his head strike for me.

Pure instinct took over. I leaped forward to escape his iron-jawed attack, heard his teeth click together behind me, crashed into Cris, heard her grunt from the impact, felt myself fall on top of her, and saw mud fly everywhere when we hit the hoof-stirred puddle in front of the door.

I rolled off her and sat up just in time for my nose to meet a fistful of mud. Blinded, I lifted both hands but got another fistful square in the face. I sat in the puddle with my head ducked between my knees, trying to protect my face with an upraised arm and trying to wipe the muck out of my eyes at the same time.

Cris said sweetly, "I just came out to tell you it's time you washed up for supper." I felt her lift my hat and plop mud on my head. I reached for her and missed. My ears told me she dropped my hat in the muddy water and stomped it. I went for the sound, but she splashed out of my way.

As soon as her squishy footsteps receded into the distance, Bill said sympathetically, "I found a clean rag in the shop. You want it?"

"Yeah."

He put a hunk of cloth in the way of my blindly groping hand and said, "Sorry, Milt. She motioned for me to keep quiet when she came up."

"Sorry, Bill, but I'm going to kill you soon's I can see to do it. You didn't need to make that remark about me having an understanding with Cris. You sucked me into saying something dumb. That wasn't friendly."

"I thought you'd say something nice, and she'd hear it and be tickled."

"Thanks. Maybe you meant well, and it grieves me, but I'm going to kill you anyway." I was still afraid to try to open my eyes. She'd got me good. Sand grated on the inside of my eyelids, and they felt glued shut by the gritty, sticky Texas mud.

"You're mighty quick," he said admiringly. "I never thought I'd see a man so nimble he could jump out of a horse's mouth before he could bite down."

Heavy sucking footsteps approached and Cowan's chuckle sounded. "I brought a bucket of water. That was as neat a takedown as ever I did see. Tell you what though, son, you need to slow down. Women like a man who takes things slow and easy."

I stopped dabbing at my eyes with the piece of rag and groped a hand into the bucket I felt him drop beside me. I flipped water into my face and said, "In one minute, just one minute, whether I can see or not, I'm going to start shooting. If I can't see, I'll just shoot at every voice I hear."

"One other thing, son. Take some advice

from an older gent. A good woman loves the land as much as a man, but she don't like to dab it on and wear it."

"Write that down, will you?" I asked, trying to get up the nerve to open one eye. "That's so good I don't want to forget it. A damn Texan thinks he's King Solomon. In the land of idiots, a half-wit thinks he's smart."

Cowan said, "Let's leave him alone, Bill. I think he's going through a sour spell. Plumb nasty."

I kept splashing water at my face while they squished away through the mud. It took me a couple of minutes to see well enough to realize my filthy hand had muddied the water I was using to wash my eyes.

A man with long hair can work up a good mad when working himself out from under a handful of mud, especially if he feels he's been treated raw, and especially if he sat in three inches of muddy water and doesn't own a spare shirt or pair of pants, and especially if a swarm of wide-eyed Mexican children gather around the well to watch and giggle. No help for it. I drew a delighted shout and a round of applause every time I roped up another bucket of water to pour on myself.

Finally, I stood, soaked and dripping, but still nowhere near clean. Spattered with mud and water, my Navy, holster, and belt lay on the stone edge of the well. That little cleanup job would take an hour all by itself.

In the dim light of dusk, I picked my way through the mud to the blacksmith shop. Judas, now held only by his reins to a snubbing post, watched me grimly while I lighted the coal-oil lamp. He listened carefully with pricked ears while I discussed his ancestry at length, shook my fist in front of his nose, and described the terrible things I'd do to him if he so much as switched his tail at me. Judas knew when he heard sincere promises. He relaxed and put on a bored expression.

The coals in the forge still put out plenty of heat, and being wet, I welcomed the warmth. Besides, I needed the fire to dry my gear. Careful not to get them too close, I arranged my leggings, moccasins, belt, holster, and pogamoggan to dry. If I fed the coals once in a while to keep up the heat, my leathers would be dry by morning, and I could oil them. I stepped outside and fished my hat out of the puddle. It seemed only yesterday that I'd stolen that new hat in Goliad. It was a sorry sight now, a clear footprint across the crushed crown. I closed the door and tied it shut.

I rigged a couple of poles to hang my pants and shirt over the forge to dry. When I walked past Judas to get to my saddle, he looked interested, so I reminded him of our previous talk. I got the fixings I needed to clean and reload my Navy, pulled a box close to the forge, adjusted the lantern, and set my naked and still mud-streaked self down with primitive dignity.

Someone tapped and pulled on the door. Without looking up I asked, "*¿Quién es?*"

Ricardo answered in English. "It is me, *patrón*. The Señor Cowan and the others wait for you to come. They prepare hot water for you to have the bath. You must hurry. Soon it is time to eat."

Still speaking in Spanish, I said, "Thanks, Ricardo. With my compliments, please give them my regrets and wish them good appetite."

"You don't come?"

"I don't come."

"Why you don't come?"

"I plan to stay here."

"Why you don't come?"

My patience ran out and I replied sharply, "Ricardo, it is not correct to ask why. You know that. Do what you're told."

I heard no sound of him departing, but the silence held so long I had time to finish cleaning and reloading the Navy, so he surprised me when he spoke again. "You are angry with me, *patrón?*"

"I am not angry with you, little brother. I am drying my clothing because I have no other. I clean my guns and my equipment."

"You don't come eat?"

"Ricardo, it pleases me to be alone."

"Yes, *patrón*."

This time I heard him leave. I removed my knife from the wet legging and carried the lantern around the shop until I found a fine-grained whetstone. As soon as the edge cut the hair on my arm without pulling, I oiled the blade and laid it beside the Navy. I didn't want the leather sheath to put rust pits in the finest knife I ever owned.

Sitting in naked majesty on the box by the forge, I thought about better days. My dress-up suit and other spare clothes had been on a fine packhorse, lost a hundred miles north of Chihuahua when Comanches nearly ran me down. A proud brave had probably cut the seat out of my best trousers and was strutting around a campfire somewhere. I'd done some sulking about my losses in that race, but I guess a man should try to look on the bright side of things. Better he wear my britches than my hair. Seemed most of my life was spent trying to make the best of a batch of bad choices.

Trying to think about other things didn't help. I sat there so mad it made my breath come fast and my face feel swollen. Laughing Milton Baynes had his feelings hurt, his pride wounded, and he didn't like any of it. Smart-talking Baynes let himself get interested in a woman who took him down hard, made him look like an absolute fool in front of everybody.

I guess sitting around naked isn't good for a man whose pride is already battered, so I got up and put on my soggy pants. At least they were warm from the forge. It felt so good to be doing something, anything, that I put on my shirt too. Just being in motion brought to mind that Milton Baynes, the wandering man, should get back to doing what pleased him most. I glanced at Judas and my nearby saddle.

Which way? East. I'd started for Louisiana, and that's where I'd go. According to Cowan, my uncle said I could come home. A New Orleans bank could probably get my brother's money to him somehow. I felt sure Ward didn't need it, but things can change in a year. I'd already lost his money once, and that was before the Army started looking for me. It was time to be about my own business. I strapped the saddle on Judas.

Somebody pulled on the shop door, found it tied shut, and kicked it a couple of times. Expecting Ricardo, I slipped the knot and let the double doors drift open. The dim lantern showed Cris holding a big cloth-covered tray.

She stood very still as if waiting for something. I went back to Judas and tightened the girth.

"May I come in?"

"Come or go as you please. I don't own the place."

"Uncle Caleb says you do, at least part of it."

"My pa's money bought it, so my pa owns it, not me. Nothing here is mine."

She carried the tray to my box beside the forge and grinned at the wet imprint of my backside. She said, "I brought you something to eat."

I pretended to ignore her while she modestly covered my imprint with her tray. I carried my leggings to the bench by the door and started lacing them on.

"Your leggings look like they're still wet."

The damp rawhide lacings marked my fingers with mud. I kept my head down, giving the job my whole attention.

"One of Uncle Caleb's riders came in this afternoon while you were working on the horses. He brought you some new clothes from Victoria."

The wet leather had stretched. I had to start over again to get the laces tight and even. Nothing works right when a man is mad clear through.

"We heated water for you. You don't have to stay muddy."

My hands were trembling. Texas has a little horned toad, a lizard actually, that spurts blood from its eyes when scared or fighting mad. In about one more minute, I felt sure I'd be up to doing it too. The thought made me stop working and close my eyes real tight for a couple of seconds.

She stepped aside when I went for my gun belt by the forge. I flipped it around my waist and dropped the Navy into the holster.

My knife went into the wet scabbard in my right legging. I brushed most of the footprint off my hat and found, without surprise, that I couldn't straighten the crushed crown.

Cris said, "I can fix that in the kitchen with steam from the kettle. Let me have it."

I put my hat on and replaced my gear in my saddlebags. When I flipped them up behind the saddle, she said, "I guess Christina was right."

My slicker was dry. I marveled grimly on how odd life is. The only piece of equipment I owned that was supposed to get wet was dry as a Texas sandstorm. I rolled it tight and tied it behind the saddle.

When I didn't answer, she went on, "We were waiting for you to come up to the house. Christina said something about Ricardo in Spanish to Uncle Caleb. He jerked as if she'd stuck him with a pin. He just swung around and looked at me. You know how people look at you, Milt, when something bad happens, and you caused it?"

I looked around to make sure I hadn't forgotten anything. Leaving things behind can cause real hardship for a man who's riding light.

"When I asked what was wrong, Christina said, 'If you want to say goodbye to *El Patrón*, don't wait any longer.' I rushed around and fixed you a tray. I almost took too long, didn't I?"

"You came to say goodbye, Cris? Say goodbye and be done with it."

"No."

I turned and looked her in the eye. "Then don't say goodbye. I will. Goodbye. Now I'm done with it."

"No, you're not."

She grabbed my sleeve. "Milt, wait a minute."

Holding his reins in a death grip to keep Judas's head still, I took a deep breath and said quietly, spacing each word, "You bother me again while I'm trying to get on this damn horse, and I'll bust you one. I never hit a woman in my life, but you got it coming. I swear you do. You hound a man past belief."

"Will you wait a minute? Will you listen to me?"

I slapped her hand off my sleeve, and she stepped back. As soon as I retied the reins, I faced her. "Talk! Go ahead and talk. Talk about mud in the face, talk about mud in the eyes, talk about stomping my hat. Go ahead. Let's hear some talk. Let's hear some talk about making a damn fool of a man in front of a crowd. I'm listening."

She spoke fast, the words tumbling out. "I took a bath. I washed my hair, and Christina helped me fix it. I ironed my only clean dress. I put on my only pair of pretty slippers. I worked all afternoon in the kitchen with Christina. I wanted to fix you a royal supper. I aired out your new clothes the man brought from Victoria. They still looked wrinkled, so I ironed them for you. I wanted to make everything just right to try to thank you for helping Win and me."

She ran out of air and took such a deep breath she almost bent over backward taking it in. Then she leaned forward and poked a finger into my chest. "I tiptoed out through the mud to tell you supper's almost ready. What do I hear? I hear you compare me to a mean horse."

She poked me again. "And what happens next? You come flying out the door like a huge frog. You land on me and crush me flat in a hole full of mud and horse droppings."

Another poke. "Then you roll off me and sit there looking arrogant and disgusted, like I'd done something dumb again, like it was my fault. It was more than I could bear."

I saw another poke coming, so I slapped her hand away before she could break a rib. I said grimly, "You are dumb, you and your brother both. Do I have to get him out of jail once? No, for pity's sake, no, it's got to be *twice*. Do you tangle me up around my horse once? No, that's not near good enough.

You got to get in my way *twice*. No, three times, by heaven. You tried to do it again just a minute ago. Is that dumb? Go ahead, answer me. Is that dumb?"

She drew an arm across her face, a fetching little impatient, distracted gesture, and I noticed her hair was still wet. She spoke softly, as if she was about used up. "Win tries to do the right thing. He shouldn't have been put in jail either time."

That was fair. I wasn't mad at him anyway, so I answered, "Forget Win. He's all right."

"It's me. I'm the dumb one," she said. "I keep getting smashed flat because I keep trying to keep you from riding away. I don't want you to go. Does that make me dumb?"

"There's nothing to hold me here."

"I hoped there might be. I hoped it would be me."

No dodging. This was plain talk. She'd shoved in all her chips and laid her cards on the table face up. Feisty she might be, but she was fearful honest too, looking scared and unhappy and close to crying.

"You sure you feel that strong about it?"

She nodded, looking down and twisting her fingers together.

I walked to the tray and lifted the edge of the cloth cover.

"Hungry?" she asked.

"Naw, but I thought I might nibble on

something, since you went to all the trouble."

Cris skipped over and lifted her tray. "Pull the box over next to the bench, and we can sit together. Won't that be nice?"

"Yeah," I said, "that'll be cozy."

TWENTY-THREE

Shortly before dark, Win and I rode up bold as brass to the Ross place. Jack Ross must have seen us coming. He stepped out on the front porch, settled his hat, rested a rifle in the crook of his elbow, and leaned his lanky frame against a post.

We pulled up, and Win said, "We need your help, Jack."

Ross ignored him, keeping his eyes on me.

I said, "I'm Milton Baynes."

The barest movement of his head must have been meant for a nod. He said, "Thought so. We met at night, so I never had a good look at you. I heard you plain enough though. You got a smart mouth, Baynes. You still looking for a fight?"

I let him wait for his answer, meeting his hard gaze with my best go-to-hell grin. "Truth of it is, I came with Win to ask a favor. From the way you talked at Win's house that night, I figured you weren't up to a fight. You been eatin' sand?"

Win's saddle creaked as he shifted his weight restlessly. "Damn it, Milt, no need to rile the man. We won't get anywhere like that."

Ignoring him, I kept my grin pasted on

and watched Ross's eyes. "How about it, Ross? You got a grievance? You got something you want to settle?"

He was tempted and made no effort to conceal it. For three or four seconds, he calculated his chances. Finally, he said, "This ain't no shootin' matter. Besides, everybody knows you're a gunman."

I said, "Win, pull your gun."

Win sucked in a breath and asked, "What? What are you talking about?"

"Pull your gun, nice and slow. Hold it on both of us. Make him lean that rifle of his against the wall. I'll hang my gun belt on the pommel of my saddle. I think Ross is aching to try me at knuckle and skull. You shoot either one of us if we go for a gun or a knife. How about it, Ross?"

Ross laughed and said, "We'll make it more even than that. Step out here, Pa."

"I'm fine where I am." The voice came from the darkness behind a front window. "You shoot my son if he goes for a gun, and I'll shoot Baynes if he does. That way I don't have to shoot my boy, and you don't have to shoot your saddle partner. Then, if we've a mind to, we'll settle with each other."

"Not an even break," I objected. "Win can't see you."

A deep chuckle came out of the dark house. "Life is hard, Baynes. You backin' out?"

I unbuckled my gun belt and hung it on my saddle before swinging to the ground. Ross leaned his rifle into the corner of the door and walked toward me. My hand went up, palm toward him. He stopped, and I said, "Wait a minute. I got to find a place to put this hat. A pretty lady brushed it up and steamed the crown back into shape for me."

A balding, grey-bearded figure appeared in the door, holding a Sharps that looked ten feet long. Rail thin, he gave me a toothless grin and said, "Gimme that lid. I'll put it in the house where it's safe."

I answered, "Old man, if you shoot at me, Win can shoot you twenty-seven times and ride clear to San Antonio before you can reload that cannon."

He chuckled and winked. "I know that, boy. Ain't no problem. Once my son bops you upside the head a couple of times, you ain't gonna be up to grabbin' for no gun. Ain't nobody gonna get shot." He stuck out a gnarled hand, took my hat like it was a basket of eggs, and backed into the house.

Ross faced me with a smirk, pointed a finger up at his own hat, and said, "Try to knock it off."

The lanky Ross had probably fooled many a Texan, but I had already given him a good close look. Most of the weight in his stringy frame was packed into solid shoulders and arms, the build of a man who could punch. He probably caught less careful men flatfooted and ended most of his fights abruptly. His kind of confidence came from plenty of quick and easy wins.

The hours I'd spent as a boy with bare-knuckle fighters in New Orleans gave me my own source of saucy confidence. My bet was that Ross was a mule-strong, hard-hitting, roughhouse fighter without a shadow of an idea about balance, footwork, defense, or punching combinations. I was also ready to bet that he'd just finished eating supper. My grin widened at the thought of his struggle to hold down his beans if I got an opening at his body.

Ross frowned, evidently getting tired of my derisive grin, and gave his invitation again. "Come on, let's see you knock it off."

He expected me to take a swipe at his hat, so I faked at his head, and he sprung the trap with a vicious right. I rolled below the sucker punch and hit him under the heart with everything I had.

Never finish with a right, I'd been taught, and never throw a single punch, always combinations of punches. And always work up and down.

So, when the blow under the heart froze him in place for a second, I followed through with a left hook to the temple, which drew his hands up and sent his hat sailing. It also set my weight just right, so I hit him under the heart again, all my 195 pounds behind it. I straightened as his hands came down again and leaned all my weight behind a left jab, catching him squarely on the nose.

Then, just like I'd been taught, instead of stepping back, I shuffled to the left and caught him with a double left jab. The perfect left jab acts much like a razor. The first should rise exactly at the same instant the elbow straightens. Thus, when it strikes, the rising fist pulls the tender skin just above the eyelids upward over a man's bony brows and tends to rip it open. Fighters like to cut adversaries under the eyebrows; blood runs into the eyes and clouds the opponent's vision. Sure enough, both my jabs caught Ross on the right eye, and blood gushed in a double stream down his cheek.

The New Orleans fighters claimed that the shock of a solid hit under the heart can interrupt a man's heartbeat for a while, the same way a hit to the belly can interfere with his breathing. One scarred veteran told me, "Stop the blood or stop the breath, makes no difference, the best of them lie down and quit. When the body falls, the head goes with it."

Ross tried to turn with me when I circled, an awkward and unfamiliar problem for him. His expression had gone blank, and I knew from experience the blows to the chest had left him with an odd sense of numbness, a frightening sluggishness he'd probably never encountered before. As I suspected, his clumsy foot movement showed every sign that he only knew how to fight when moving straight forward.

My moccasins were perfect for the boxer's shuffle, keeping the weight close to the ground without pointless and vulnerable hopping around. Ross's high-heeled boots gave him a terrible problem setting his weight properly to punch.

Desperately, he fired his best and most reliable weapon, the powerful right, but he could just as well have mailed a letter to me beforehand so I'd be ready. He set his feet and drew back his fist, warning me that the blow was coming. I timed it easily, let it whip over my shoulder when I ducked under it, and threw all my weight behind my own right. It caught him squarely on the upper lip with all his weight coming forward straight into the blow. An ax striking seasoned wood makes the same sound.

Ross's feet flew up in front of him, and it looked like he landed on the back of his neck. He lay still for a long count of five before he stirred. Then he rolled over and slowly came to his knees, head hanging. Finally, he raised his head and looked around. When he found me, he straightened up on his knees and held his right hand with the palm toward me while he groped at his mouth with the other hand.

His glassy eyes were round with surprise and pain. The poor devil had sprung a sucker punch, hit thin air, and caught six solid punches before he could recover his balance and get into the fight. His second try with his trusted right missed, and his mouth ran into an express train right of mine.

I felt mighty smug. Not many fighters I'd ever talked to were cool enough to count their own punches. He'd eaten seven of my best. I could hit no harder.

He pulled his sleeve across his right eye and looked at the broad stain of blood. Then he rubbed a finger under his nose and watched blood drip from the finger. His eyes lifted to mine, and he asked in a thin, strained voice, "What did you hit me with?"

I opened both hands in front of his face and spread my fingers wide, showing him both palms and backs, the traditional gesture of bare-knuckle fighters, the standard proof that I had no concealed roll of coins, brass knuckles, or other device to magnify punching power or to cut. The idea behind the gesture was the same as a gambler letting other players see the seal on a new deck of cards.

"Pa?"

"Nothin' but straight fistfightin', son," the

old man answered from the doorway. "Damned if he ain't slick. I ain't never seen one like him before."

"Baynes?" Ross's voice was returning to normal.

"Yeah."

He took a couple of deep breaths, now gently probing his chest where I'd hit him twice in the same place. "You come here asking a favor. I'm gonna give you one. I'm gonna let you quit. You don't have to fight me no more."

"That's good. I'm tired of it."

"Me too." He carefully explored his face with hesitant fingers before he added, "You can rest up for a minute or two. Then we'll go in the house and talk."

"I'm George Ross," the old man said, passing my hat to me and extending a hand. We'd no sooner shaken hands when he turned to Win. "I'd be obliged if you'd bring the water bucket from over yonder. I'll get Jack a towel."

Win started to dismount, discovered his forgotten pistol in his hand, and put on a sheepish expression. I turned away so he wouldn't know I saw it. In private, I'd tease the pants off him later. George stalked out of the house with a towel, dipped it in the water bucket, and rinsed Jack's face.

Jack Ross's voice came out relieved when he said, "Hey, now that's better. I thought you'd knocked my eye out there for a minute, Baynes. I couldn't see nothin' on that right side but a blur. I surely do feel better." He laughed. "Did ya'll see me feeling around trying to find my eyeball?"

I said, "I need a needle, some thread, and some carbolic." George spat tobacco juice and said, "We got 'em. Come on in the house. I'll light a lamp."

I picked up Jack's hat, and we filed through the front door. We settled around a table, and I put six stitches along the lower edge of Jack's eyebrow. As soon as I finished and wiped the blood away, I tested his nose between thumb and forefinger.

"Not broken," I commented.

Jack said, "Hell, I could have told you that. I got good bones. My nose bleeds every time I get in a scuffle, but it don't mean nothin'."

Win said, "Let's talk business."

I nodded. "Yeah, we want you to help us with a chore, Jack." I looked from him to his pa. "Would you mind if we put out the light?"

Jack leaned forward and blew out the lamp. "Like I told you, Pa, light irritates him, turns him snotty. What's the big job you want me to help with, men?"

Win went straight to the point. "Sheriff Mullins has put Milt and me on the dodge. He's got no proof we've done anything wrong, but I can't get any work done and keep running from the law at the same time. We want to get signatures enough to force a recall election, get Mullins out, and get an honest man in the office. Milt and I can't run around getting signatures with the Army after us. Will you help?"

"Who you want to be the new sheriff?"

Win answered, "I don't care, Jack. I don't know anybody well enough to pick a man. Folks have been real careful not to pester me overmuch with neighborly visits since I moved here."

The smell of coal oil from the hot lamp spread through the still air in the dark room. I could see the dim outline of Ross's hand as he gently explored the new stitches in his face. The silence held while Ross did his thinking.

The old man surprised me when he said harshly, "Talk."

Jack shifted his weight uneasily.

George Ross spoke again. "Speak up, son. This here's a chance might never come again. These boys ain't the law. They're in trouble too. A favor begets a favor. Talk. Make a deal."

Jack's hand came away from his new stitches, and his fingers tapped the table rapidly. Again, silence fell while he made his decision. Finally, voice shaky, he said abruptly, "I'm one of the riders."

Win's question came slowly. "The riders?"

Jack drew in a deep breath and held it for a moment. It came out with a groan, and he said, "It started out to be a way for us to run off drifters. The whole country was filling up with trashy, thieving, gun-toting drifters. We teamed up with that damned sheriff. Then it got to where we decided some folks who'd been around here for a while didn't measure up. We'd knock 'em around and make threats. Most of 'em moved on. Then Mullins started talking about killing a few people."

Win asked softly, "Who's in on it, Jack?"

Jack blurted, "Hell, everybody. Mullins, Buckner, Horton, Sullivan, Cottingham, Felix, everybody's in on it. Even Felix's hired hand, Wilson, is part of it." He turned his head toward my dark corner and added, "Baynes, you killed Horton and a snake named Dunwoody. They was the ones tried to hang Win. You burned Dunwoody along the ribs with a bullet when you stopped the hanging."

His fingers resumed their nervous tapping, just the kind of noise that drives me crazy. I had to fight off the urge to slap his hand away from the tabletop. Finally, he picked up the bloody towel and dabbed at his face. I stretched my jaw and heard it pop. His fidgety finger tapping had caused me to grit my teeth without noticing what I was doing.

I asked gently, "Who did the Lanmon killing?"

He said, "Horton, Dunwoody, Wilson, Mullins. I wanted out when Horton and Dunwoody tried to hang Win, but Mullins said he'd kill me, and the others talked me out of quitting. Everybody said there wouldn't be no more of that kind of stuff. When they killed the Lanmon family and arrested Win, me and Cottingham got together and backed out. Then all the others, everybody, told Mullins to go to hell. We were out of it.

"Even Buckner and Sullivan in town backed out; they said they never had no killin' in mind from the first place. Felix and Wilson got out too. Wilson said to hell with it, he was leaving the country. I think he did too, just rode off. He said he never had no idea of killing nobody and never fired a shot, but just being there, just seeing the Lanmons cut down was the worst thing ever happened to him."

Softly, I said, "So the gang's split up. Wilson claimed he was there when the Lanmons were killed but had no part in it. Horton's dead. Dunwoody's dead. Mullins is the only one of the killers still around?"

Jack shifted his weight again, causing his chair to creak. I heard him take another deep breath before he answered. "Yeah, that's right. Look, Baynes, we ain't killers. We didn't plan nothin' like that. That damn Mullins is crazy. We didn't know that at first.

He likes it. He actually likes killing people. How does a man get that way?"

Win asked, "You think those other men would help us get rid of him?"

"Sure they would, if they could keep it quiet what we been up to. We're all scared we're gonna get hung for the Lanmon killings. We were part of the gang, but it ain't fair, Win. Mullins didn't tell us nothin' before he pulled that stunt on you and your sister. We didn't hear about the Lanmons either until after it was too late. It don't seem fair to blame a man for what he don't even know about. Does being part of the gang when something like that happens make us guilty too? Mullins says if he goes down he'll take us all with him."

Win asked, "What do you think, Milt?"

I said, "I'm no lawyer, but I don't think a man can be guilty when somebody else commits a crime. Seems to me, if you men get together, Mullins has no chance. You get embarrassed and look like fools, but the drifters you abused have moved on, so who's going to press charges? Mullins, though, he should hang."

George Ross's chair scraped, and the sound of him spitting into a tin can was plain in the quiet room. He said gruffly, "My boy didn't have nothin' to do with burning your barn, Mill. We could sure help build you another one, though. Me and Jack been thinkin' too much about you bein' a damn Yankee and not enough about actin' neighborly."

"Matter of fact," Jack said, "I been givin' some thought to it. I been meaning to come calling, friendly-like. You got an awful pretty sister, Win."

"You're too late," Win said flatly. "She's spoken for."

"No offense intended," Jack said in a surprised voice. "I didn't have no idea. Who?"

"Milt."

"I should'a known. It figures. You have all the luck, Baynes."

"Yeah," I answered, "both good and bad."

Win chuckled and said, "You tell her what he said, Jack. Then step back quick and watch what happens."

I said, "Be fair. Just go ahead and shoot me."

Jack asked, "What do we do first? How we gonna do this?"

Win said, "If you men got together and went to the army officer in Goliad, that would probably be the end of it. He'd arrest Mullins. We'd need a regular election for a new sheriff, or maybe that lieutenant would just appoint a new man. That's the way it seems to me. What do you think, Milt?"

I said, "I think we're going to find out if a bunch of Texans have any real grit. How long will it take to get them together, Jack?"

TWENTY-FOUR

"Win?"

"Yeah." He lifted his hat from his face. When he saw me staring through the binoculars, he came to his feet beside me.

"There's a soldier coming. Looks like he's riding alone." Win pulled his hat brim lower over his eyes. "I guess I'm still half asleep. I can't see him yet. Where?"

"He's riding toward us straight as an arrow, and he's got a white flag tied to his gun barrel. When I first saw him, he had his rifle on his hip. Now he's waving it back and forth. He acts like he knows we're here."

Win's voice was grim. "I see him now. Wonder why Jack Ross isn't with him. You suppose something's happened to him?"

"Certainly not," I said sarcastically. "He probably just forgot."

"You think the soldier's a decoy? You smell a trap?"

"Don't think so. Haven't seen anything else move for over an hour. You know what? I think it's Jonas."

"We going to sit here and let him ride up on us?"

"Yeah. I'd rather face his kind than have him following me."

Win snatched off his hat and smoothed his hair. "If we're going to have a parley, we might as well have coffee ready. I'm going to put a couple of sticks on the fire."

I put the binoculars back in their case and handed them to him. "I'll talk to him. You do the watching. I don't want to be surrounded by the U.S. Army while we chat."

"All right. You still think that's Jonas coming?"

"Sure of it. I could see him plain enough before I put up the glasses. I'll wave him in."

I stepped out in the open and raised an arm. Jonas saw me at once. He stopped waving his rifle barrel back and forth and reached up to stretch the white cloth out at full length. I responded with the Indian peace gesture, raising my right arm high, palm of my hand toward him.

I waited in the open until he reined to a stop ten feet from me. "Remember me?" he asked, his grin showing he knew damn well I did.

"You mind if I put this rifle away, chief?"

"Name's Milt. Be obliged if you did."

He untied the knot, stuffed the white cloth into his coat, and slid the rifle into its scabbard. His eyes drifted idly, casually along the wood line behind me.

"Why you riding around waving your laundry, Jonas?"

"Come to take you in, chief. I come peaceable. Where's that little redheaded jailbird friend of yours?"

"He's probably putting on his apron and white gloves, getting ready to serve refreshments. Want some coffee?"

"Whoee, I should'a known. All the comforts of the plantation."

He slid from the saddle, keeping his hands in sight. Then he dug out his tin cup and started forward, leading his horse. We matched steps into the woods, neither of us being quite willing to turn his back to the other.

Win met us at the fire. "Looked all around. Didn't see anything." He nodded to Jonas and asked, "Where's Jack Ross?"

"My lieutenant like him so much he want Mr. Ross to stay close by. He send me instead. He say, since you take my word one time, maybe you do it again."

I asked, "You bring a message, Jonas?"

"I do. I surely do. The lieutenant send his compliments. He invite you two gentlemen to come to a big powwow going on in Goliad. Wants you to be guests of the U.S. Army."

"He wants us to go in and be arrested?" Win asked sharply. Jonas shook his head. "Lieutenant McKenzie say he want to talk to you. You come talk under the white flag. I take your guns, and you come in under the protection of the Army."

I said, "I like the protection of my Navy

better than your Army, Jonas."

I poured coffee into his cup and handed it to him.

His eyes flicked at my holstered handgun, and he chuckled. "Mr. Colt do make a fine Navy, don't he, chief?"

"Name's Milt."

Jonas took a sip of coffee and grinned up at me.

"That part about us taking your word sounds like we got you in trouble," I said. "I'm sorry about that. I truly am."

Jonas burst into laughter and quickly put his cup on the ground to keep from spilling his coffee. "No trouble, chief. The lieutenant say I done good. No trouble at all."

Win asked, "What's so funny?"

Still chuckling, Jonas said, "The sheriff say I tie him too tight and gag him so hard he nearly choke. He say I got in his way and cause the chief here to get the drop on him. That sheriff, it a good thing he locked in that cell right then and can't get hisself out. He cuss me mighty heavy. He cuss me up and down, front and back."

Win said, "I don't see anything funny. You shouldn't have to take that."

"Wise up, Win," I said. "This man laughs to cover anger. He can be in his most dangerous mood when he's smiling."

Jonas sipped his coffee and went poker-faced. "My lieutenant don't want no little

279

Negro soldiers talking back to no big important white men. He say soldiers, they got to
put up with a lot." He ducked his head, but
I caught his grin.

I said, "There's more. Stop holding out.
Tell the rest." He rubbed his ear and grinned
at me. "You got me, chief. I shouldn't say
nothin', but . . . well, now I was feeling
mighty low-down, and the lieutenant dismiss
me, so I was dragging my poor cussed-out
bones up the jail stairs. The lieutenant, he
think I gone. He reach his arm through the
bars and blap, blap, blap. He done slap the
sheriff across the face with his gloves, back
and forth. Lieutenant McKenzie, he say, 'If'n
you cuss one of my men again, I'll horsewhip
you to death.' "

I picked up the coffeepot and poured another round. "Sounds like our favorite sheriff
had a hard day."

"Chief, I figured the smart thing was to
stay away from the lieutenant. He was wall-
eyed mad as ever I seen him, and I wasn't
supposed to hear none of that nohow."

I gave Win a glance. He picked up the binoculars and walked away without comment.

Jonas nodded in Win's direction and said,
"Good man. He gonna take a little look-
around?"

"Something about being on the dodge
keeps a man cautious."

He spread his hands, palm up. "Nobody

280

come but me, chief. This here ain't no trap. Come right down to it, the lieutenant don't think I need help to bring in such as you."

I winked and grinned straight into his hard black eyes. It was about as easy as winking at the twin bores of a loaded shotgun. "You ever watch a man do card tricks, Jonas?"

"Yeah, I seen lots of tricks, chief."

"My name is Milt. Well, you know how they do it. They get you to watching one hand while they do something with the other. I'm watching you while Win looks to see if your lieutenant is doing something with his other hand."

"You all right, chief. You smart. But you ain't got no worry. You keep your Navy. Lieutenant McKenzie say to bring you in straight up. He say to ask for your guns but to be polite about it, so you just keep your Navy if'n it make you feel snug."

I called, "Win, come on in."

When he came back through the trees, I said, "I think we ought to go with Jonas. You agree?"

Win looked at Jonas and asked, "Your lieutenant say he wouldn't try to hold us?"

"He say you ride in under the white flag. That mean you ride out that way too if'n you please."

Win gave me a sour smile and said, "If they put me in that Goliad jail a third time, I'm going to get mad."

Jonas said, "Ain't gonna happen, not this time. But you outlaws ought'a know, it be better you come. I's doin' you a favor to tell you. It be better to be in jail than to have Lieutenant McKenzie after you."

"Why should we be scared of him?" I asked.

Jonas grinned at me. " 'Cause next time he might not tell me to bring you in straight up. Mostly, I just bring back a little dab, something easy to carry. The lieutenant, now, he be satisfied if'n I bring in . . ."

He glanced at Win. ". . . a red scalp and . . ."

He looked at me. ". . . maybe a legging, with the leg still in it."

I said, "Win, it's our civic duty to go in with Jonas." He jerked his head to give me a surprised look. "What are you talking about?"

"If the lieutenant sent Jonas after us, I'd have to kill him. I think McKenzie would miss having such a cheerful man in his outfit."

"I ride in front," Jonas said. He laughed at our surprised expressions and added, "I knows you won't shoot me in the back. You don't know nothin' 'bout me."

When we rode into Goliad, we found a line of tables in the shade of the "hanging tree" in front of the courthouse. Every table had at least one man, busily writing, seated at it. Jack Ross walked over as we dismounted and said, "We had a big talk with Lieutenant McKenzie. He won't let anybody leave until we write down all we said, so I couldn't come get you. I took his word you'd be treated right."

I looked at the pairs of blue-coated soldiers positioned around the courthouse building and the street corners. "Looks like the Army has taken over the town."

Jonas led us to Lieutenant McKenzie, who was seated at one of the tables. A sandy-haired man with long sideburns, his face showed the deep leathery wrinkles of a fair skin exposed to too much sun.

He looked up at our approach and returned Jonas's salute. "Any trouble, Private?"

"No, suh."

"Good work. Report to your sergeant. Dismissed." McKenzie's voice echoed the flat, routine confidence of those long accustomed to instant obedience.

Jonas saluted again and moved away.

McKenzie glanced at me without offering to shake hands and said, "You must be Baynes."

I pulled up a chair from beside his table and another from nearby. Dropping one chair beside Win, I sat in the other.

McKenzie said sharply, "I didn't invite you to sit."

I answered, putting on my friendly grin, "I've learned to expect lack of courtesy since

I've come to Texas, McKenzie. No need to apologize."

His pale blue eyes bored into me for a silence of fully five seconds before he pulled a couple of short black cigars from his blue coat. "Cigars, gentlemen?"

Win accepted, but I said, "No, thanks. Every time I try one, it gives me a headache."

I sat through another long silence while he and Win lit up and blew smoke at each other. Finally, McKenzie's attention seemed to drift back to me, and he said, "A poor beginning. I'm Lieutenant Angus McKenzie. I presume you are Mr. Baynes, sir?"

I nodded. "I am, sir, Milton Baynes, at your service.

He rose and extended his hand over the table. I came to my feet too, and we shook hands over his table. He turned to Win and went through the same ceremony. Seated again, he said quietly, "Several citizens requested a conference today. I have asked them to record in writing some of their statements to me."

"For the record, of course," Win said. "That sounds familiar."

McKenzie eyed Win for a moment. "Yes, I'm told you were an officer, Mr. Mill. You understand perfectly." Turning back to me, he said, "It seems clear that you men have been involved in several violent events recently. Are you willing to discuss these matters?"

I said, "Certainly, sir. Not knowing exactly what is of interest to you, shall I start at the beginning and tell you of my innocent and hapless involvement in somebody else's fight?"

McKenzie's stern features never changed, but I thought I detected a glint of humor in his eyes. Something told me he was surprised, that he expected my speech to be hardly above the level of grunts and snarls.

He said, "That would be most accommodating, sir."

"It's a long tale involving considerable vexation and much disappointment with local civil authority in Texas, sir. It's such a long story I'm inclined to give it a title. How does TEXAS VEXATION sound?"

He leaned forward and said softly, "Look, Baynes, you have shown me that you can speak the English language as well as I. You have also shown me you can be as arrogant a horse's ass as I. Will you please tell me your version of what's been going on around here? Will you do that without flourishes?"

I came to my feet and stuck out my hand. He rose and we shook hands again. I took a seat, leaned back, and started talking.

TWENTY-FIVE

Win and I spent the rest of the afternoon and most of the evening at the hotel writing. The next morning, when we handed over the stack of handwritten sheets of paper to McKenzie, I asked, "What can you do about Mullins?"

He gave me a disgusted look. "Not enough."

"What?"

"You heard me. Everybody thinks they know he's guilty of murder, but nobody saw him do anything, nobody heard him admit anything, and nobody gave me any proof. All I got was useless talk. All the witnesses they quote have vanished or are dead."

"You going to leave him in office?"

"No. In cooperation with Judge Bilbrey, I've declared the office vacant. I've got direct and conclusive statements from witnesses to prove he led a vigilante group which abused citizens. Mullins claims he's going straight to the commanding general of the military district of Texas with a formal complaint."

Win asked, "Will complaining do him any good?"

McKenzie gave us both a grim smile. "My orders are clear. He's wasting his time."

"Who takes over as sheriff?"

"You want to make a nomination?"

"No."

"One thing, Baynes, about the Horton and Dunwoody killings. I need a statement from Miss Mill, since you claim she was an eyewitness to the whole incident. Where is she?"

"Hid."

"It would help clear everything up if I could talk to her and get her written statement."

"You need for her to come here?"

"That would be best. If I can talk to her and see her do the writing, I'll have no trouble certifying her statement with my own signature."

"You can do that?"

"Look, Baynes, you've heard the expression noncommissioned officer, haven't you?"

"Sure."

McKenzie ran the back of his hand across his brow and blinked. His eyes looked tired. He spoke with the patience of a military man who found most civilians incredibly ignorant.

"Noncommissioned officers are sergeants and corporals. They carry heavy responsibility. They provide most of the leadership needed to get military tasks accomplished. Commissioned officers do that kind of work, too, but they have additional duties. They are commissioned by Congress. That commission confers certain powers on officers which can not be delegated to sergeants. Because of an officer's commission, his signature carries a special significance in certain legal matters."

"So you need to see Miss Mill?"

"I do. As the sole eyewitness, other than you, she is the only one left to verify or refute what you say."

After we left McKenzie, Win went back to the hotel, and I dropped by Judge Bilbrey's office. When I mentioned what I planned to do, he invited me over to his house to talk about it, said his wife would be interested.

Mrs. Bilbrey met us at the door. Feeling as comfortable as a dog with a broken tail, I stood on the front porch with my hat in my hand, wearing a sheepish grin. Bilbrey introduced us as if we'd never seen each other before. The first thing she said to me was, "I see you're still wearing that gun."

I said, "It's the only way I can keep my leg warm, Mrs. Bilbrey."

She said, "Call me Susan."

Over tea I outlined my plans, and Susan insisted that her house was the perfect place for what I had in mind. She also demanded that Cris stay with her rather than at the hotel when she arrived in Goliad.

I said goodbye to the Bilbreys and walked down to the hotel. After I dragged him off the bed, Win and I saddled up and rode toward Cowan's to get Cris. We made good time, so we arrived at dusk, a time of slanting light I always found magnificent. I stopped Judas for a while when we came in sight of the place.

Win pulled rein beside me and asked, "What's the holdup?"

"Just an odd feeling, Win. I was riding along and looked up, and there it was. Everything looks so familiar, I guess I almost got a feeling like I was coming home. Haven't felt that way for a long time."

Win sat relaxed in the saddle for a moment before he shrugged and said, "You could do worse. Uncle Caleb says you own part of it anyhow. With him around, you'd have a chance to learn all about how to make the best use of the place. You and Caleb seem to get along. He took a liking to you right off."

I said, "Yeah, we get along. He missed the best spot to build a house though. Look yonder, in those woods, that's the best location. The house would catch the south breeze and be sheltered from the north. If a man dug a well and found good water there, it'd be perfect."

He said, "You sure you need more than a hat for a roof and a saddle for a pillow?"

Judas impatiently made a move to bite my knee, so I put him forward at a walk. Win came along, holding his mount beside me. I asked, "Cris got any rings?"

"Yeah, she's got one. She doesn't wear it much."

"Which finger does it fit?"

"Ring finger."

"Which hand?"

"Left."

"Could you get it for me without her noticing?"

"I guess so. Sure. Why?"

"Why don't you just do it without asking why?"

He gave me a sly go-to-hell grin. "I don't know. I just won't. So tell me."

I tried to sound offhand. "I thought I might make her a new ring. The old one will give me the proper size. I've got some gold coins. That blacksmith of Caleb's has all kinds of tools. He knows how to make stuff like that. He said he'd show me how."

I was afraid he'd laugh, but he didn't. He simply asked, "What kind of a ring?"

The question was so thickheaded I wanted to pop him in the mouth. "Just a little round ring, a regular little old plain gold ring, that's all. I can't make anything fancy, wouldn't have time if I could."

"Where did you get gold coins?"

"I always carry some."

"Where? We didn't find any when you were hurt. Cris even washed your clothes."

"I sew them into my leggings."

"All this talk about digging wells and

290

building houses and making rings, you trying to tell me something, Milt?"

He'd been playing dumb to irritate me. I could see that now. He must have decided to stop acting dense. "Yeah, I guess I been circling around trying to."

"You asking me if it's all right for you to propose to my sister, to ask my sister to marry you?"

I said, "I thought I might feel you out to see if you had any strong notions about it, yeah."

"You ask her. It's fine with me."

I sighed with relief. "That's good. What do you think she'll say?"

He didn't answer for a moment, so I turned to look at him. He was grinning at me and shaking his head.

"What's funny?"

"I can sure tell you got no sisters, Milt." He chuckled, proud of his little joke. Then he said seriously, "I'd say, if you're not awful damn sure what she'll say, you got no business asking her to marry you. That's just one man's opinion. No offense intended."

We rode the rest of the way to Cowan's in silence. In the midst of the din of barking dogs, the old man shouted a greeting and waved us to dismount. He shouted, "Get yourself cleaned up. Supper's almost ready."

I went upstairs to wash up and put on a fresh cotton shirt, leaving my leather one

291

lying on the bed. When I came down the stairs, Cris was the first person I saw. She just walked right up as natural as a prairie morning and put her arms around me. First time in my life a thing like that ever happened. Something swelled in my chest at that moment, made me too proud and pleased to talk, even made it hard to breathe.

We sat down together at Cowan's long dining table, and he crowed, "We got some first-rate Mexican food tonight. You and me got to make real Texans out of these two redheads, Milt."

He gave me a broad wink and plucked a green pepper from a bowl in the center of the table. "Ever eat jalapeño peppers, Milt?" Cowan bit off half the pepper and closed his eyes with delight.

I took one and bit off a more conservative quarter. "Yeah, we have these in Louisiana too. They're a special treat only available in warm climes. Delicious."

Win and Cris both took a pepper.

Win asked, "Are they hot?"

Cowan laughed. "Mild with a touch of spice, son. Food for the gods." He popped the second half of the pepper into his mouth and reached for another.

Win bit off half a pepper and chewed expectantly. When Cris's hand started to her mouth, I caught her wrist and gently forced it down. I gave a tiny shake of my head in

292

answer to her questioning glance before I released her. I took another small bite of my pepper and joined Cowan in looking perfectly normal.

Win's chewing slowed, and he took a swallow of water. His glass didn't make it to the table before returning to his mouth. He emptied his glass and reluctantly lowered it. Sweat beaded his forehead above blinking, watery eyes. His face reddened as he glanced desperately around for a moment before reaching for Cris's water glass.

Cowan boomed cheerfully, "What say? Good, huh?"

Win drained Cris's glass of water and sat breathing through his mouth behind his hand.

Cris turned to me and said, "What can he do? Tell me, Milt. This isn't funny anymore."

I said, "Give him a spoonful of sugar."

She dug a spoon into the sugar bowl and handed it to her suffering brother.

He looked a question at me through eyes leaking tears down both cheeks, and I said, "Take the sugar. It'll stop the burning in about one second. Water won't help."

He stuck the spoon into his mouth and almost instantly took a deep, relieved breath.

Cowan leaned forward and said with wonder, "My own nephew, and he ain't outgrown needin' a sugar tit?"

Win, wiping tears off his face with the back

of his hand, said in a hoarse voice, "I'll never sit down to eat with either of you bastards again without wearing a gun."

Cowan said smugly, "Don't cuss in front of your sister. It ain't wholesome nor respectful."

Cris looked from Cowan to me and said, "I still don't think you two are good for each other."

Christina came in carrying a huge platter of meat.

Win asked hoarsely, staring at Cowan, "Rats again?"

Cris protested, "Win, please!"

He shifted his bloodshot gaze to me. "Or hairless dog?"

Christina smiled and said, "Cabrito, señor."

"What's that?" Win asked.

"Barbecued goat," I answered.

"I didn't ask you," Win snapped. "I asked Christina."

She nodded and smiled.

"Goat?" asked Win and Cris together.

Christina looked around in wide-eyed surprise. "Of course. What else? It is cabrito."

Cowan grinned at me and said, "Pass your plate, Milt. Welcome home."

TWENTY-SIX

Bill Longley came to the shop just as I started the bellows to heat up the forge. He shook hands and said, "I'm going home to Evergreen, Milt."

I nodded. "Nothing like going home."

He shifted his feet with the lanky awkwardness now so familiar and said, "Mr. Cowan's talking about trying to drive cows to Kansas next year. Talk is they pay hard money up there. I'd like to go on a drive like that, just to do it. But I think I'm a farmer at heart. I'll be a good farmer someday if I'm left alone."

I said, "Anybody who sees you practice with those Dance pistols would be warned to act civil. I wish you the best."

He looked at the gold coins I'd laid out and winked at me. "She's almost too pretty to be real, and she's a perfect lady. Hope everything works out for you, Milt."

"You too, Bill."

"Adios."

"*Vaya con Dios.*"

I stood for a few moments watching him ride away. The blacksmith came to stand beside me and said in Spanish, "He has much sadness, comes to anger too fast, and has no fear. Fate is not kind to such young men. Few live to grow old."

His comment called for no answer, so I gave none. I watched Bill as long as I could, troubled by a feeling I'd never see him again. Something about his narrow frame, sitting so straight in the saddle, seemed terribly lonely. Bill Longley needed a steady friend to ride with, needed one badly.

When Bill vanished in the distance, we turned back to our work. Making a gold ring didn't take as long as I thought it would, nor did it take as much gold. While we were at it, we made a plain gold disk with a little hole in it for a chain to go through. I used a small hammer and chisel to cut MILT on one side of the pendant and CRIS on the other.

The ring wasn't one of those narrow dainty ones. I wanted it to have a wide thick band. Seemed to me it ought to be substantial, made to last a long time. Still, it looked such a tiny thing. I couldn't get it past the first bend in my little finger.

We were finished a couple of hours before noon. I washed up and walked over to the big house. Cowan sat at his long dining table, ledgers spread in front of him. He glanced up and said, "Let me see what you done."

I handed him the ring and pendant. He rose, went to a window, and examined each carefully in good light. "Ain't never seen no gold worked up any better. This here doodad needs a chain. You got one?"

"I'll buy one first chance I get. I just wanted to give her something today."

"This the day you're doing the askin'?"

"Yeah."

Cowan raised his voice only slightly. "Christina."

"Yes?" She must have been only a step or two from the door to appear so suddenly.

"Bring me my little wood box from upstairs."

She vanished without answering.

Cowan sat idly drumming his fingers on the table, setting my teeth on edge. I never understood why so many people like to make useless noise when quiet is so much more restful.

Christina returned in seconds and placed a beautifully waxed black box on the table in front of him. When he opened it, a pair of chains on each side straightened to hold the top upright. "Where's Cris?" he asked, poking around with a blunt finger.

Christina said, "In the sewing room, señor."

"Good."

She flashed a smile at me and vanished silently, as always.

"This is the one. Thought I'd never find it." Cowan held up a thin gold chain.

"You got to put a price on it for me, Caleb. I don't know about things like that."

"It's worth more than you can pay, son. This here's a family matter. I give this here to my wife more'n thirty years ago. She was a lovin' sister to Cris's mother. They're both gone now, so rightfully, this goes to Cris anyhow. If she says no to you, then you give this back to me." He ran the chain through the pendant, joined the clasp, and handed them to me.

"Think she'll like it?"

"It don't make a damn, boy. If she don't love you, she ain't gonna accept it if it's the prettiest thing in the world. If she loves you, she'll pretend it's the prettiest thing in the world even if she hates it. You'll never know in this life whether she really admires it or not."

"She doesn't like my long hair. You got somebody around here can cut it without making me look like a Comanche left me for dead?"

"Christina!" Cowan bellowed.

She appeared again after a few seconds.

"Set up a chair in the patio. Get the scissors and stuff. Milt wants to get his ears lowered."

He snapped the black box shut, came to his feet, and headed toward the stairs. "See you at noon."

I fiddled around a minute or two, so Christina would have time to get things ready. When I wandered out on the patio, a wooden chair stood beside a small table with a comb, scissors, and a sheet on it. I saw no sign of her, so I sat down to wait.

Light footsteps sounded behind me, so I turned, knowing Christina always moved without sound. Cris walked up, slapped the sheet around my neck, grabbed the scissors, and said, "It'll be easier if you undo your braid."

"I thought Christina was going to do it."

"Uncle Caleb told me to get down here and cut your hair. Did you want her to do it?"

"No, uh, I guess not." I started pulling the braid loose. "Not if you don't mind a few ticks and fleas."

She made a shuddering, disgusted noise. "Milt, why do you always say something that gives me gooseflesh? Every time I ask you an ordinary question, you give me an answer that sours my stomach."

"I just have a skill at delightful conversation," I said modestly.

She chuckled and ran a comb through my hair a couple of times. "Are you familiar with the story of the big strong man who . . . ?"

"No, I never heard of Samson. No, I don't want to hear any story about a man losing his strength along with his hair. I've seen too many who did."

"Why did you decide to cut your hair?"

"Susan Bilbrey said you wanted me to."

"I didn't say that, exactly. I told her I thought you'd look more handsome if you did."

"That's the same thing."

"No, it's not."

"Sure it is. You want me to look handsome, don't you?"

"Well, I'm sure that's your business, not mine."

"That so? Well, now that's a sharp disappointment."

"I haven't the wildest idea what you're talking about, Milt. Do you want to keep the part in the middle?"

"Fix it the way you like it. Seems to me the way I look ought to be important to you."

She started snipping away with the scissors and didn't answer for a while. "Why should I care what you look like?"

"That's a thing that's mystified men for centuries."

"What? What has mystified men for centuries?"

"Trying to figure what causes women to fall in love with us."

The scissors stopped. "Are you telling me you think I'm in love with you?"

"Certainly. You are, aren't you?"

"I haven't given such a thing a moment's thought."

"That so? I've been thinking about it a lot."

She started snipping again. "About being in love with me?"

"No, about you being in love with me."

"Milt, do you feel all right today?"

"Feel great. You see, it wouldn't make any sense at all for me to ask you to marry me unless I was sure you were in love with me. That's what Win said, and it seemed like clear thinking to me. So, once I decided I was sure you were in love with me, I figured there wasn't anything to keep me from asking you. I thought it all out so as not to make a mistake."

The scissors clattered to the stone floor of the patio. I leaned over, picked them up, and held them over my shoulder for her, but she walked around in front of me. She snapped, "Stand up."

When I did, she stepped around me, sank into my chair, and asked, "Are you asking me to marry you?"

"Can't you tell?"

Her eyes narrowed. "I'm not going to ask that question again, Milt. Answer me."

"Yes, I am."

"You're supposed to kneel. Kneel down and ask."

"Aw, I'm not going to do that. I'd feel foolish."

"All right. Ask standing up with a sheet

around your neck and half your hair on the floor."

"Will you marry me?"

"Yes, Milt, I will."

I dug into my pocket. "Good. That's settled then. I made you a little trinket, kind of to seal the bargain."

"Bargain?"

"Uh, the agreement, the uh, engagement."

I put the chain over her head and let the pendant fall to her breast. She clasped her hand over it for a moment and took a deep breath with her eyes closed. Then she lifted the pendant and turned it over and over, admiring both sides. She looked up at me with huge eyes and said, "Milt, aren't you going to kiss me?"

"I want to in the worst way, but how can I when you're sitting in a chair, and I'm dancing from one foot to another?"

Cris sprang up and held out her arms to me. It was the prettiest and sweetest gesture I ever saw. I held her for quite a while without speaking, held her so tight I could feel her heart beating.

TWENTY-SEVEN

I thought we'd ride to Goliad, so Cris could write out the statement that Lieutenant McKenzie wanted. Then Win, Cris, and I would go to the Mill ranch and pick up her things. We'd ride back to town, get the marrying done, and that would be that. I figured Cris and I would ride back to stay at Cowan's, and I'd start building a house. Easy. Uncomplicated. I thought the deciding to get married would be the hard part; the doing of it seemed simple enough. I suppose a man can be dumb that way until he goes through it himself.

My little brother, Ward, got married in a saloon about fifteen minutes after having a bullet crease in his cheek sewed up. It worked fine. Everybody had a good time. In his case, though, his wife was the only woman involved. In my case, a bunch of other women got interested.

Maybe a crowd of Goliad ladies felt bad about the way they'd snubbed Cris. Somehow, by some kind of magic, she stopped being a damn Yankee and turned into a sweet little neighbor, sister to that nice Mr. Mill. Anyway, all kinds of kinks got in the rope, and everybody but me had a week's work to do.

A man can go in a store, buy a suit, and walk out wearing it, unless he's picky about a half-inch change in the sleeves or some such. A woman can't do that. She either has to tear out most every stitch to make a store-bought dress fit, or she has to sew the garment from scratch. Either way, it takes several days. I guess all men are built pretty much alike, and all women are put together completely different from each other.

The first day after we got back to Goliad, I think it was a Monday, I bought a new suit and shoes and shirt. That took about thirty minutes. The rest of the day, I sat around counting my fingers. Cris and Susan and some other women worked themselves into a fine dither planning how to decorate the Bilbrey home for the wedding and thinking up difficulties.

I could see how Cris would want something special for a wedding dress. That made sense. But I didn't see the need for every female in town to have a new dress, and it seemed there were a hundred other thorny problems I didn't even know existed.

I suggested to Cris that I'd be more useful helping Win at the ranch, and we agreed that I could come back Saturday when things would be ready.

I went by to tell Judge Bilbrey that I'd be out of town for a few days. While we were talking, I mentioned the map that Emilio drew for me. The judge expressed interest, and I ended up showing the ink-on-leather drawing to him. He offered me ten dollars for it, and I accepted. Later, on the way out to Win's, I stopped by Emilio's home, met his family, and gave him the money.

The boy's eyes nearly popped out at the sight of a ten-dollar gold piece. He swelled up and couldn't stop grinning when I told him the judge wanted him to come by and sign his name on the leather map, that the judge called it a work of art and planned to frame and hang it on his office wall.

When I rode up to the Mill place that evening, I hailed the darkened house. Win walked out and shook hands. I asked, "You still got enemies? You still keeping the lamps off at night?"

He nodded and handed me a piece of paper he pulled from his pocket. "Maybe there's still enough light to read that."

The note said,

YOU AND BAYNES WILL DIE WHEN YOU LEAST EXPECT IT.

I asked, "Where did this come from?"
"Found it stuck to my front door."
"Maybe it's old, Win. Maybe somebody wrote this before Ross got everybody together and went to the Army. Seems to me things are a lot better now. You should see the

305

Goliad ladies clucking over Cris."

He asked, "You think the lions are ready to lie down with the lambs?"

"No, not exactly. I'm just saying that a lot of scared men aren't scared anymore. Once a man owns up to doing something dumb, he usually doesn't go right back to doing it."

Win led the way into the house and said, "You may be right, but since I came home and found that note I quit early to cook, and I eat in the dark, just like my outlaw friend taught me. You hungry?"

"Sure."

He ladled beans onto a plate and shoved it across the table to me. I took a couple of bites and said, "You're going to miss your sister."

He chuckled in the darkness. "I take it you don't like my beans as well as hers. She's good company, too, Milt, although you set her to spitting and clawing like a scorched cat at first. She was scared of you."

"Yeah, I'm pretty scary. You been looking around for a replacement cook?"

He hesitated for a second before replying, "Not yet."

"A slow answer like that is usually a lie."

His chuckle sounded again in the increasing dark. "Did you know Lanmon had a spinster sister?"

I said, "Hell, Win, I didn't know anything

much about him but what you told me. We said howdy one dark night. Next thing I knew, he was shot down."

"Well, I didn't know it either. She's a teacher up in Victoria. I met her when we came through Goliad. She was here to see what to do about his property. Eva asked me if I'd look after the place while she decides what to do."

"Eva, is it?"

He answered slowly, "Yeah." After a quiet pause, he added, "I'm taken with her to tell the truth, and she seemed kinda friendly. More than ordinarily friendly, if you know what I mean. Maybe I caught her eye. I mentioned that I might be visiting up to Victoria pretty regular, what with my only sister likely to be living in those parts. She seem to like that idea, said I should come calling."

I waited, grinning in the darkness, until he spoke again. "She's a mite taller than I am."

"Hell, Win, everybody's taller than you."

He snickered with me and said, "Everybody but Cris."

"She'd be bigger than you, but she's mean. Meanness can stunt your growth."

"There you go again. When are you going to stop saying things that get you in trouble? How do you come up with stuff like that when any fool can see you love her? She's got you for good. No wise jokes will change anything."

I laughed. "You're right, Win. Man don't get over the plague. Once you catch it you just live with it as long as you can."

"You did it again, another smart remark. You pop out with sly little cuts one after another. Suppose I told her you said that."

"You won't. I trust you. You know she'd kill me. If you got that mad at me, you'd shoot me yourself and get all the satisfaction. I even gave you a pistol."

We had a good laugh together. After a quiet spell, he spoke again.

"You were snickering a while ago when I said Cris was scared of you at first. Well, you do scare people. There's just something about you. You don't seem to realize it."

I snorted, but Win ignored me and went on. "In town, the men still walked a cautious path around you, but they came to me and did a lot of talking. Milt, I think Mullins left that note. The men in Goliad all think there's something wrong with him. Ross says the man's lost a wheel on his wagon, can't talk about anything but killing you. He sees you as causing all his trouble. I'm part of it too, but you're the main one. Bruce Cottingham came by and said the same thing, says you broke a spring in Mullins's head, and now his clock won't keep time."

I chuckled. "I can make cute comparisons too. Mullins is a ship without an anchor. The lieutenant took his job away. Now there's nothing for him to do but drift away. Now we've compared him to a wagon, a watch, and a ship. What's next?"

Win sat morosely quiet, obviously not taking much enjoyment from my attempt at humor. I added gently, "Relax, Win. He's probably already left the country. I don't expect to see him again."

"I think you better be watchful."

I dropped the laughing act and spoke straight. "I figure I'm even with him. He set men on me and pounded me good and took my money. I thumped him and his men and got my money back. We're quits the way I see it. If he disagrees and comes at me, I'll kill him, and that'll be that. Right now, thinking about him won't bother my sleep."

"Think, Milt! Look what you've done to the man. You rode in, a complete stranger with an outlaw reputation. You took up for me and Cris and saved my life. Then, you killed two of his best men. Next, you broke me out of jail and left him lying in the dirt with a busted head and broken ribs. You finished? Hell no. You came back again, made friends with the judge and his wife, and broke me out a second time, only this time you left Mullins locked in his own jail and looking like the biggest fool in Texas. The Army came in, and I'll be damned if you don't make friends with the lieutenant. By this time you'd made friends with Ross and

309

got Mullins's own gang to turn against him. Then your buddies, the lieutenant and the judge, kick him out of office. He's got every reason to want to kill you, Milt."

"He's got every reason to move on, that's what he has."

Win sighed in disgust, but I guess he gave up on that subject, because he asked, "You come to sit around and talk, or do you plan to help out around here?"

"I thought I might make myself useful if you can find some easy chores for me to do. A man about to get married needs to save his strength."

"Then we might as well hit the hay. It's easy to go to bed early when there's nothing to do but sit around in the dark."

We worked around the place for a couple of days, but I started getting lonesome to talk to Cris. I told Win that maybe I better get back to town. He put on a dumb, surprised expression and asked, "Why? You don't have anything to do till the wedding on Saturday, do you?"

I shrugged and grinned. "Never can tell."

Win said, "You go on, Milt. Thanks for the help. I'll be along tomorrow."

Judas got me to Goliad before noon. I still felt strange riding into town in broad daylight. Pa and my brothers always teased me about being such a cautious man, and my short time acting like an honest-to-goodness outlaw hadn't done anything to change my habits.

I rode straight to Judge Bilbrey's house and visited with Cris for a while. I could have sat around all day enjoying a new habit Cris had picked up; she just naturally seemed to like putting her hand on my wrist while we had coffee together in the Bilbreys' breakfast room. But the house was full of nosy women, and I could see she was busy with woman talk and her sewing, so I got Judas to carry me down to the store.

I had bought my new suit there. Sullivan had gone through the sale as if he expected me to shoot him between the eyes any second. At the time, I had told him we were quits. I guess he'd had time to think about it and decided to believe me. When I walked in to buy a penny's worth of candy, he acted friendly, even told me his headaches from our set-to in the saloon had finally gone away, that he hadn't had one for a week.

I had one foot in the stirrup, getting ready to swing into the saddle, when Mullins shot me in the back. The bullet struck me like a sledgehammer over the left shoulder blade, slammed me against Judas, and snapped my foot out of the stirrup. Another shot struck my hip and knocked me sideways a split second before I reached for my Navy. When my hand got there, the Navy was gone. I jumped for the porch of the store and landed on my belly.

Mullins rode up to the hitching rail and

leveled his handgun, aiming deliberately. I rolled desperately and heard another shot strike the boards beside me just as I rolled behind a stack of boxes. His horse came halfway up on the porch, feet slipping on the slick boards, and shied when it slammed against my boxes. Another shot hit the boards. The stack tipped over on me, and I rolled off the porch, taking the boxes tumbling with me under the plunging feet of the frenzied horses at the rail.

I looked up too late to try to spin away from the next bullet. Mullins looked down his sights at me with the fixed glare of a madman and pulled the trigger. The hammer fell with a clear dead click — a misfire. He screamed like a wild creature, high and shrill, and drew back like he was going to throw the pistol at me. But he didn't. Instead, he holstered the handgun, and pulled his rifle from its boot.

Somebody shouted his name and Mullins jerked his head in that direction. In the middle of trying to watch him and avoid horses' hooves, I spotted my Navy and dove for it, hoping the horses wouldn't stomp me to death. I heard Mullins fire, but when I rolled to my knees with my Navy in hand, he wasn't aiming at me. He was pointing his rifle down the street.

When he threw a glance my way and saw my pistol coming up, he spurred his horse straight at me. I jumped from my knees, trying to avoid the charging animal, but the horse's shoulder smashed me off my feet again, which maybe was lucky. I felt the wind from the passing barrel as Mullins swung his rifle, trying to crush my skull. He missed with his swing, but he almost got it done anyway.

On the way down, my head crashed into the hitching post with a crack almost like another shot, and I found myself on my hands and knees. One of the horses jerked loose from the hitching rail, spun around, and kicked me square in the belly, driving the air clean out of me, and knocking me over backward. The terrified animal kicked me on the leg before I could roll away. Then it went down the street trying to buck off its saddle.

I tried to stagger to my feet, Navy still in hand, but my numb leg buckled. From the ground, I aimed carefully at Mullins as he continued to spur his horse, trying to get away now. Never was a steadier aim taken by a shakier man, but the hammer fell silently. I eased it back and tried again. Another misfire.

Mullins galloped down the street and out of sight. I managed to get up and limp over to lean against Judas, good old Judas, the best gun horse in the world, standing still as a statue. I was just getting some air back into my lungs when Sullivan stepped out on the porch and yelled, "He shot a soldier!"

I hopped on my good leg to the downed bluecoat and looked down into the eyes, already fixed and unblinking, of the nice man. I backed away and glanced at my Navy. When Mullins's bullet tore the weapon off my hip, it ruined a fine handgun; the frame was bent. The hammer jammed before it reached the firing caps. My Navy would never fire again.

A crowd of people seemed to gather in an instant, but I guess I was a little fuzzy, not being used to butting hitching posts. I dropped my ruined Navy in the dirt, picked up my flattened hat, walked back into the store, and leaned heavily on the counter.

Sullivan ran back in from the street and asked, "What're you doing in here?"

Looking back on it, I admit to some pride that my voice didn't even quiver when I said, "I want to buy a pistol. I want a new Navy Colt, but a good used one will do fine. You got any?"

TWENTY-EIGHT

"What're you talking about? You're shot, man. Three or four times!"

"Colt Navy," I insisted. "You got any?"

Sullivan's manner changed in a blink from excited to forced calm. He said, "Right, I got three or four brand-new ones. I'll get 'em out. You can pick one while we wait for the doctor. He should be here any minute."

He kept talking like he was trying to soothe a frightened child. "You just lean on the counter. You won't hurt a thing. That's a strong counter, solid oak."

A small key opened a glass-covered case, and he laid a couple of pistols on the counter in front of me. "One has a regular pair of walnut grips. The other one is fancy with ivory grips."

Sullivan's head jerked toward someone standing in the door, and he snapped, "Go get the doctor. Git! We got a hurt man here."

I picked up the one with walnut grips. Ivory is pretty, but it attracts too much attention for a quiet man and costs too much money. When I eased back the hammer, the action felt a little stiff, but a new gun feels like that at first. A gun needs breaking in just like boots. Very carefully, I put pressure to the trigger. As soon as the hammer fell, I recocked the new Navy and tested the trigger action again — smooth pull, no creep — nice familiar balance in the hand, just like my old one — smooth bluing without rust pits or scratches.

"Nice. How much you asking for it?"

"Well, uh, I figured to ask twenty-two dollars, but I could let you have it for twenty."

My left leg cramped every time I tried to put weight on it, and my right hip felt bruised clear to the bone. I couldn't figure how I was going to walk if I needed to limp on both sides. A drop of blood splattered on the counter. Sullivan grabbed a dust cloth and wiped it away.

I said, "Pardon me."

He answered solemnly, "Think nothin' of it."

I shook my head sadly. "It sure is a pretty thing, but I'd hate to pay that much." I rubbed my face and looked at a bloody palm. Blood was running down my face; I must have split my head against that hitching post.

Sullivan hustled a few steps away and hurried back with a new white towel. He handed it to me and said, "You got a place bleeding there just above the hairline." He leaned on the other side of the counter and continued, "Maybe I could take eighteen, but I'd ask you to tell everybody you paid twenty-two. I don't want to sell 'em that cheap as a rule."

I rubbed my face with the towel and held it to the sore spot where I'd rammed into the post. I fished out a twenty-dollar bill and laid it on the counter. "My holster tore. I guess it got old. I been wearing it since I was sixteen."

He trotted away and came back with a couple of holsters. "These here were made special for the Colt Navy. Got a black one and a brown one. Take your pick. Three dollars."

"How about the Navy and the holster for that twenty?"

"Deal. Baynes, don't you want to sit down? I don't know what's keeping that doctor."

I unbuckled my gun belt and discovered a fingernail turned back. Once I noticed it, it started hurting worse than all my other bumps and scrapes. "Throw away the old holster and slip the new one on my belt, will you? I'd be obliged if you'd load that Navy for me too."

Lieutenant McKenzie spoke from the door. "The doctor is coming down the street right now. How bad are you hurt, Baynes?"

Sullivan slid my belt with the new holster on it across the counter. I slipped it around my waist and buckled it awkwardly, favoring the hand with the sore finger. "I got hit in the back and in the hip. I think the one in the hip glanced off my handgun. Ruined it.

317

The handgun, I mean, not my hip."

McKenzie walked to me and looked at the back of my leather shirt. "I see the hit, but I don't see any blood. Unlace that shirt and let's take a look."

Sullivan said, "He got kicked a couple of times and probably stomped a bunch of times too. He rolled around under three or four spooked horses."

McKenzie pulled my shirt back, and I pulled out the pogamoggan which I carried looped over my shoulder. When I dropped it to the counter, Sullivan picked it up and said, "Well, I'll be damned, look at that. I never saw such a wicked-looking thing."

The poor devil was right. He never saw it hit him when he walked out of the saloon, and he was goofy afterward. He rubbed his finger across a lead mark on the leather covering the rock. "Looky here. The bullet hit this thing."

McKenzie said, "I don't see anything but a mean-looking bruise."

Sullivan said, "The bullet hit that club and glanced off. That's the luckiest stunt I've seen in my life, Lieutenant. He got shot at four or five times point blank and never got hit."

"You going to load that Navy for me?" I asked, shrugging my shirt back into place. My finger touched something and I sucked air between my teeth. McKenzie looked a question at me, so I added, "He's helping out. I got a sore finger."

McKenzie asked, "You're not hit anywhere else?"

I shrugged and answered, "My left leg feels swollen big as a log. My right hip feels terrible. I'm not holding a towel on my head for fun. I feel hit enough for one day."

A red-faced man carrying a black bag shoved his way into the store. He asked bluntly, "Where you hit?"

McKenzie answered, "Take a look at his back on the left side, his left leg, and his right hip. He's also got a bleeding head wound."

I snapped, "I hate to disappoint the crowd, but I don't like to be displayed."

The doctor snapped back, "Sullivan, draw the curtains and shut the front door. You're closed for a few minutes. Lieutenant, bring that chair over here. Good." He looked me in the eye and said, "Pull down your britches and sit down and shut up."

So I unbuckled my gun belt again and laid it on the counter. With my britches down around my knees, I sat in the chair while the doctor took a look at my leg, hip, back, and the top of my head. When he finished, he said, "That's as bad a bruise on your leg as I've ever seen. Why that leg didn't break is a mystery. You probably got some torn muscles there. The hip isn't serious. The back wound is merely another bruise. We can put some stitches in that head wound now."

I held up my finger and said, "This hurts the most."

He wrapped a tight bandage on my finger and said, "It won't hurt but a few more minutes. It won't bother you after that if you don't bang it around. I need to shave a spot on your head before I stitch it."

I shook my head. "No you don't. I'm getting married this Saturday. I got to be beautiful, and I already had my haircut, thank you."

He chuckled and nodded. "No problem as long as you don't lose your hair. If you get bald, you'll have a big scar to explain."

I pulled up my britches, gritting my teeth at the pain from the leg, and asked McKenzie, "Who was that soldier?"

"His name was Soft Talker," the lieutenant said. When I lifted an eyebrow, he added, "Many of my Negro scouts took Seminole names."

"My lady liked him," I said softly. "She said he was a nice man. I got business for a few days I can't postpone, but I'll even the score for him. I'll find the man who killed him."

The lieutenant said sharply, "Don't interfere. My trackers are on his trail right now."

"Win Mill found a threatening note when he went home, McKenzie. That crazy man

320

might go after him too. Do you suppose you could send out a couple of men to make sure Win's all right?"

He nodded and snapped, "Done." He jerked open the door and walked out without another word.

That Saturday, when I rode Judas from the hotel to the Bilbrey house, gritting my teeth and riding awkwardly with a sore leg, I looked up and found myself facing ten heavily armed men. My uncle, Rod Silvana, eased his horse up beside Judas and said in Spanish, "We received your letter that you were in trouble. It seems you have handled it yourself."

I said, "No, sir, not quite yet. I've got one more snake to kill, but I'm putting that off to do something more important today."

He grinned and said, "I understand. We will talk later."

Twenty bluecoats stood in ranks in front of the house. Lieutenant McKenzie called them to attention and saluted me when I dismounted. He walked up close and said quietly, "We'll be leaving after the ceremony. Our job here is done. One of my troops has a personal gift for you. It's a very private kind of gift, for you alone."

I gave him a lifted eyebrow, so he added, "You will understand when you see it. The soldier tells me we can trust your discretion.

The soldier says you are a man of honor."

Win came to town with an army escort, which tickled him.

All of Goliad came to Judge Bilbrey's house to see Cris and me get married. Cowan, Christina, Ricardo, and half the crew from Fort Cowan came riding in like a small army. They couldn't all come inside, but the ladies had planned for that. The ceremony took place on the front porch, so the crowd in the front yard and the street could see.

Judge Reid Bilbrey performed the rites. Susan was matron of honor. Cowan gave away the bride. Win was best man, and he had to go through the usual pretense of losing the ring. Everybody had a good time.

Judge Bilbrey loaned me his fancy buggy. Cris agreed to spend the first night with her wild husband under the sky instead of a roof, so we planned to stop somewhere along the road to Fort Cowan.

We got pelted with rice on the way to the buggy. I pulled away at a spanking trot. At the edge of town a single bluecoat caught up with us. Corporal Jonas grinned down at me as his horse trotted beside the buggy. He pointed at his new stripes to be sure I didn't miss them.

Jonas leaned far over in the saddle and gently laid a beautifully beaded leather pouch in my lap. He gripped my hand for a long moment before he straightened in the saddle and gave Cris a smart salute. His horse swerved away, and I looked back to see him join a departing line of bluecoats.

I gave the reins to Cris and turned away from her to loosen the drawstring of the leather pouch. Inside was a patch of skin about the size of the palm of a man's hand. Flowing from the patch was a lock of slick blond hair. An image of a man flashed into my mind, a blond man leaning back in a chair and smiling while I got the beating of my life.

I pulled the string to close the pouch and put it in my coat pocket. Cris asked, "Well, what is it?"

She surrendered the reins, and I settled back with my arm around her. "Cris, I don't want to keep secrets from you. It's a warrior's gift to a warrior. I think you would hate it, and it would make you unhappy. Would you mind if I didn't tell you?"

Cris Baynes snuggled her head against my shoulder, gave me a sweet smile, and said, "You vowed to protect me. Do your duty."

So I never told her, and she never asked again. She never knew how I came to be so sure the Lanmon family and Soft Talker were avenged.

At least, she pretended she didn't know.

McCORD ON McCORD

My grandmother started life as Stella Cowan. The Cowans trace back to John Locke and his father, General Matthew Locke, and through Jane Rutherford to her father, General Griffith Rutherford. William Jones Cowan, my great-grandfather's uncle, joined Colonel James Walker Fannin's regiment, and his name appears on the monument with the others who lost their lives at the Goliad massacre. Benjamin Francis Cowan, my great-grandfather, was "furloughed" home after he spent three weeks in the "Gangrene Camp" from wounds inflicted by General Grant's artillery at Petersburg in 1864.

My great-grandfather on the McCord side, a Dallas millionaire early in this century, hired detectives to trace the McCord family tree. Told that an English ancestor was hanged for poaching in the king's forest, he dumped the enquiry, spent his money, and left his progeny to earn our daily bread. Our genetic poaching skills diluted by time and intermarriage with the less gifted, McCords regressed to becoming engineers, architects, teachers, and mechanics. But the dubious heritage still persists — some of us practice law, and I write novels.

Handed a BB gun at age five and told to keep marauding sparrows from dining at our chicken troughs, my interest in weapons came alive, and I later took eagerly to competitive rifle matches and hunting.

Boyhood years as an amateur boxer, competing in three weight divisions as I grew, taught me that true defeat comes only to those who quit. Then twenty years as an infantry officer put me in close contact with the best men our country can produce.

To those critics who say Western heroes are too tall and wide to be believed, I say, "I've seen their real-life sons and daughters tested. When I write about their imaginary fathers and mothers in my fiction, why should I make them less worthy than their real, superb, living sons and daughters?"

The history of the American West draws me like none other. Books on this subject must be held just right, else romance and adventure pour out in your lap, soak through your chair, and drench the carpet. Mexicans fight Mexicans, Indians battle Indians, Irish railroaders dynamite rocks to fall on competing Chinese workers and the Chinese return the favor, white men feud, and everybody brawls with everybody in all kinds of weather on every type of terrain. The challenge of settling the West didn't appeal to weak or timid men and women, and its story doesn't seem credible to them now.

To mark human perversity, survivors often married their enemies' kinfolk, creating the most interesting and varied bloodlines on earth and the most fascinating and exciting people anywhere. To research and write a Western novel requires me to visit spectacular places, read spellbinding references, and talk to enthralling people. It's heavy work.

The employees of Thorndike Press hope you have enjoyed this Large Print book. All our Thorndike and Wheeler Large Print titles are designed for easy reading, and all our books are made to last. Other Thorndike Press Large Print books are available at your library, through selected bookstores, or directly from us.

For information about titles, please call:

(800) 223-1244

or visit our Web site at:

www.gale.com/thorndike
www.gale.com/wheeler

To share your comments, please write:

Publisher
Thorndike Press
295 Kennedy Memorial Drive
Waterville, ME   04901